ELEMENTAL SOLUTION

BOOK 4 ELEMENTAL GAMES

TAMAR SLOAN

HEIDI CATHERINE

SEQUEL HOUSE

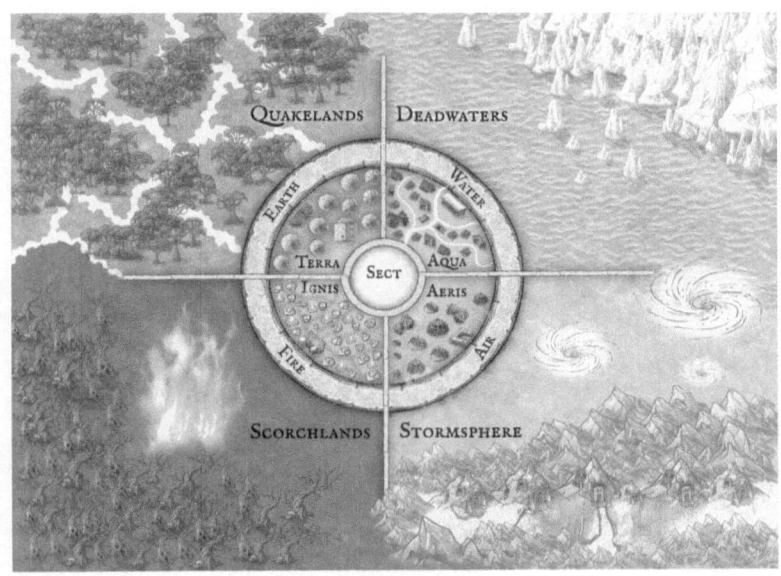

ONE

AURA

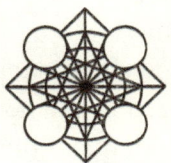

Aura pushes down a blaze of emotions as she enters the control room with Hayze. So much happened in the short time they were gone.

They gave Atmos the farewell he deserved, sending his ashes swirling into the air to be carried away by the currents of the breeze.

And they made a difficult decision...

It's time to form an alliance with the leaders. Which is something they never thought they'd do. But it's better to make your enemy your friend than to lose every friend you've ever known.

Pace's head snaps up when he sees them. "Great. You're back. Are you ready to start the Games again?"

Tempo touches him on the arm, then goes to Aura. "Did you take care of Atmos?"

Aura nods. "We carried him to the roof and released his ashes."

"I could have flown them up to the clouds." Skylus scowls from the corner of the room.

"The wind did that for us," says Hayze. "Besides, you're safer on the ground for now. Another storm is moving in over the Quakelands."

"It looks like a big one," Aura adds.

"Are we safe in here?" Tempo glances nervously at the ceiling.

"This building's designed to withstand anything," says Geo. "Including a hurricane."

"The storm will take a while to reach us," Aura points out. "And it might change direction and not reach us at all."

"I've been going through the different Game scenarios." Geo skims his fingertips over the colored buttons on the control panel, not in the least bit concerned about the storm. "I've found one I'd like to try next."

A wave of apprehension washes over Aura. It may be the leaders who are trapped in the Games, but Jewel is in there with them. And they all know by now that no Game is a good Game.

"I'm not re-starting them." Skylus steps forward to join them. "And you can't do it without me."

"The leaders showed us no mercy," Pace reminds her. "The Games are the best weapon we have right now. We have to restart them."

Aura glances at Hayze and he gives her a subtle nod. It's time to tell the others what they decided.

"A weapon's not what we need." Hayze speaks slowly as he chooses his words.

"Then what do you suggest we use?" Pace huffs. "A hot cup of tea and a hug?"

"Something like that," says Aura.

Pace tilts his head in confusion.

"We need to form an alliance with the leaders," Aura

explains. "Mother Nature's the one who's in control here. We need to work together to fight her, or we'll all be overcome."

"We have our powers," says Hayze. "Yet we've had little opportunity to use them to help everyone who's battling the elements out there."

"Tempo and I stopped the rain in Terra." Pace puts his arm around the girl he loves.

"Which was fantastic." Aura smiles widely, hoping she and Hayze will be able to convince them. "And that's something we could do a lot more of if we weren't wasting time playing games."

"It's not a game." Geo sits back in his chair and crosses his arms. "And we never agreed to play. Nor can we trust the leaders."

"People!" Skylus holds out her hands and sighs deeply. "*We* are the leaders now. Don't you see it? While they're trapped in virtual reality, we're the ones in charge. And we can leave them in there as long as we like."

"Is that why you don't want to restart the Games?" Tempo's face fills with horror. "You want to leave them suspended in the darkness forever?"

Skylus shrugs. "I mean, if it's for the good of the world, then why not?"

"Because it's unethical," Hayze growls.

"What are you proposing?" Geo returns his hands to the control panel and looks at Hayze.

"That we restart the Games in freestyle mode," says Aura. "Then we can negotiate with the leaders without them turning on us. We can't keep them in there forever."

"Nor can we leave them in the nothingness indefinitely," Hayze adds.

"That's right." Aura nods in agreement. "But letting them

out before we have a solid agreement would be dangerous. If they're suspended in the Games, they have to hear our case."

"And what exactly is our case?" asks Tempo.

"We want a peace deal," says Hayze. "The leaders have the trust of the Quadrants. And we have the powers to make a real difference. If we work together, we can create a far better future than anything we could achieve alone."

Tempo rubs her chin as she considers this.

"We could make them tell us where Jewel is as part of the deal," says Geo, not forgetting his counterpart from Earth.

This seems to convince Tempo, whose eyes light up and she nods at Pace. "We can't leave Jewel behind."

"Okay." Pace wipes his hands down his Water suit. "But if they try any funny business, we pull the plug."

"Agreed," says Tempo. "Let's talk to them. For Jewel."

Aura sighs. As much as she also wants to rescue Jewel, they're missing the point. They're doing this for everyone in all four Quadrants, not just their friend.

"I'm not keen," says Skylus, her nasally tone as smug as ever. "We have Geo, so Jewel is superfluous to requirements. Let's not waste time on her if we don't have to."

Aura clenches her hands into fists to stop herself throwing a fireball at the girl from Air. Her selfishness knows no bounds.

"What if we negotiate a succession plan?" Hayze rakes his hands through his dark blond mop of hair as he tries his best to smooth the path ahead. "One where we take over when the leaders are no longer able to rule."

This sparks Skylus's interest. Her brows shoot up as she glances at Cyclonis's pod. As the oldest of the four leaders, and the most unwell, he's certain to step down from his post first, which would make her the first to take over.

"Fine." A sly smile twists its way to her lips. "Let's do it. But this time, you need to give me a chance to speak."

Unease snakes its way into Aura's gut, even though they're all in agreement to restart the Games. The problem is they all have different reasons, which isn't a strong foundation for a successful alliance.

But it's a start.

They're far more aligned than they were before Aura and Hayze took Atmos to the roof. They can work with that.

Geo presses the back of his hand to the control panel. The sensor reads his Earth tattoo. It beeps and lights up with a soft, emerald glow. Skylus puts out her hand and does the same, followed by Hayze and Pace.

The beeping silences and the screens on the wall in front of them light up, revealing Jewel and the four leaders lying on the hard dirt in the center of the arena. They sit up, blinking as their eyes adjust to their bright surroundings. Aura knows exactly what that feels like. And she hopes never to experience it again.

Jewel looks up and smiles, and Aura knows she's smiling at her, letting her know she's okay. Aura's heart pangs with sorrow as she silently promises her friend once again that they'll find a way to release her from this nightmare.

"We're ready to talk," says Infernos, getting to his feet and turning in a circle. "What do you want from us?"

Hayze raises his brows at Geo, who presses a button and nods for him to speak.

"We want to work with you," says Hayze. "Not *for* you. *With* you. We'll help you tame the Elements, and you'll help us unite the Quadrants. No more using people without their agreement for your own purposes. That ends now."

Infernos looks to Avalan and Oceania who stand beside him, leaving the unconscious Cyclonis at their feet. They nod at each other and Aura's heart swells with hope that it could be as easy as this.

"We also want a succession plan," Skylus adds, leaning forward to ensure her voice can be heard.

"Not now," Aura hisses, feeling all the hope leak out of her chest. "Let Hayze handle this."

"You said I could talk," Skylus snaps back. "That was me talking."

"Did you say succession plan?" Oceania asks as the agreeable expressions on the leaders' faces sour. "That sounds more like you want us to work *for* you, not *with* you."

"No," says Hayze firmly. "We want to work together. Skylus was talking about one day when you're no longer able to fulfil your roles. At that point, we'd like to take over."

"You mean when you kill us?" Infernos growls. "Which I imagine will be sooner rather than later if we agree to this."

"They don't need to kill you," Jewel points out. "They could just keep you in here forever. It's much cleaner."

"We won't do that," says Aura, wishing Skylus had kept her big mouth shut. "We sincerely want to work with you. This is a genuine offer."

"But you don't trust us." Avalan narrows her eyes. "If you did, you wouldn't be talking to us in here. You'd release us and we could discuss this in real life."

"Of course, we don't trust you," snaps Pace. "What reason have you given us to trust you?"

"We want to know where Jewel is," Tempo adds. "Tell us that and maybe we'll start to trust you."

"Jewel's right here." Avalan takes a step closer to the Earth girl, who immediately shuffles back.

"You want an alliance," says Oceania, diverting the topic away from Jewel. "Yet it's clear you don't trust us. And you're also forgetting one thing."

"What's that?" Pace asks, taking the bait.

"We don't trust you either," Oceania replies, crossing her arms.

There's a loud groan and Aura scans the screens, hoping Geo hasn't secretly launched a scenario in the arena.

"It's Cyclonis." Tempo points to the screen on the far left. "Look, he's waking up."

Sure enough, the Air leader has pulled himself into a seated position and is rubbing his chest where Atmos threw a drone propeller, only narrowly missing his heart. Assuming he has one.

"Cyclonis!" The other three leaders rush over, crouching beside him with joyful expressions that leave Aura confused. The leaders have never been close, their feuds famous across the Quadrants. She wouldn't have expected them to be quite so ecstatic to see he's recovered. Perhaps it's the fear of Skylus taking over in his place?

"Where are we?" Cyclonis looks around, his face turning pale behind his long, gray beard. "This is the arena. We're..."

"Yes," says Infernos, his leather suit creaking as he squats. "They put us in the Games."

Cyclonis notices Jewel hovering to the side. "How many of them are in here with us?"

"Just Jewel," says Avalan. "The rest are in the control room. Aside from Atmos, of course."

Cyclonis smiles, sending a shiver down Aura's spine to realize he's happy about having killed the boy from Air.

"Well, thank you." Cyclonis directs his gaze at the screens as he speaks to them. "My body recovered much faster in the pod than it would have if you hadn't put me there. I feel quite rejuvenated. I'm going to enjoy this."

He stands and stretches out his arms.

"You've been in here for a while now," Jewel tells him. "And let's just say that you haven't enjoyed it so far."

Aura's assaulted with the memory of Cyclonis falling from the floating platform over and over again. It was a blessing for him that he missed it. A blessing that she no longer wishes had been granted after the lack of remorse he just showed for what he did to Atmos.

"Your timing is perfect," Infernos says to Cyclonis. "I was—"

"We haven't finished our negotiations," Hayze interrupts, trying to regain control of the situation.

"What negotiations?" Cyclonis asks.

"We were talking about forming an alliance," Aura explains. "For the good of the world, we need to figure out our differences and work together."

"Work together," Oceania repeats, looking Cyclonis directly in the eye. "Do you understand? We need to work together."

He nods at her, then looks to the other leaders, who also nod.

"What's happening?" Tempo asks quietly. "Something's happening."

Aura swallows, her hand instinctively entwining with Hayze's.

"Stop the Games!" Pace shouts. "They're up to something."

The four leaders turn their backs on each other and run for the edges of the arena. Cyclonis's purple robes flow behind him as he heads for the purple seats. Infernos, in his leather suit, dashes toward the red section and Oceania makes a beeline for the blue.

But Avalan hesitates at Jewel's side, seeming reluctant to leave her.

"Stop the Games!" Hayze urges Geo. "Hurry!"

Geo is hunched over the control panel, frantically scanning the buttons. "I don't know how. It's different in freestyle mode.

I can't just end the scenario. Help me look for the right button!"

Aura looks back at the screens, seeing Avalan reach out for Jewel.

"I'm s-sorry," she says, her voice cracking with emotion. "I'm really so very sorry."

"So am I." Jewel puts up her palms to use her powers against her leader.

"Do it, Jewel!" Pace shouts. "Buy us some time!"

"I love you, Gemma," says Avalan before she turns and runs. "Please, if you want to live, you have to trust me."

"Who the heckus is Gemma?" Hayze asks, not taking his eyes off the panel as he continues to scan for the right button.

"Jewel, stop her!" Aura shouts.

Jewel turns her face, her eyes searching and her hands shaking as she lowers them to her sides.

"I'm sorry, Aura," she says as tears pour down her face. "I can't stop her."

Aura steps closer to the screens, a hand of her own held aloft as she reaches for her friend, wishing she could give her a hug.

"Why?" she asks.

Jewel shakes her head, not giving a response.

Oceania is the first to reach the stands and throws herself down on the closest blue seat in the first row.

"What's she doing?" Skylus asks. "She's sitting."

"Oh, my sweet fractal," Hayze breathes. "She's not sitting. She's waiting."

"For what?" Pace asks, looking up from the control panel to see Infernos take the same seat in the red section.

"It's like the room with the coloured walls," says Hayze. "The one we were in when we thought we were stopping the Games."

Aura gasps to realize he's right. "They each need to sit on a corresponding seat in their own section. That's why they wanted Skylus in there with them. They needed a fourth person to stop the Games."

"That's *not* why they wanted me." Skylus pouts. "They have Jewel in there if they needed a fourth."

Aura remains silent, not needing to convince Skylus to know she's right. Jewel may not have prevented Avalan from running away, but that's a far cry from stopping the Games herself.

Cyclonis runs to the purple seats with surprising ease and sits down, leaving only Avalan still in motion.

"Try any button!" Pace gasps. "We have to stop the Games before they do!"

Geo presses buttons at random, but nothing happens. The screens remain lit, showing Avalan closing the gap between her and the final seat in the green section of the stand.

She reaches it.

Sits down.

And the screens go blank.

TWO

HAYZE

Hayze and the others don't need drones to keep the leaders contained. The moment Avalan, Cyclonis, Oceania, and Infernos leap out of their pods, they freeze.

Six teens face them, their arms raised and palms exposed.

Earth.

Air.

Water.

Fire.

Each a force of nature held in the hands of the weapons the leaders themselves created.

Avalan takes a step forward, her face twisted with far more than anger. It almost looks like...pain.

Yet Hayze still tenses his arms. "You may want to recollect there's more than one way to ensure your compliance," he growls, throwing her words back at her.

She freezes as her eyes narrow. "You don't want to do this."

Pace snorts. "Feels pretty good from where I'm standing."

"Especially when you had no intention of forming an

11

alliance with us," Tempo says, scowling. "You were waiting for Cyclonis to wake up so you could end the Games."

The leaders were smart enough to have a way out. Four seats they had to reach to be free.

Skylus drops her hands, making Hayze's stomach tighten. Whose side is she on now? "You only wanted me with you so you could use me. I was your ticket out."

Cyclonis glares at her. "You're the reason we always had to be careful. The power's gone to your head."

"Except you're weaker than us," Skylus continues as she takes a step forward. "Except we could end *you*."

Hayze isn't sure whether Skylus realizes she just proved Cyclonis right by saying that, but there's no time to point it out. She looks like she wants to tear the leader apart.

Aura swings an arm sideways to block her and Skylus stops. "You did that even though we just offered you an olive branch."

"You forcibly put us in the Games," Infernos spits. "You don't get to be upset that we did what we had to do to get out."

Hayze crosses his arms. "Are you even listening to yourself?"

Infernos clamps his mouth shut, realizing he just verbalized exactly what the teens have been fighting for.

Cyclonis strokes his beard as he gazes at Skylus. "Yes, you are powerful," he admits. "More powerful than we anticipated."

Pace snorts again, no doubt because the statement encapsulates the predicament the leaders have found themselves in.

"But you still need us," Cyclonis continues. "And you're right, Skylus. You're the most impressive of all."

Hayze's lips press into a tight line. What is the Air leader up to?

Skylus flicks her braid, then lifts her chin. "Yes, I am."

"And the only one I would consider as my successor," Cyclonis says, leaning subtly away from the other leaders. "You and I must work together. To show the Quadrants which is the greatest Element of all."

Aura gasps. "He's trying to buy you!"

Worse, he's trying to divide the teens. And Cyclonis has gone straight for their weakest point—Skylus's ego.

"Don't fall for it," Hayze growls. "It's an empty promise."

"Worse than that," Skylus says haughtily. "It's a lame offer. The best he can hope for is to be *my* second in command."

Hayze almost chuckles. Cyclonis underestimated Skylus's ambition and confidence, inflated as they are. She won't be settling to be anyone's equal. She's too far above that.

Cyclonis's hand returns to stroke his beard, but Hayze doesn't miss the way the old man's lips twist. His creation is beyond his control.

They all are.

Oceania raises her hands, palms up, her eyes beseeching as she looks at Hayze. "You've seen what will happen. Why we needed a Solution."

"What is she talking about?" Tempo asks, tensing.

Pace glances between Hayze and Aura. "You saw something in the high-tech room, didn't you?"

Aura swallows, then nods. "We saw Eterna's predictions."

"Of three scenarios," Hayze says. "If we don't do anything, if we tear down the walls of the capitals and Quadrants, or if we do what they ask us."

Geo stills. "And?"

"Devastation is the outcome of the first two," Aura says, her shoulders dropping. "Everything we know, everyone we love, is gone."

Hayze glares at the leaders as he speaks. "It's only in the

final scenario, where we tame Mother Nature in each of the Quadrants, that anyone survives."

Avalan inclines her head. "It's the only way."

The other teens are silent as they digest this. Hayze tries to stop the images from flashing through his mind, from stealing his breath all over again. And fails. There was...nothing. No green. No movement. No life. All taken by fire, air, water, earth.

Unless those with the ability to tame them stop it.

Pace's face is pale as he turns to Hayze. "But..."

"Our families," Tempo whispers. "Our people."

"All gone," Avalan says, her voice a battering ram through the tense air. "Forever."

"The Quadrants don't need anarchy," Oceania says softly, as if she can sense how bruised the teens must be after being hit with the truth. "They need stability."

She's saying the people beyond the Sect need the leaders just as much as they need the teens.

That they're all part of the Solution.

"At the price of freedom," Pace says, his hands now fists at his side as he no doubt thinks of the Alliance, another stakeholder into this murky mix of injustice and good intentions. "Those in the capitals win, everyone else be damned."

Infernos scowls. Oceania's shoulders slump. Cyclonis has stopped stroking his beard, now simply clasping his jaw as if trying to keep silent. Avalan closes her eyes, and who knows what that means.

A tense second passes and her eyes snap open, their dark depths still and hard. As if she's reached a decision. She gazes at the teens, her chin held at a regal angle. "We will form an alliance with you."

The announcement draws gasps from both sides. Cyclonis's hand falls away, revealing a slightly slack jaw. Skylus's mouth pinches as if she just sucked on something sour. Oceania looks relieved. Geo lets out a slow sigh.

Hayze has no idea how he feels.

"How do we know we can trust you?" Pace growls.

Tempo's already shaking her head beside him as if the question's rhetorical.

Infernos crosses his arms over his red leather vest. "How do we know *we* can trust *you*?"

"Because we haven't acted like morals are optional," Pace spits back.

Infernos flashes his teeth but doesn't respond as silence stretches out.

All Hayze knows is one word hangs in the room.

Stalemate.

The teens don't trust the leaders. The leaders don't trust the teens.

And turns out, there's no Solution without trust.

Avalan takes a small step forward, putting Hayze and the others on edge. "I know how to prove you can trust us." She looks at Aura. "I'll show you I want peace."

Aura stares back, waiting.

"I'll show you where Jewel is."

It's Oceania who draws in a sharp breath as her startled gaze snaps to Avalan, revealing two things. That this is significant.

And conversely, Aura's unmoved by the statement.

"You'll need to do better than that," she states flatly. "You'll need to bring her here."

Avalan inclines her head. "She already is."

This time, it's Cyclonis who looks at the Earth leader in surprise, revealing a third nugget of information.

The other leaders don't know where the Earth girl is.

Aura must realize it too because she narrows her focus even

more intensely on Avalan. "When Jewel's here in this room with us, then we can talk about an alliance."

Avalan shakes her head. "I must take you to her. It's the only way."

"Convenient," Hayze says, crossing his arms. "No deal."

Yet Avalan doesn't take her eyes off Aura. "Jewel is special. This must be done right."

Hayze tenses. He doesn't like the sound of that. "Done how?"

Avalan finally looks at him. "Aura touched Jewel from the beginning. I'm sure you understand that."

He glares back. "Aura's heart is as beautiful as she is."

"And Jewel saw that. Aura is the one she loves and trusts."

The words trigger a memory from only minutes ago. One Hayze didn't have time to process, but now seems more important than ever. "You told Jewel you loved her in the Games. Why?"

"I love you, Gemma," Avalan had said before she turned and ran. *"Please, if you want to live, you have to trust me."*

And who the fractal is Gemma?

"I love all my people," Avalan answers smoothly, already turning back to Aura. "This has always been about saving them. Which is why I'll let you meet Jewel."

Throughout these strange negotiations, the other leaders have remained silent. Hayze glances at each of them in turn—Infernos, Cyclonis, Oceania. They all look...pissed.

They don't like that the teens are being offered knowledge they've never had access to.

"Fine then," Aura says, probably realizing the same thing. "Take us to Jewel."

Except Avalan shakes her head. "I will only take you, Aura."

"No!" Hayze roars. "No deal!"

"This must be done right," Avalan responds calmly. "Aura's the only one I'll take."

Pace takes a step forward, his body vibrating with fury. "Do you think we're stupid? Do you really think we don't realize this is a trap?"

"Aura's powerful and you know it," Tempo adds. "You're trying to divide us just like Cyclonis did."

Avalan's back to looking at Aura as if this all depends on her. "You trust me enough to come with me. I'll trust you with the truth I've kept from every soul in this room and beyond."

Dread is coating Hayze's insides like black tar. "No."

This time he whispers the word.

This time, he acknowledges what he's up against.

Just as he expects, Aura turns to him. She looks up, the decision already heavy in her blue eyes. "It's the only way we'll know the truth."

"Aura..." Her name escapes on a groan. She can't do this.

"And that Avalan can be trusted," she adds.

It's how they can take the first step toward an alliance. A Solution.

Hayze shakes his head as he keeps his gaze locked on her. "It's too dangerous."

Aura arches a brow. "Compared to what you've done?"

Run into an inferno.

Convinced Pace to lock him in ice so Aura used her powers.

Returned to the Games more than once...

Hayze snaps his mouth shut with an audible clack.

"I need to know Jewel's okay," Aura whispers.

And Avalan is aware of that. She's using it to her advantage.

He never stood a chance against this attack.

Hayze leans down and brushes a kiss against Aura's forehead. He breathes in deeply, drawing her scent into every ounce of his body. "If she tries anything, singe her ass," he snarls, angry at fate for forcing this on him.

Aura pulls back, her lips twitching as she gazes up at him. "And then I'll run straight back to you."

"That's the only bit of this plan that I like."

Pushing up on her toes, she places a sweet kiss at the corner of his mouth. Avalan's already at the door by the time Aura pulls away. With a last, pained look, she walks away.

Hayze locks his muscles as every cell screams for him to follow her. They're stronger together. They always have been.

He watches, frozen with both fear and fury as Aura leaves the room behind Avalan.

Either taking the first steps toward peace.

Or toward the moment she'll forever be stolen from him.

CHAPTER
THREE

AURA

Aura tries to hide her trembling as she follows Avalan from the room.

She's surprised Hayze agreed to let her go alone. But he knows she can look after herself. She's far more powerful than the petite Earth leader with her headdress made of feathers and flowers.

Yet sometimes power comes from knowledge, not strength.

And Avalan knows something Aura's desperate to find out.

Where Jewel is.

They pass through the outer room. Its walls glow with lines of scrolling data that not long ago had shown Aura and Hayze exactly what would become of the world depending on which path they take. The memory makes Aura shudder with its hopelessness.

"This way." Avalan sweeps ahead without a backward glance.

Aura quickens her pace to keep up. "You said Jewel was here. How far?"

"A person is only as far away as your heart allows," says Avalan so softly her voice is barely audible.

Aura narrows her eyes as she tries to figure out what's going on.

Avalan doesn't answer. Instead, she presses the tattoo on the back of her hand to a sensor beside a wall panel that's lit up in green. It slides back, revealing a darkened room.

"After you." Avalan steps back and motions for Aura to enter.

Aura draws in a breath, not trusting the Earth leader but aware if she wants answers, she has no choice but to do as she's told.

"Don't be afraid," Avalan says when Aura walks into the darkness, blinking as a gentle glow casts into the room. It's only a small space and mostly empty, aside from a desk in the middle with a chair.

"What is this place?" Aura asks. "Where's Jewel?"

"This is my private office," says Avalan. "All the leaders have one. If you get your wish and take over from Infernos one day, you'll be assigned one too."

"It's not my wish to take over." Aura clenches her fists. "We just want a better world than the options we were shown. Hayze and I believe that's possible."

Avalan nods as she sits at her desk, not appearing the slightest bit interested in what Aura has to say. She taps at some buttons and blurry images appear on the walls.

"Not this again," says Aura. "I don't want to see the future. I want Jewel."

"And I'm giving her to you." Avalan taps another button and the images come into focus.

In the middle of the wall directly ahead, the face of a little girl appears. With large dark eyes and skin the color of midnight, Aura recognizes her immediately as a younger version of her friend from Earth. Jewel is smiling at someone, her chubby arms outstretched as if pleading with them to pick her up.

"I don't want memories of Jewel," Aura says. "I want the real Jewel."

Avalan nods. "Just watch. Then we can talk."

Feeling robbed of the opportunity to find her friend once again, Aura lets out a sigh, watching as a man comes into the frame.

"There's my sweet Jewel," he says, scooping her up and covering her face with kisses. The girl giggles as she presses her little body to the man who can only be her father.

More images fill the other walls and Aura turns in a circle as she takes in the dozens of scenes being displayed at once, all of Jewel's life as a child. Every moment has been documented. First steps. First tooth. First time she slept without her father rocking her in his arms.

Aura's heart expands with love for her beautiful friend to see that her curiosity and kindness were traits that were with her from the start. And it seems she got them all from her doting father, who showered Jewel with attention as if he thought he could make up for her lack of a mother by being everything to her at once.

As the footage rolls on and Jewel grows bigger, so does the list of questions nagging at Aura's mind, which is ironic given she came here with Avalan to find answers.

When Jewel reaches what Aura guesses is about six years of age, the images blur, leaving only one clear memory that expands until it fills the entire wall. There's nothing remarkable about the scene. Just Jewel and her father at their kitchen table, sharing a small loaf of bread. Aura notices the way Jewel's father slices the bread to disguise the way he gives her the larger half.

Aura swallows, watching closely, hoping she's wrong about what she suspects she's about to witness. This was around the age Jewel had said she was when her father died. Having just seen the strong bond between father and daughter, the thought of them being pulled apart sends tears trailing down Aura's face.

The footage begins to shake as Jewel's father mouths one very clear word.

Quake.

With no time to get to a safe zone, Jewel dives under the table. Her father follows, pulling her into his arms, shielding her with his broad frame.

But the quake is catastrophic and soon the footage is shaking so violently, the image of the frightened girl and her protective father are replaced with a pile of rubble that was once their happy home.

Aura looks down at the white tiles beneath her feet, unable to bear the devastation.

"You must watch," Avalan warns, her voice laced with steel. "Don't look away."

Aura lifts her gaze, wincing as she waits for the small girl to emerge from the rubble, forced to live out her days without her beloved father by her side.

Yet no girl emerges.

The footage changes from day to night and back to day again. Eventually a group of people arrive to pick through the rubble, pulling away sheets of metal and timber and forming neat piles until they reach what they're looking for.

Two broken bodies.

Two bodies that no longer hold the spark of life.

One of a father.

And one of a small girl.

"But that's not possible," breathes Aura. "No! Jewel lived.

Her mother came back for her. She raised her after her father died."

Avalan nods, tapping some buttons on her desk. The image on the wall morphs into another of Jewel sitting on the lap of a woman who has her back to the camera. Jewel's house has been restored, identical to the one in the images Aura just witnessed that were taken before the quake.

Aura strains her neck, trying to catch a glimpse of the woman's face, fearing that she's figured out who it is.

"Are you Jewel's mother?" she asks Avalan when the woman in the image fails to turn around. Why else did Avalan tell Jewel in the Games that she loves her? Aura doesn't buy Avalan's excuse that she loves all her people. She's never told Geo she loves him before.

"Please," says Avalan, not removing her eyes from the screen. "Just watch."

Little Jewel leaps from the woman's lap and throws herself on the floor and wails. "I want Daddy."

"Daddy's gone," the woman says.

"Daddy's not gone," Jewel protests.

"Gemma!" The woman gets up from her chair and turns to crouch beside Jewel. "It's you and me now."

Aura's hands fly to her mouth as the woman turns, and it's not because she just called her little girl Gemma.

It's because she recognizes the woman immediately.

And it's not Avalan.

"Rateen," Aura murmurs, realizing she had it all wrong. "Jewel's mother is Rateen."

Avalan nods and the walls fill with dozens of images again, this time of Jewel growing from a girl to a young woman with her mother by her side. As the years pass, a bond between the two is forged, and the tears that rock Jewel to sleep at night dry up.

Aura watches with interest, desperate to ask the questions that are fighting inside her to get out. But Avalan has made it clear that first she must watch. And it's now as she witnesses Jewel experience some of the more delicate milestones of becoming a woman that she understands why Avalan had insisted Aura came here alone.

She was respecting Jewel's privacy by inviting only her closest friend to learn the truth.

But what is the truth? Rateen isn't even real, she said so herself. She's Eterna, the mighty machine that predicts weather patterns and forecasts if humankind will perish or thrive. And why is she calling the girl Gemma—the same name Avalan had called Jewel in the Games.

"Who's Gemma?" Aura asks, recalling Jewel's reaction to hearing that name. It was so strong she'd given up her fight and allowed the leaders to end the Games, knowing it would leave her trapped in the nothingness she detested so much.

Avalan simply points to the screen. "That's Gemma. It means Jewel in Latin."

Before Aura has the chance to ask what *Latin* means, the images come to an end when Jewel wakes on her eighteenth birthday. As they vanish, the walls of Avalan's office glow in the same way they had when they'd first stepped into the room.

The Earth leader rises from her chair and goes to Aura, her eyes searching her face as if assessing how much she understands.

Aura shakes her head. "You still haven't told me where to find Jewel."

"I was hoping that would be enough," says Avalan. "That you'd see..."

"I saw a little girl raised by a loving father." Aura takes a step back, needing some space. "I saw her lose that father along with her own life. But then she was alive again. Which makes no sense. And her mother was there, yet I know for a fact her mother is nothing more than a simulation."

"That's right." Avalan nods, smiling through tears. "That's what you saw."

Aura shakes her head. "I still don't understand."

Avalan sighs, reaching out and touching Aura on the arm. "Your earlier instinct was right. I'm Jewel's mother."

"But how?" Aura shakes her arm, breaking the contact as she tries to process this. "It was Rateen I saw in the footage."

"I can't thank you enough for being my daughter's friend." Avalan reaches for her again but changes her mind and allows her hand to drop.

"Start from the beginning," growls Aura, her patience snapping as she raises her palms. "Put what you showed me into words. Tell me what's going on or I'll raze this entire Sect to the ground to find out for myself."

Avalan swallows. "I was only young when I became leader. My father died and I was forced to take over long before I was ready."

Aura nods, aware of that much in history already. The leadership for the Quadrants is often passed down through bloodlines and Avalan was one of the youngest leaders the world had ever seen.

"I wasn't ready to take over because I was pregnant," Avalan continues. "I had to choose between being a mother to my child or being a mother to an entire Quadrant who desperately needed me. I couldn't do both, so I made the only choice possible."

"You abandoned Jewel," says Aura, with a bitter taste on her tongue. "You left her for her father to raise."

Avalan nods. "I sent them to the Quakelands for their own safety. If people knew she was my daughter, she'd be a target for any rebels. Even Jewel had no idea who she was. I wanted her to have a normal life until she was of an age I could come for her so she could take over."

"Jewel was supposed to lead the Earth Quadrant?" Aura asks, not sure why she's surprised when she can so easily imagine her friend rising to such a challenge.

Avalan nods. "I had cameras installed so I could check on her progress. Her father did a wonderful job. Except I hadn't counted on one thing."

"Mother Nature," says Aura, letting her palms fall.

"That's right." Avalan straightens a feather in her head-dress. "The only force more powerful than a mother is nature herself. Eterna had failed to predict how big the quake was going to be as it tore through the Earth Quadrant, taking out the two people I loved most."

Aura steps forward, listening keenly as Avalan reaches the part of the story that makes the least sense.

"I felt so guilty," Avalan continues, more tears flowing freely. "How can I protect my people when I allowed my own daughter to perish?"

"But she didn't perish," says Aura, unsure why she's feeling sorry for the woman who abandoned her friend at birth. "She lived. You sent Rateen to raise her."

"Rateen is a simulation," Avalan chokes out. "You said as much yourself."

"But I saw her with Jewel." Aura looks back at the blank wall. "She raised her. A simulation can't raise a child."

Avalan locks her gaze on Aura. "They can if the child is also a simulation."

"No!" Aura takes a few steps back, bumping into the wall as she tries to take this in. "Jewel is real."

"She is to me. And she is to you." Avalan nods. "And I can't tell you how much that means to me."

"No." Aura shakes her head, refusing to believe what her gut is telling her is true.

Avalan's words make sense. It explains why Geo woke up in his pod in Earth alone. Why he said he'd never seen Jewel in all his years growing up in the Quakelands. Why Calla was so confident they would never find Jewel's body. Why everyone except Jewel managed to escape the Games. And why Jewel had an innocence about her that set her apart from everyone else.

"I had to see how my girl would grow up," says Avalan. "I missed her entire childhood. I couldn't miss the rest of her life as well."

"But it wasn't her," says Aura. "It was never her."

"It was her." Avalan crosses her arms looking more like a vulnerable mother than the leader of a Quadrant. "I programmed her with all her own qualities using sophisticated artificial intelligence technology that could accurately map her development. The Jewel you met in the Games is the very same girl my daughter would have grown into."

"No," Aura says once more. "People aren't just a result of who they were born to be. We're just as much the result of our experiences. You don't know how Jewel would have grown up if her father had finished raising her instead of a simulation who didn't even know her real name."

"I always thought of Jewel as Gemma," says Avalan. "It was my own special name for her. It made me feel bonded to her to use a name that nobody else did."

"You're Rateen." Aura's eyes widen. "You programmed her based on yourself."

"I...I...I..." Avalan's face swims with emotions as she tries to unpick the confession she accidentally just made. Then she gives up and shrugs. "Can you blame me for wanting to raise my daughter myself?"

"But if Rateen's a simulation, why not make her look like you?" Aura asks. "Why choose the body of an old woman?"

"I didn't want Jewel to know she's my daughter," Avalan says. "She still doesn't know. I wanted her to have a normal life without the pressure of being a leader's child."

Aura clenches and unclenches her fists, desperate to talk to Hayze so they can figure all this out together. Despite it making sense, this whole story seems impossible to believe.

"I've trusted you with my most guarded secret," says Avalan, lowering her voice. "I proved you can trust me by giving you Jewel. And now I need something from you."

"You didn't give me Jewel!" Aura cries. "You took her away! You just told me my best friend isn't even real."

Avalan nods. "And you can't tell anyone. Nobody else knows."

"Not even the other leaders?" Aura finds it hard to hide her surprise.

"No. And you can't tell them," says Avalan. "You can't even tell Hayze."

"I don't keep secrets from him." Aura crosses her arms. "No deal."

"But you must," Avalan insists. "Because...well, because of the second thing I have to ask of you."

"What?" Aura glares at the Earth leader. "I haven't even agreed to the first."

"I need you to tell Jewel." Avalan claws at her hair, sending a feather floating to the floor. "Nobody can know about this until Jewel does."

"What do you mean?" asks Aura.

"You need to tell Jewel she's not real." Avalan's fingertips flutter from her hair to her throat.

"But how can I do that?" Aura presses her back to the wall, wishing it would swallow her.

"She still lives in the Games," says Avalan. "And you're the only one she trusts. It has to be you. Once she knows, we can tell everyone else. But only then. I owe my daughter that much."

The trembling in Aura's body returns. She can think of nothing worse to tell someone she loves. That not only the world Jewel grew up in is a fake, along with the woman she thought was her mother, but...

Jewel is also a fake.

Artificial intelligence.

Not. Real.

This knowledge is going to break Jewel's heart.

The heart that doesn't even exist.

CHAPTER

FOUR

HAYZE

Hayze paces. He grits his teeth so forcefully it hurts. He jams his fingers in his hair hard enough to make him grimace.

And with every step and grind and tug, he doesn't take his glare off the three remaining leaders.

Cyclonis, Oceania, and Infernos stand near the pods. Cyclonis is sitting on the chair Hayze offered him, his face gray and drawn. Oceania is pale and still. Infernos looks pissed.

Hayze asks the one question he's battered them with since Aura left with Avalan. "Where did they go?"

Cyclonis sighs as he wipes his hand down his face. Oceania's eyes dart to the door, as if she wishes she went with them.

"The answer is the same, boy," Infernos snarls. "We don't know."

Pace shakes his head, shifting his weight as he leans against the control panel, arms and legs crossed. "Clearly we don't believe you."

Except Hayze does. The other leaders have no idea where

Jewel is. Yet he keeps asking the question he knows they don't have the answer to. It's part frustration. Part reminder for the leaders that they've never been united.

Part desperation.

He reaches the door and pauses, his weight balanced on the ball of his foot. One swipe and he's out of this suffocating room. One swipe and he's on his way to answers. One swipe and his heart will have room to beat again in his constricted chest.

Yet he remains in suspended animation. He's gone through this agonizing debate as many times as he's stood here.

"Just go," Pace says. "It's been too long."

Hayze spins to face him, temptation a physical pull on his insides. His friend's words echo the fear that's a noose of steel around his ribs.

Tempo moves closer to Pace. "We can't trust the leaders. You have to find Aura before it's too late."

Hayze takes a step back. He doesn't need to look over his shoulder to see where the sensor is. He knows exactly where it is.

One swipe.

Yet, he doesn't move another muscle. Even as remaining immobile hurts because he wants to move so badly.

"We need to trust them," Geo says, his voice strained.

Skylus lifts her chin. "Isn't that what an alliance is about?"

Trust the leaders. That's something Hayze certainly doesn't do. Returning Aura will be the first sign that a foundation has been laid.

Which is why he's still here. Leaving this room would clearly state he has no faith in their promises. It would destroy the alliance before it began. But it's more than that. Leaving this room means he doesn't trust Aura.

"Aura can look after herself," Hayze says, hardening his voice along with his resolve. "She's Fire."

That knowledge is the gossamer thread keeping him in this room.

Pace pushes away from the control panel, his face flushing red. "They have drones! They've been preparing to control us since the moment they began the Games."

"Does it look like we're controlling you now?" Infernos snaps.

Skylus smiles. "It's pretty clear who's in control here."

As much as her superiority complex is annoying, it provides Hayze a small measure of relief. Skylus is right. They're in control here.

Even though it doesn't feel like it.

"They wouldn't have gone far," Oceania says softly. And with little conviction.

Hayze glares at her. "How could you have a teen in the Games and have no idea where they really are?"

She flinches. "Avalan told us Jewel was in a pod in Terra."

Geo shakes his head. "She lied to you." He scans the control panel. "She lied to all of us."

Pace crosses his arms. "I want to know what she has to hide." He arches a brow at Oceania. "Don't you?"

She tugs her shoulders back and lifts her chin. "We all want the same thing—to save the Quadrants."

"You've certainly shown you're willing to sacrifice for that," Tempo says bitterly.

Hundreds of teens have died in the Games. How many more have been created, fated to wake up on their eighteenth birthday in a world they've never seen before? How long would the leaders have continued in the search for their Solution?

"And it worked," Infernos points out with a growl. "It

worked so well, we're now your prisoner, waiting to see if an alliance is possible."

"It's possible," Oceania says, her voice quiet but hard. "It has to be."

Or they're all doomed.

"If Aura and Avalan come back," Pace points out.

"*When* Aura and Avalan come back," Cyclonis snaps. He straightens, winces, but doesn't falter as his steely gaze sweeps over the teens. "Whatever Avalan's motivations for keeping Jewel's location a secret, they were founded on love."

"He's right," Oceania says. "Avalan cares for this world. She's tireless in her quest to save it."

"Some people will sacrifice everything for love," Hayze says, keeping his voice low and steady.

So they wait in the room.

Giving the leaders time to digest that he's not only talking about what the Earth leader is capable of.

The alliance means nothing to him if Aura's not by his side. He will raze the Sect to the ground looking for her. He even flexes his hands for good measure, nursing the heat that pools in his palms.

The loud wailing that suddenly pierces the air has everyone leaping to attention. The teens raise their hands, ready to defend or attack. All around them, the walls flash with color, alternating between red, blue, green, and purple.

The leaders' responses only heighten Hayze's alarm.

Oceania's hand presses to her throat. "All four?" she whispers in horror.

Cyclonis's face turns grim as he pushes to his feet, wavers, then steadies himself.

"Move," Infernos snarls, shoving his way to the control panel.

Pace scowls as Tempo places a calming hand on his shoulder. Hayze strides over, grabbing the leader's arm. "What does it mean?"

"It's an alarm," Infernos answers, turning to glare at him. "The Quadrants are in danger."

"The storm," Hayze breathes. The one Eterna predicted was closing in on the Scorchlands and the Quakelands.

"All four?" Oceania repeats, blinking at the walls as they cycle through the four garish colors.

Infernos punches a couple of buttons and the noise and flashing stops. "It's a supercell storm."

Cyclonis joins the Fire leader, one arm cradled over his chest. "Eterna predicted they would come."

Tempo frowns. "What's a supercell storm?"

Oceania shakes her head, then walks toward the door. "A storm like we've never seen before. One large enough to eclipse all four Quadrants." She stops, glancing back to look at each of the teens in turn. "One so powerful only you can stop it."

Skylus smiles as she adjusts her flawless hair. "With pleasure." She goes to join Oceania, but Hayze shoots out an arm to stop her.

"We're not leaving without Aura."

Skylus simply leaps, tucks herself into a ball as she sails gracefully over his arm, and lands on the other side. "Some of us are more than willing to fulfill our destiny."

Geo rubs his chest. "We have to go, Hayze. You saw what the storm is going to mean for our Quadrants."

Hayze scowls, hating the images that assault his mind. He presses his fingers to his temples, wishing there was time to understand all of this. Eterna only showed them two Quadrants being decimated and devastated. Yet this storm is about to envelop all four.

"Come, Cyclonis," Skylus orders. "We have people to save."

The old man's lips thin deep inside his beard, but he skirts around Hayze to join her. "You had better stop every single soul from dying," he growls.

Oceania turns to Pace and Tempo. "Please. We have to help our people."

They both still, clearly torn.

Geo expands his chest. "Even without Avalan, I'll do all I can for the Quakelands."

Hayze rushes to the door, conscious that tiny flames are crackling over his arms. The others leap out of the way, giving him a clear path. He draws in a steadying breath as he stands in front of it, completely unsure of what his next move is.

They can't abandon the Quadrants.

But he can't leave Aura behind at the mercy of Avalan. There's no way of knowing if the Earth leader took advantage of Aura's desperation to find Jewel.

Pace's brows twitch, wanting to frown even as compassion softens his face. "You stay, Hayze. We can go."

Except it's Hayze and Aura's parents who are among the vulnerable. Aura wouldn't want him to stay.

This is what they've fought for—to save lives.

There's a faint whoosh as the door slides open behind him.

Then his name's said in a familiar, surprised voice.

Hayze spins around, not quite believing that Aura's only inches away. She smiles faintly. "Still alive."

Clasping her to him is instinctive. An action he doesn't even know he does until she's pressed tightly to his chest, his heart hammering against his ribs. "Aura. Are you ok—"

"We must hurry," Avalan says from the main room beyond. "This storm is everything Eterna predicted it would be."

Aura tugs his hand as she steps back, stopping a few feet in. The others follow, going a few shades paler as they look around. The screens are alive with images, surrounding them in color.

Four sections, four Quadrants.

One monstrous storm blanketing the western horizon, reaching from north to south, moving with a speed that looks far from natural.

"It's massive," Tempo whispers, her eyes wide with horror.

"We must go," Avalan says. "Each Elemental Solution to their Quadrant."

Skylus is already stalking away, assuming Cyclonis will follow her, which he is. "I don't have time to wait for you," she says, still not looking back. "I'll meet you there." She rises from the floor as the door across the room opens. In a flurry of purple, she's gone. Cyclonis runs after her, cursing.

Oceania waves to Pace and Tempo, also moving to the door. "Come, I know a shortcut to the Deadwaters."

Pace scowls as he doesn't move. "We don't need you."

Oceania angles her head, suddenly looking lithe and regal. "I know shortcuts in Aqua you could never dream of."

Tempo glances at the walls showing the Deadwaters. The sky is dark and angry, the ocean below mirroring the gray restlessness.

Pace curses. "Show us the way."

Oceania breaks into a run, Pace and Tempo close behind. Avalan glances at Geo, who nods silently. Wordlessly, they leave for the Quakelands.

Hayze looks around, reeling. Everything's happening so fast. He frowns as his mind finally catches up. "Where's Jewel?" The whole reason he remained behind was because he was told it was the only way to learn the truth about the Earth girl.

Aura turns away as she tugs his hand toward the door. "There's no time. We need to get to the Scorchlands."

"This way," Infernos orders.

Hayze has taken one step when he stops. "No deal." They're not going anywhere with the Fire leader.

Infernos arches a brow. "Navigating Ignis is something you have time for?"

Hayze doesn't answer the rhetorical question. He has no intention of navigating the streets he's unfamiliar with. He was going to use the rebel tunnels. But if Infernos follows, he'll discover they exist.

"And just like Oceania, I know a shortcut."

Hayze glances at Aura, wishing there was another way.

"We don't have a choice," she says, the same reluctant acceptance mirrored in her eyes.

Time is marching forward.

Just like the monstrous storm.

Infernos strides through the door. He knows the decision has been made. "This way."

Hayze and Aura break into a run as they follow him. To their surprise, Infernos heads up the stairs and out onto the roof. There, he takes a sharp left and disappears from view. Hayze and Aura don't hesitate as they do the same, both conscious the world they've burst into is darker and wilder than the one they left.

The clouds are low and ominous. The wind is fierce and feral.

Mother Nature isn't planning on holding back.

Although the roof appears to continue, the metal drops out from under their feet. Their gasps are cut off as they land on hard cement only a second later. Hayze and Aura keep running, realizing a descending set of stairs is hidden, just like the real Sect is, behind an illusion. One that leads straight to the wall dissecting the Fire Quadrant from the Earth Quadrant.

"Hurry," Infernos snaps over his shoulder, now a few feet

ahead along a broad stone path. Thick walls reach up on either side for several feet, hiding them from the people below.

This must be how the leaders have been secretly navigating the Quadrants all along.

Hayze grits his teeth. He tucks his head in. And streaks ahead.

Aura's right beside him, also unwilling for the Fire leader to keep calling the shots. They now know the shortcut is the wall itself. Infernos just became redundant.

All that's visible is the stretch of stone ahead and the sky above. The further they run, the darker it becomes. The more the wind whips. The greater the urgency grows.

Hayze doesn't care if Infernos falls behind. In fact, a part of him hopes he does. The leaders are going to need repeated reminders of who holds the power in this alliance.

They run until their breaths are panting gasps. Until the sky is shades of menace and threat. Until the wind is howling down the enclosed top of the wall, whipping them with dust and debris.

The wall ends at a set of stairs. Hayze and Aura run down them, bursting through a door and into the Scorchlands.

Or what's left of them.

CHAPTER
FIVE
AURA

The Scorchlands normally looks like a graveyard of nature with its charcoaled tree trunks dotting the barren landscape as far as the eye can see.

But right now, it's a whirlpool of ash and dust. Circling and swirling in a dangerous dance, the tiny particles sting Aura's eyes, forcing her to squint as she covers her face with her hands.

"It's so dark," says Hayze from beside her. "And there's no fire like Eterna predicted."

"We need Skylus," Infernos growls. "To calm the wind."

"Well, you're stuck with us instead," says Aura, aware of just how much Skylus would have loved to have heard Infernos's words.

"We need to make sure the people stay inside..." Infernos's voice trails off as it's stolen by the howling wind. Aura peeks out from behind her hands to see he's moving in the direction of her village.

Fighting her disappointment, Aura accepts they came here for nothing. Eterna is playing games of her own. This is a massive dust storm, not the catastrophic fire they were shown. The people don't need to be told to stay in their bunkers. That's exactly why they built them. Their homes withstand almost anything except lava, as they discovered in the Games.

"Come on." Hayze puts a hand on her back, speaking directly into her ear. "The bunkers are the best place to wait out a storm like this."

Aura threads a hand through his as they run, using her other to shield her eyes. The wind buffets them, making them unsteady on their feet as they fight against it.

They reach the wall that's doing its best to protect the village. But it's a useless effort as dust and ash fly over the top, turning the air a murky gray as almost all rays of light are blocked out. Infernos is nowhere to be seen, leaving Aura with the harsh realization he only came with them as a way to escape the Sect.

Hayze coughs and Aura squeezes his hand, afraid if she lets go she'll lose him in the clouds of dust.

"Can you see the gate?" he asks, gaining control of his breathing.

"This way." She leads him forward with nothing but the memory of the footsteps of her youth to guide her.

Her instincts prove right, and they find themselves at the gate that opens onto the village. They walk through, finding the air slightly clearer on the other side, the particles whipping them made more of dust than ash. The streets are empty, with people already locked safely inside their bunkers.

Only one solitary man stands partway down the street ahead and Aura narrows her gaze, trying to see who it is. They need to get him inside before this storm gets any worse.

Pushing against the strong wind, Aura and Hayze move down the road, doing their best to shield their faces. Aura's forearms sting as tiny pebbles blast her, but she presses on.

Infernos was right about one thing. They do need Skylus here. She's the only one who can put a stop to this furious wind.

They reach the man and Aura rubs her eyes as he turns to face them.

"Infernos," gasps Hayze, just as shocked as Aura that the Fire leader hadn't vanished the first opportunity he got.

It's only then that Aura notices Infernos is holding a small boy in his arms. He presses the terrified child to his chest, shielding him from the storm.

"He didn't make it inside," Infernos shouts. "Nobody could hear him knocking."

Shame washes over Aura along with the relentless wind. She thought the worst about the Fire leader, when he put himself at risk to make sure his people were safe. It seems Infernos really does care about them in his own twisted way.

"We need to get him into a bunker." Aura pulls on Infernos's arm. Being young, the boy's skin is delicate and the tiny stones peppering him are taking their toll. "Come on."

Hunching down, they stagger to the nearest bunker and Hayze bangs on the metal door with his fist. The peephole blinks, telling them someone is watching from the other side and Aura glues herself to him as they wait for the door to open.

Except it doesn't.

"Let me," growls Infernos, pushing in front of Hayze to glare down the peep hole as he bashes on the door again.

There's a loud scrape of metal as whoever's inside pulls back the bar keeping the door secure and it swings open, banging on its hinges as the wind catches it.

"Hurry!" an old man calls, motioning for them to enter.

Infernos rushes inside with the boy. Aura and Hayze follow, helping the man to secure the door. It takes all three of them pushing against the wind to close it.

It's not until the metal bar is back in place and the bunker is sealed that Aura realizes how intensely the wind had been howling. The muted hum of the storm inside the bunker is such a stark contrast it has Aura's fingertips fluttering to her ears in the fear she's gone deaf.

The sound of flint striking stone echoes in the bunker as a flame sparks to life and a woman with silver hair places a candle on a table. Soft light flickers, revealing the destruction the blast of wind caused. But nobody is hurt and that's all that matters.

"My leader," the old man says, dropping into a deep bow in front of Infernos. "How may we be of service?"

Infernos shakes his head. "It's me who is of service to you."

"That's Alinta's boy." The woman takes the child from Infernos's arms. The boy snuggles into her, whimpering as she makes some cooing sounds and rocks him gently.

Aura now knows why they needed to come back here, even if the storm wasn't one made from fire. If they hadn't, this boy would have perished. And they needed to bring Infernos. If they'd come alone, these people would never have opened their door.

"You're Ember's boy," says the man, a flicker of recognition passing over his face as he studies Hayze. "You've changed since I saw you last."

"The world is changing," Hayze replies. "To survive, we need to change with it."

Aura nods pointedly. "And we need to help each other."

The man holds up his palms. "I told you. I didn't recognize him at the door. Or you."

"My name's Aura," she says. "I'm Vesta and Brando's daughter. Thank you for opening your bunker to us."

He nods curtly, turning his attention back to his trusted leader. "I would offer you a drink, but..." He motions to the overturned possessions in his modest home.

"Now that the boy is safe, I must leave," says Infernos. "There could be others."

The bunker rattles violently, vibrating in its dug-out surroundings.

"The wind is increasing," the old woman says. "You should wait for the storm to pass."

"Hayze," Aura whispers. "Is it getting warmer in here?"

"It does feel a little warm," he says, going to the peep hole and pulling back the cover.

Even if Aura wasn't an expert on all things Hayze, she'd know what he's seeing outside isn't good. His every muscle stiffens as the breath catches in his throat.

"What is it?" Aura goes to him, putting a hand on his back.

He steps aside, his face pale as he motions for Aura to look for herself.

She presses her eye to the peep hole and squints as she focuses, gasping as she sees what startled Hayze.

Glowing embers are falling on the village. So many of them that it looks like a hailstorm made from fire. If anyone's left outside now, they'd be burned in a matter of moments. It seems Eterna isn't playing games. And if her prediction is right, many lives are about to be lost.

"What did you see?" Infernos asks.

"A fire has sparked." Aura pulls back as Infernos takes her place at the peep hole.

Hayze nods. "And the wind's fuelling it."

"We're safe in our bunkers," the woman says, still clutching the small child to her chest. "We've seen plenty of fires here before."

Aura bites down on her lip. It's true the Scorchlands is accustomed to fires. But this one is different. With wind this strong, it could easily turn into the biggest firestorm the Quadrant has ever seen.

"We need to go outside," says Hayze. "To see what we're dealing with. Aura and I can stop the flames before they reach the village."

"Nobody can stop a fire with their bare hands." The man shakes his head in amusement and disbelief.

"How about a person who can make fire with their bare hands?" Aura puts out her palm, allowing a small flame to spark to life.

The man's smile is instantly wiped from his face.

"Sorcery!" the woman gasps, stepping back and shielding the boy from Aura in the same way Infernos had protected him from the raging wind. "Get away from us."

"It's not sorcery," says Infernos, turning to stand beside Aura. "The leaders have worked tirelessly for many decades to find a Solution to the growing crisis the world is facing. Aura and Hayze are an important part of that Solution."

The woman narrows her eyes at her leader, while her husband moves to stand a little in front of her.

"Aura and Hayze have learned to harness Fire." Infernos's face fills with the same pride a parent might show for their child. "And by working closely together, we can restore the Fire Quadrant, making it a safe place to live once more."

"It's impossible," the man says, still skeptical despite what he just saw.

Aura lets the flame in her palm extinguish, then moves to the candle in the center of the table, putting out that flame too. The bunker descends into darkness and Aura waits a few seconds before re-lighting the flame.

This doesn't seem to set the couple at ease and they continue to eye both Aura and Hayze with suspicion and fear.

"They won't hurt you," Infernos tells them. "They're the Solution."

They remain frozen in shock, their trust in their leader seeming to have a few blind spots.

"And we're a Solution that needs to get the heckus outside," says Hayze, motioning for Aura to join him again at the door.

"Fine by me." The old man shuffles forward and pulls back the bar, keeping the door closed. "Be gone."

Once again, the door flies open with a bang and each of Aura's senses are assaulted by the storm as they cower in the limited shelter of the doorstep.

Her ears are deafened by the howling wind.

Her vision is clouded by the swirling dust.

Her breath is tinged by the sharp taste and scent of burning ash.

And every inch of her exposed skin prickles as the intensity of the heat caresses her with unwanted hands.

Despite her body screaming at her to get back inside, Aura and Hayze step out into the storm. The door behind them slams closed, and she turns, surprised to find Infernos has followed them outside.

"I stand by all my people," he shouts. "And that includes you."

If Aura wasn't acutely aware of the heinous acts this man has committed, she might be taken in by this. But this is the same man who not only tore Aura away from her family but risked her life alongside seven others in the Games.

Six.

Six lives, she corrects herself.

Because Jewel isn't real.

She glances at Hayze, relieved there's been no time to talk to him about what Avalan told her. She doesn't want to keep secrets from him, let alone one this big. But how can she possibly tell him anything before she has a chance to talk to

Jewel? Avalan was right when she said Jewel should be told first.

"Are you ready?" Hayze shouts over the wind as he holds out his palms.

"I'm ready!" Aura calls back, putting out her own hands as she prepares for the battle ahead.

"Stay close behind us," Hayze says, turning back to Infernos. "We'll do our best to keep you safe."

They step up onto the street and Aura focuses on drawing the fire from the air as they move. Embers hiss and fall at their feet and they inch forward, walking in the direction of the intense wall of heat ahead.

"Look!" Infernos shouts from behind them.

At first, Aura thinks it's the enormous wall of fire that's climbing over the wall surrounding the village. Then she realizes he's pointing to his left. She turns and sees the bunker closest to the flames is caving in. Bowing to the intense heat, it collapses in on itself, devouring any unfortunate inhabitants who may have been hiding inside.

"That's not possible," Infernos growls.

But this isn't a regular fire. The intensity of this firestorm is too great, fuelled by impossible winds no human could have predicted.

"Get the people out!" Hayze shouts, turning back to the bunker they only just exited and banging on the door.

Infernos runs to the home beside it, shouting as the door opens, warning the people to flee. Aura does the same at another bunker, only to find the door remains firmly closed.

"Infernos!" she shouts. "Over here!"

He races to her side and knocks. The door instantly opens as the startled inhabitants stare at their leader.

"Get out!" Infernos orders. "The bunkers aren't safe! Tell as many people as you can. Gather in the street. Hurry!"

Aura hates that the leaders had a point back in the Sect when they said the people trust them. This is their value in working together. But how can they rely on four people who have double crossed them more than once?

Hayze appears at Aura's side, panting as Infernos takes off to warn as many people as he can, swiping at flying embers as he moves.

"Only one house opened their door for me," says Hayze. "And they wouldn't listen. They won't come outside."

"I know who'll listen." Aura grabs Hayze's hand and they run toward the homes they grew up in. Their parents will open their doors. They won't wait for their leader before they leap into action.

They break apart as Hayze races to his parents and Aura to hers.

She knocks on the bunker's door so hard, the skin on her knuckles breaks open and bleeds. "Mom! Dad! Hurry!"

The door opens a crack, and the wind does the rest of the work, slamming it against the opposite wall.

"Aura!" her parents shout in surprise.

"It's not safe in there!" She pulls at their arms, hauling them out into what must seem even worse danger. "The bunkers are caving in!"

Her parents go with her, their faith in her unquestioning.

"Warn your friends," Aura pants. "Tell as many people as you can!"

Aura finds Hayze in the chaos as another bunker near the wall succumbs to the intense heat and collapses. She can only hope whoever was inside managed to get out. Terrified residents run down the street with their hands on their heads, trying to stop their hair from catching fire as they cough and splutter in the blazing temperatures.

"We need to create a safe zone!" Hayze shouts. "A place the fire can't touch!"

Aura nods even though she's not sure what that's going to look like. She stands beside Hayze and they concentrate hard, raising their palms and drawing the heat and embers up and around them, leaving them standing in a protective bubble.

Grimacing, Aura works hard to expand the shield.

"Infernos!" Hayze shouts, his voice flying away in the wind. "Bring the people to us!"

Aura isn't sure how Infernos could possibly have heard Hayze, but it seems he did.

As their bubble of safety grows, the people of the Fire Quadrant run into it, falling to the ground in relief as they draw clean, cool air into their lungs and nurse their burns.

"I am Fire!" Hayze shouts, his hands waving wildly as they create more space for anyone seeking refuge.

"I am Fire!" Aura imagines the shield expanding down the street, welcoming the people in with the comfort of a mother's embrace.

The handful of people they're protecting soon grows to a dozen. Then more come to them, including their parents, until there are hundreds of people gathered in the street, not understanding what's keeping them safe but prepared to accept it all the same.

"Where's Infernos?" someone calls out.

Aura tries not to be distracted by this question. If she lets her concentration slip, this entire group of people will meet a fiery end. She waves her palms, drawing the heat and smoke of the firestorm out of the air, sending it to a faraway place where it can do no harm.

Finally, Infernos stumbles into the bubble of safety. He's covered in ash, his leather suit torn and melted, hanging off him in shreds, his dark hair completely scorched away.

The people rush to help him as he falls to the ground, praising him as their leader and the last of the village to make it to safety.

Aura doesn't respect Infernos.

But she does respect what he just did.

"Hold steady," Hayze warns, sensing her distraction. "It's about to pass over us."

Aura's hands shake as the power surges in her palms.

"I am Fire!" she shouts again, hearing Hayze echo her words.

They pour everything they have into their shield, keeping it intact and the people safe as the roar of the firestorm surges over them. The sound is deafening. The heat is oppressive. The panic is palpable.

But Aura and Hayze remain calm.

Because they are Fire.

They are the Solution.

Which is nothing to be ashamed of.

Aura's never felt more proud.

SIX

HAYZE

T he absence of heat is like a vacuum, sucking away the remnants of the firestorm's fury, leaving behind only a haunting stillness. Hayze lowers his arms as Aura does the same and they execute a slow turn. Neither of them says a word. Their throats are too dry. Their bodies too exhausted.

And their minds too astounded.

The village has been razed to the ground. The bunkers that have protected the people of this village for as long as it's existed are gone. The cement domes were supposed to be indestructible. The level of heat needed to incinerate dozens of homes is unimaginable.

Yet, it happened.

And Hayze and Aura ensured there were minimal casualties as a firestorm born in hell itself swept through.

Infernos staggers to his feet, his dark face streaked with ash, reminding Hayze he and Aura weren't the only ones saving lives. No one would've left their bunker without Infernos. The leader blinks, looks around, then grins.

"We did it!"

Hayze does the same. He blinks. Looks around once more.

Then breaks into a smile.

Aura leaps into his arms the same moment he opens them. They clasp each other, laughing freely and joyously. Hayze spins on the spot, the world of ash and dirt blurring around them.

When he stops, Aura clasps his face, gazing up at him as she smiles. "We did it."

They are the Solution.

A slap lands on Hayze's shoulder, and he releases Aura and turns, expecting to see his father. Except it's Infernos, a flap of leather hanging open at his shoulder. He nods at both of them, moisture glinting in his eyes. Hayze and Aura nod back. The stillness amplifies, grows heavy.

Something is rising like a phoenix from the ashes of the firestorm.

The fragile beginnings of an alliance.

"Sweet blazes, what was that?" someone croaks behind them.

Hayze turns to answer, only to be enveloped in a fierce hold from his mother and father. There's a cry and sob and Aura's hugging hers. A wave of relief courses through the people of the village as they rush to hold loved ones. Children cry as they cling to their parents, men and women check and double check their partners are unhurt.

Aura slips under Hayze's arm and he draws her in close. They watch the people, *their* people, rejoice and celebrate. Hayze has never felt prouder. Like he's found his purpose.

They are Fire.

Hayze's mother wipes her tears, leaving dark streaks across her cheeks, then turns to where her bunker once stood. "Our home," she whispers.

It's a puddle of cracked cement.

Another woman behind her looks around, her hand to her mouth. "There's nothing left."

As the joy of surviving ebbs, the realization they've lost everything is sinking in.

Infernos raises his arms as he turns in a slow circle. "You have the most important things of all—your lives and each other."

"As always, you speak the truth," Aura's mother murmurs, bowing her head.

The other villagers nod, some couples linking hands, a few mothers and fathers drawing their children close. Even Hayze's parents can't begrudge the leader the truth of that statement.

"And you're alive because your leaders sought to ensure we will never be at the mercy of Mother Nature again," Infernos continues, his voice confident and commanding. He waves an arm in the direction of Hayze and Aura. "We created the Elemental Solution."

Every face turns to them, eyes wide in soot-streaked faces. A soft murmur rises.

"They saved us."

"They protected us from a fire hot enough to collapse bunkers."

"They're the Elemental Solution."

A mixture of hope and awe, maybe a tinge of worship, lights every face gazing at them. Hayze's breath catches in his throat, unsure how to react. This feels good. Like the beginning of a new era.

And yet it doesn't quite fit.

Infernos lowers his arms. "My people, now is the time to take this second chance with gratitude and enthusiasm. Go forth and find tunnels that haven't filled with crumbled cement, they will be your shelter. Rebuilding the bunkers will be the first priority."

For the first time, Hayze thinks of the rebel tunnels. Infernos has no idea Hayze's parents and a handful of others could make their way as far as the Sect. What will the rebels do after the revelation of the Solution?

In fact, it's Hayze and Aura's parents who rush forward the moment Infernos is finished. "We need to talk to our son—"

Infernos raises a hand. "We must return to the Sect." He ushers Hayze and Aura away. "There is much to be done."

They have to find out if the other teens were successful in saving their Quadrants.

They have to discuss what this means.

Hayze looks over his shoulder, wishing he could communicate this to his parents, even as he knows he can't. His father is holding his mother as they both watch him with the one person they'll never trust—the Fire leader.

The man Hayze just sided with to save their lives.

"We're proud of you, Aura!" her father calls out.

"We love you so much!" her mother adds, a blazing smile on her face.

Aura waves back and blows them a kiss before glancing at Hayze. She knows this is hard for him. That he's torn.

"Hurry," Infernos says, his voice low. "We have to get back."

Hayze frowns. "What's the rush? My parents need our help." And some reassurance he hasn't aligned with the enemy.

Even though he thinks he may have...

Infernos flashes an angry glare. "Your village is one of many across the Quadrants. Your parents aren't the only ones whose lives are at stake." Guilt flashes through Hayze, a hot fire of emotion trying to rival the firestorm. He turns to his parents. "I'll be back," he promises. "I love you."

His mother smiles a little. His father scowls a lot. But there's no time to think about it because Infernos has broken into a jog. Hayze and Aura do the same, and as the man keeps up the steady pace, Hayze realizes he was never going to lose the Fire leader in the frantic run here. Infernos is clearly fit.

The run back is vastly different to the journey here. There's no dust. No desiccating heat. There's...nothing. The Scorchlands have been *scorched*. The wall surrounding the village has collapsed. The black forest beyond has disappeared, incinerated as the firestorm swept over it. The ground is hard and cracked, black and parched. No scattering of charcoal. No ash. The heat was so intense the whole forest was razed into oblivion. It's like it never existed.

The sights seem to fuel Infernos because he increases his pace. Hayze and Aura are right beside him. If this is what happened to the Scorchlands, then how did the other Quadrants fare? The images Eterna showed them of the Quakelands are fresh in Hayze's mind. Was Geo able to save the people on their safezones? And Skylus in the Stormsphere? And then there's the Deadwaters, a place Aura now lives with the memories of. A supercell storm would be catastrophic there. Were Tempo and Pace able to quell it?

They reach the massive wall which keeps Ignis separate from the Scorchlands, discovering dozens of people are already here. They were crouched and tucked at the base of the gates, but the moment they see Infernos, they leap to their feet. "It was the worst firestorm so far!" someone cries. "Infernos, you must help us!"

Infernos holds up his hands, and the people stop. "I know. We were at the center of it."

A man shakes his head. "You couldn't have been. You wouldn't have survived. Our bunkers blistered!"

A teen next to him nods. "Ain't seen nothing like it in my life!"

"I wouldn't lie to you," Infernos says. "Visit the village yourself and see. It's proof we have a Solution."

Hayze and Aura glance at each other as they stand behind him. What's left of their homes is a testament to the dangers the people are facing, but also what the two of them are capable of.

They're the two people standing between these people's lives and death.

"Please, let us in," an old man begs, indicating toward the closed gates of the capital.

"My children," cries a woman. "At least take my children!"

A man scowls as his hands clench and unclench. "You can't keep us out forever." There's an energy to him that has Hayze wondering if he's part of the rebels.

Infernos stiffens. "Those who have earned it are always welcome in Ignis."

That has Hayze going still. His parents worked tirelessly all his life and weren't able to buy their entrance. Even after selling their child before he was even born...

"Now return to your villages," Infernos says, raising his voice. "Or return to the village I just told you about. There, you'll marvel at the wonders of the Elemental Solution."

He spins on his heel and strides toward the wall. Hayze and Aura hesitate, but then follow. Hayze tells himself their powers are useless in the face of these people's desperation. That their role is to protect and save on a much larger scale.

Sweet fractal. He's starting to sound like the leaders!

Infernos scans his hands over a sensor that Hayze can only make out now that he knows it's there and a door opens.

Infernos steps through, hurrying Hayze and Aura behind him, then slams it shut.

Shutting off the very people Hayze assumed he was fighting for.

"We'll find a way," Aura whispers, clearly as uneasy with what they just turned their backs on as he is.

Hayze takes her hand as they ascend the stairs that will take them to the top of the wall. "We have to."

The moment he reaches the top, Infernos breaks into a run again. Hayze is happy to follow, now keen to get back to the Sect. Aura's right beside him, the same determination he's feeling tightening her features.

They're fighting to save the people, just like Infernos is.

But they're also fighting for a world where there are no walls.

They've just entered the Sect when Tempo gasps. "You're back!"

Pace envelops Aura, then Hayze in a hearty hug and Tempo does the same. "Well?" Pace demands, pulling back. "What happened?"

"We protected the village," Aura says, growing an inch as she straightens. "There were very few casualties."

Pace whoops as he punches the air. "Us, too! No supercell storm ever stood a chance as we kept the ocean flat as glass."

"Impressive," Hayze says, trying to imagine what that would've looked like. Wind battering, rain pelting, yet a sea that refused to be ruffled by any of it.

"So is saving that many lives from a firestorm," Tempo says, smiling hard. She glances over her shoulder. "Or a storm *and* an earthquake."

Geo's a few feet away, standing back, although he's grinning. "We went underground once I excavated a cave. One the earthquakes couldn't touch."

Hayze grins right back. "Frenius." The people would've been safe from everything Mother Nature was throwing at them. He sees Skylus is to Geo's left. "And the people of the Stormsphere were safe?"

She smoothes her robes. "Of course they were." She flicks a glance at Cyclonis. "And he actually got there in time to see it."

The leaders are to the right, standing side by side. Cyclonis nods. "I certainly saw that the Solution we created was exactly what we intended it to be." Although the words are a reminder of the trials and tribulations that brought them to this moment, he's grinning. Widely.

Avalan steps forward and extends her arms, her crown of flowers and leaves and feathers practically vibrating with pride. "You saved hundreds, possibly thousands of lives."

Hayze's own pride swells, despite all the reasons this is far from perfect. His parents are alive. So are Aura's. So are the people in their village. Right now, that's a victory.

And the leaders were part of that triumph.

With a happy gasp, Tempo throws herself into Pace's arms. He lifts her until her feet leave the floor, then spins as they both laugh. Skylus's tinkling giggle joins them, quickly followed by Geo's chuckle. The leaders smile. Oceania's eyes mist over. Infernos impulsively grabs Cyclonis in a tight clasp.

Hayze draws Aura into his arms, their own joy weaving its warmth around them. He wishes they were alone so they could really celebrate this. Then try to understand exactly what this means.

Maybe this alliance is the answer.

Maybe this is the Solution.

He ducks down, conscious there's still a piece missing. "What about Jewel?" he whispers. Not only should she be here to celebrate this, but she's now as essential as the rest of them.

Air only has Skylus, they can't afford for Earth to be one down, too.

To his surprise, Aura stiffens. "I can't tell you," she whispers back, her hands fisting against his chest. "Not yet."

Hayze draws back an inch, as if the words just wedged themselves between them. "You can tell me anything."

Aura simply gazes back. It takes him a few seconds, but he realizes what she's not saying. He kept his role in the rebels a secret from her. And he did it because he thought it was the right thing to do.

Is that what Aura's doing? The right thing is to keep a secret?

He lets out a breath and unwinds his body, drawing her in close. "I can wait," he murmurs against her hair, telling himself he doesn't have a choice. He has to trust Aura.

Aura wraps her arms around his waist and squeezes. "Thank you."

He wants to tell her she needs to be safe, but he's conscious the leaders have fallen quiet.

Avalan claps her hands to get the other teens' attention as they continue to celebrate, her face still soft with happiness. "You must rest," she says, indicating toward another door. "Tomorrow is when the real work begins."

Hayze frowns. "There's another storm coming?" So soon?

Oceania shakes her head. "This is far more important."

More important than what the teens in this room just achieved?

"You're evidence that the Solution works." Avalan inclines her head, her dark eyes glinting with something Hayze can't place. "Which means it's time for Phase Two."

SEVEN

AURA

"Phase Two?" Aura instinctively steps closer to Hayze.

Avalan nods. "That's right."

"We're not going back in the Games," growls Geo.

"That's right." Tempo nods as Pace puts a protective arm around her. "So, if that's what you mean, you can forget about it."

"That's not what she means," says Oceania, smiling sweetly. "The Games have served their purpose for you. There's no point sending you back in there."

"Then what do you need from us?" Skylus asks. "How may our vital skills be of service?"

Infernos clears his throat. He glances at the other leaders, who nod, giving him permission to speak on their behalf.

"You proved today just how valuable you all are," he says. "You truly are the Solution we've been searching for all these years."

Aura can feel the tension in Hayze's body as they wait for the Fire leader to get to the point.

"Which is why we need to begin Phase Two," Infernos continues, his face still blackened from the fire and his clothes torn. "First light tomorrow, after we've had some well-earned rest."

"What's Phase Two?" Hayze asks, glaring at the Fire leader. "We can't agree to a plan if we don't know what the fractal it involves."

"This is supposed to be a partnership," Pace growls. "Withholding information indicates you still think you're in charge."

"Patience." Infernos holds up a hand. "I'm about to tell you."

"Then get on with it," Pace snaps. "Like you said, we all need rest."

Aura shoots Tempo a sympathetic look. They're all tired. It's no wonder their patience is being stretched to the limit.

"As you've become aware, there are others who came before you," Infernos continues. "Two volunteers from each Quadrant have been entered into the Games for many years now."

"We didn't volunteer," Geo points out. "And neither did they."

Infernos waves a hand. "Your parents volunteered you. That's the same thing."

Aura opens her mouth to argue further but closes it again, deciding it's more important to listen than to continue an argument they'll never agree on.

"Every single year, all eight teens failed the Games," Infernos says. "Until this year, when almost all of you harnessed your powers."

Sadness hits Aura as she remembers Atmos and how easily the leaders cast him aside when he failed to control his Element.

"So, what's Phase Two?" Hayze asks again, his fists clenched at his sides. "Get to the point."

"It's the acceleration phase." Oceania steps forward.

"I was just getting to that," Infernos snaps.

"Yeah, pretty slowly," Pace grumbles.

Oceania smiles. "In the acceleration phase, we call on all the teens aged thirteen and up who are currently in waiting. And we put them in the Games now."

Aura's jaw falls as she takes this in. "But that's..."

"Forty teens in total," Infernos finishes, doing the math for her. "If we have the same success as last time, with one dud per cohort, that will provide us with thirty-five new Solutions."

"No!" Skylus shoots several inches off the floor and glares at Infernos. "*We* are the Solution. Nobody will ever be as powerful as us. You saw for yourselves that I'm the only one who can harness Air."

"This isn't about us," growls Geo.

"Exactly," says Aura. "It's about those unsuspecting kids they're talking about putting into the Games."

Hayze nods. "We won't agree to this. It's cruel. Nobody will ever be taken from their home against their will and subjected to that ever again. Not on our watch."

Cyclonis shakes his head, running his fingertips down his long, gray beard. "You saw for yourself today what's happening to the world. How long do you think you're going to be able to contain the Elements to keep everyone safe? The next storm will be worse. And the one after that will be worse again."

"That's right," says Avalan. "There will come a point where one of you doesn't survive."

"You may be powerful." Cyclonis looks at Skylus as she returns to the floor. "But you're still human. You won't live forever."

"Then we find another way to do this," Hayze insists. "Which is what we've been saying all along."

Aura nods, as proud of Hayze as she always is. "We need to find a kinder way forward. An honest way."

Infernos chuckles. "Have you learned nothing this whole time?"

"What do you mean?" Pace asks. "I think it's pretty clear we've learned a lot. More than you have if this is what you're seriously suggesting."

Infernos shakes his head. "The whole idea of the Games is for the volunteers to believe their lives are at risk. If we're *honest* then nobody will harness their powers. It will be nothing more than a scary computer game."

"You're the ones who called it a Game," Pace mutters. "And stop calling us volunteers! We never asked for any of this."

"Why don't we call for actual volunteers then?" Oceania suggests.

The other three leaders' heads turn sharply toward her. Clearly, that wasn't in the script.

"We can only put eight participants in at a time anyway," Oceania continues, pointing to the pods. "Let's call the forty teens here and explain we need volunteers to help us with a very important mission. And we see who offers their help."

"You mean tell them half the truth?" asks Aura.

"That's a step up from the total lies we were told," says Tempo.

"You like this plan?" Hayze's brows shoot up in surprise.

Tempo shrugs. "We did well today, but the leaders are right. Next time we might not be so successful. We need more help."

Aura can't help but wonder if Tempo came close to losing Pace in today's storm. If there were more teens with Elemental powers, it would significantly reduce the risk of them coming to harm. She looks at Hayze, her heart swelling with love yet still knowing that's not reason enough to put other innocent lives at stake.

"We can't agree to this," says Geo. "Consent is non-negotiable."

Aura and Hayze nod their agreement. Trust may have been built with the leaders during the storm, but it appears they're still miles away from reaching an alliance.

Cyclonis holds up a hand. "It's time to rest. We'll decide what to do at first light."

Aura wants to object, but the ache deep in her bones tells her he's right. It's hard to think straight, let alone make such important decisions when she's this tired.

"There's a room with bunks you can use," says Oceania.

"Where will you be?" Hayze narrows his eyes.

"We can rest in our offices," says Avalan. "Surely, after all we just went though, you don't think we'll abandon you?"

Hayze sighs, looking at Aura, who nods her agreement. The leaders aren't going anywhere. They're just as exhausted as they are.

Oceania leads them out of the pod room and through a series of doors to a room with four sets of bunks and a small bathroom beside it. It's only basic but luxurious compared to anything they've had access to recently.

There's a loaf of bread and a bowl of fruit on a table at the side of the room, and the teens share it out while negotiating time in the bathroom to get cleaned up. Nobody speaks about what the leaders proposed, even though it's clear it's the only thing any of them can think about. Talking is for the morning. Now is for recharging.

Skylus is the first to fall asleep, having flown up to one of the top bunks and rolling over to turn her back to them all. Geo crawls into the bottom bunk opposite her and pulls the blanket over his head.

Aura snuggles in beside Hayze on one of the bottom bunks, while Tempo climbs up the ladder of another set, swatting Pace away playfully when he tries to follow, telling him she needs her rest.

Hayze curves himself around Aura and she presses her back to his front, not having felt this content since they spent the night together in Calla's treehouse.

Within minutes, everyone is asleep.

Except Aura.

Her eyes sting with fatigue and her body begs for a reprieve from the non-stop action she's put it through, but she knows she must hold onto consciousness for a little longer than everyone else.

Because she has a job to do.

She needs to talk to Avalan. It's time to tell Jewel the truth. If a group of consenting teens are added to the Games tomorrow, Jewel is going to wonder where they came from. And why she's still there. This has gone on long enough. Jewel needs to know not just how she's different, but why.

Then Aura can tell Hayze. Keeping this secret from him is torture. The fact he so willingly trusted her when she said she couldn't tell him what happened to Jewel only made it infinitely worse. It's a reminder he's a better person than she is. Because she almost walked away from everything they have when she caught him keeping secrets from her. But that was before the Games. Back when they were different people. She'd like to think she'd trust him now.

She wriggles forward and Hayze tightens his grip on her, moaning softly in his sleep. Trying again, this time she manages to move a little away from him, then waits a few minutes before shuffling forward again. She could wake him and explain where she's going. But then he won't sleep worrying about her and he needs his rest. There's no sense in both of them having a sleepless night.

Eventually, she manages to get herself out of the bed and tiptoes out the door. If she can find Avalan, she'll be back beside Hayze before first light. She might even manage a few hours of precious sleep herself.

Using the soft glow from the screens that line the walls of the hallways, Aura makes her way to Avalan's office, hoping she has the right room. Knowing the sensor beside the door will be useless, she knocks quietly.

The door immediately slides open and Avalan greets her with a smile.

"I knew you'd come," she says. "Jewel was right to choose you."

"Choose me?" Aura asks, allowing herself to be ushered into the small room.

"As her friend." Avalan puts a hand on her arm. "She could see the kindness in your heart."

"Jewel's not real," says Aura firmly.

"Then why do you care so much about telling her the truth?" Avalan asks.

"Because..." Aura doesn't have an answer for that. Telling Jewel shouldn't matter. Perhaps this is more about closure for herself?

"You care because she's real to us," Avalan says gently. "And that's all that counts."

Aura nods, remembering what a good friend Jewel was to her in the Games. This isn't about Aura. It's about Jewel. However she was created, she's part of this world.

"How does this work?" Aura asks. "I need to be back before Hayze realizes I've gone. I don't want him to worry."

"Would you like to leave him a message?" Avalan asks.

"Is that necessary?" Aura tilts her head. "Isn't this just a case of pressing a few buttons so Jewel can hear me? I've talked to her while she's been in the Games before."

"Oh no, no, no, no, no, no!" Avalan tuts. "You can't deliver news like that over nothing more than a speaker. That's far too impersonal."

"But how else can I talk to her?" Aura rubs at her tired head, wishing she could think more clearly.

Avalan marches to her desk and presses a button. The wall of her office that displayed images of Jewel the last time Aura was in here rises into a cavity in the ceiling, revealing a small room with a pod.

Aura takes a step toward the door she only just came through. "I'm not going back into the Games. We never agreed on that. You said I had to tell Jewel. That's all. You never said anything about this."

"Aura, my sweet girl." Avalan returns to her and looks her directly in the eye. "There's nothing to fear. Jewel has returned to her home. She's back with her mother. When I connect you to her via the pod, that's where you'll go. No Games. Just Jewel, waiting for you to tell her the truth. Then you can come straight back here."

"Hayze is waiting for me," Aura insists. "I'm sorry, but I can't do it. You'll need to tell her yourself."

"That's your choice." Avalan nods. "Just let me show you something first."

Before Aura can agree or disagree, Avalan presses another button and the wall beside them lights up with an image of Jewel. She's sitting outside a small home with tall trees all around her in a perfect virtual replica of the Quakelands. Tears are streaming down her cheeks as she peers in the direction of the forest.

"This is live footage," says Avalan.

"What's wrong?" Aura asks. "Why is she crying?"

"She's waiting for someone," Avalan says.

"Rateen." Aura reaches out a hand, wanting to give her friend a hug. "She still thinks she's her mother."

"No," says Avalan. "Not Rateen."

"Aura." Jewel holds out her own hand, mirroring Aura's stance even though she can't see her. "Where are you?"

"I'm here," Aura whispers. "I'm right here."

Jewel shakes her head. "You left me."

"Can she hear me?" Aura asks in surprise.

"No." Avalan walks over to the pod. "But if you'd allow me to connect you, then she could."

Aura takes another step away. "But Ha—"

"Hayze is asleep." Avalan puts a hand on the membrane of the pod. "You can record him a message if it makes you feel better. But I assure you that you'll be back before he wakes."

Aura returns her gaze to the image of Jewel on the screen and her heart tears in two. She can't leave Hayze. But how can she leave Jewel thinking she abandoned her when nothing could be further from the truth? If only she had some sleep, she could think more clearly.

"Aura," Avalan prompts. "It's your decision."

Jewel breaks down into sobs, holding her head in her hands and collapsing to the dirt in front of her virtual home.

It's too much. This whole situation is just... Too. Much.

Aura forces her trembling legs to walk to the pod.

She needs to trust Avalan.

If she doesn't, she'll spend the rest of her life haunted by the image of Jewel calling out her name.

"Okay," she tells the Earth leader. "I'll do it. Send me to Jewel."

EIGHT

HAYZE

Reality filters in slowly as sleep releases its hold on Hayze. He hears Tempo's muffled giggle followed by Pace's attempt to shush her. He registers the absence of smell he now associates with the sterile Sect. Soft light caresses his eyelids, telling him it's morning.

Then he feels the cool sheet beside him.

Hayze shoots out of bed. "Aura!" he gasps, looking around frantically.

They fell asleep holding each other. It was the perfect ending to a tumultuous day where they achieved so much, yet started something they had no idea existed.

Phase Two.

"Where is she?" he roars. The bed they shared is now empty.

The other beds in the room either contain his friends, blinking and confused, or are just as vacant.

"Where is she?" he demands again, sprinting out of the room.

"Hayze!" Pace calls behind him, but he doesn't slow his

frantic run down the corridor. He shoves through doors, uncaring of the noise he's making. He wants the leaders to wake up.

He wants them to know they've unleashed the fury of Fire.

Bursting into the main room, Hayze discovers Avalan is already waiting for him. Still and steady as an ancient tree, she gazes at him. "Good morning."

"You know where she is," Hayze growls, breathing hard despite the short run. Adrenaline is firing through his veins, heating his whole body. Avalan has one chance to bring Aura back to him or the feathers in her headdress are about to be little more than ash.

"Aura's talking to Jewel," Avalan says calmly. "She left you a message so you wouldn't worry."

She steps to the side as the screen behind her flickers to life, revealing Aura. She has dark circles under her eyes, her shoulders are curved and tight, her face a shade too pale. Exactly the way she looked last night.

Exhausted but beautiful.

"Hey," she says, gazing at him as if there isn't the distance of the unknown between them. "I'm going to talk to Jewel so this can all be resolved." Aura's lips lift an inch. "And then I'll be back, telling you everything I know."

Hayze takes an involuntary step forward. Where the fractal has she gone?

"I just have to do this first. The right thing." This time Aura smiles, the soft, breath-taking smile only he's ever been graced with. "I love you."

The screen goes blank, taking on the same neutral glow all the others have. Avalan steps back into view, inclining her head. "See? She's fine."

Hayze scowls. "How do I know that's real?" They've assumed so many things are real and they've been far from it.

69

"Because virtual reality can't mimic that kind of emotion," Avalan says. "There's a nuance to deep human connection that we have yet to capture with artificial intelligence."

The door behind Hayze bursts open and he already knows it's Pace and Tempo.

"Where's Aura?" Pace demands.

"What have you done with her?" Tempo half-shouts.

Avalan glances at Hayze. He sighs, rubbing his forehead. "Apparently Aura's gone to talk to Jewel. She'll be back soon."

Pace unwinds as his gaze darts between Hayze and Avalan. "Okay." The single word is weighed with caution. Pace is echoing Hayze's sentiments.

He'll play along until Aura's back, as promised.

Or they have the slightest proof the Earth leader is lying.

Geo bursts in a moment later, Skylus floating serenely behind him. Avalan smiles at them graciously. "I'm glad you're all here. Aura will be joining us as soon as she's finished talking to Jewel, which means you'll need to be the welcoming committee."

Hayze's eyes dart around the room. "Welcoming committee?"

Last night's conversation comes back in a flood.

The acceleration phase.

We call on all the teens aged thirteen and up who are currently in waiting. And we put them in the Games now.

Hayze's muscles tighten, ready to fight for what's right. "You haven't agreed no one will be put in the Games without their consent. There is no acceleration phase."

His answer is the sound of Infernos's booming voice. "Come, this way."

And the clatter of dozens of feet slapping on stairs.

The door opens. "This," Infernos says with flair, "is the true Sect."

A large group of teens fill the room, all wide eyed and open-mouthed. A portion are wearing the blue suits of Water, some are wearing the strategic straps of Earth, others are wearing the purple robes of Air. And the remaining quarter are wearing the red leather of Fire.

"Hayze?"

He spins around. The girl gaping at him is someone he knows well. "Pyra?"

She smiles widely, running and throwing her arms around him before he can move. "Hayze!"

He clasps her back, in part automatically, in part to be polite.

Pyra was a friend growing up. She used to help him paint.

She's also the one who betrayed the rebels to Infernos.

She pulls back, grinning. "I'm so glad you're here."

Hayze is saved from responding because Cyclonis claps his hands sharply. "Welcome," he intones, clearly going for the sober, wise look as he raises his hands like a messiah. "It's a pleasure to have brought you here."

The teens are still blinking and looking around. They're surrounded by a level of technology they didn't know existed. Right now, they have some sense of how Hayze felt when he woke up on a raft, alone. But at least their world still exists. And they know how they got here.

Oceania nods, beaming. "You are very special, young people."

A girl in Air robes sniffs delicately. "I've never been special," she whispers.

"And yet you always have been, Indra," Cyclonis says, his eyes soft as he turns to her.

Her gaze snaps up at the use of her name. "You know who I am?"

It's Infernos who nods. "We've been watching you since the moment you were born."

Hayze grits his teeth. The leaders have been part of these teens' lives long before that.

"That's a bit creepy," someone mutters.

Hayze glances over, registering a thin boy in a Water suit. His dark hair flops over his eyes, which are darting around as his body practically vibrates with tension.

"Kai," Oceania says softly. "I understand you're scared."

"I'm really not," he mutters back.

"But there's no need to be," she continues. "You're safe here."

Hayze steps forward, deciding to stop hedging. "You'll never have to do anything you don't want to do." He throws a glance at each of the leaders, daring them to say otherwise.

"Exactly," Avalan says smoothly. "We've brought you here to offer you a wonderful opportunity to help your Quadrants."

Pyra draws in a breath, looking at him like she's now hanging on every word. Hayze pretends he doesn't notice. He's not sure how he feels about the girl he assumed was a friend. A friend he trusted.

"Sure you have," Kai mumbles under his breath. "I'm just here because you promised food."

An Earth boy throws a fist into the air. "For the Quakelands!"

The teens from the other Quadrants scowl at him. "For the Deadwaters!" a Water girl cries.

"For the Stormsphere!" Indra quickly follows.

"For the Scorchlands," Pyra snaps.

Cyclonis beams at the show of patriotism, no matter how divided it is. "And you can do something very special for your Quadrants."

The teens fall silent, seeming to realize they're about to learn exactly why they're here.

"As you know," Avalan says, her dark gaze roaming over their faces. "The storms, the quakes, the fires are getting worse. The Quadrants are in trouble. Even the capitals are no longer safe."

The silence thickens. A few teens swallow, some drop their gaze to stare at their feet. They live the hardships of the Quadrants. They see, breathe, taste the poverty and desperation.

"Which is why a Solution was necessary," Oceania says, smiling softly. "You."

Some teens draw back in disbelief, including Indra. Some scowl like Kai. Many lift their chins in pride and interest. Including Pyra.

Avalan nods slowly. With emphasis. "You've been gifted with the power of the Elements."

The same shock and skepticism and excitement ripples through the teens.

"I really am special?" Indra whispers.

"I can wield Fire?" Pyra gasps, gazing at her hands.

Kai crosses his arms. "Not possible."

The leaders turn to Hayze and the others simultaneously. "Show them," Avalan orders quietly.

Hayze bristles, but Skylus has already complied. She floats a couple of feet off the floor, then executes a graceful turn. The teens collectively gasp, which only encourages her. She twirls faster, her robes arcing out like petals of a purple flower. Indra claps enthusiastically and the other Air teens join her.

Tempo angles her chin, unwilling to be outshone. With a wave of her hands, she forms a floating bubble of water. The teens fall silent again. Beside her, Pace grins, creating his own shimmering orb. They glance at each other, then move closer together. The two bubbles lengthen, becoming floating rivers.

The two strands weave around each other, twining and glistening. An impossibility that's undeniably real.

With a quick snap of Pace and Tempo's wrists, the dual strands unwind and shoot over the teens. Another flick and the water explodes out, making them duck. But it's soft flakes of snow that float down, melting on motionless heads and open mouths.

For the first time, Kai's speechless.

Geo steps forward, then promptly drops to press his hands on the floor. Ripples expand from his palms, quickly growing in size as they roll toward the teens. They gasp and grab hold of each other, the snowflakes forgotten.

They're now standing on shifting ground.

The ripples grow to small, pulsing waves. The teens bob as if they're standing on the surface of the sea. They look fascinated and terrified.

Geo stands abruptly, smiling a little as the floor stops moving. He steps back, tucking himself a little behind Skylus. He's finished with his show of powers.

All eyes turn to Hayze.

He hesitates, feeling like this is all moving too fast. The teens need to understand what the Games involve before seeing the impressive stuff.

Yet everyone's waiting.

And the Quadrants need help.

So he closes his eyes. Clenches his hands.

And *becomes* Fire.

Hayze hears the shocked intakes of breath. Hears Pace whisper 'nice one' as he steps back, no doubt taking Tempo with him. He knows he's now a human torch.

But all he does is feel.

The heat surrounding him. The heat within him. The heat

he controls so others can see the ferocious strength of Fire, but not lose their eyebrows.

Smiling a little, he unclenches his hands. The next round of gasps is a foot further away because the fire just grew. He twitches his fingers. The heat curls around him. He pictures the flames weaving and dancing, twisting and curling in shades of crimson and blood and sunshine.

A quick clenching of his hands and it all disappears. Hayze opens his eyes to see the teens all looking at him, mouths agape. Pyra's the first to move, lifting her hands up high as she bursts into a round of applause. The other teens join her, now looking like they'd sign their souls over to the Games.

Which is exactly what Hayze didn't want.

Infernos pats the air, asking everyone to be quiet. "To be able to do this, you'll need to take part in the Elemental Games. Safe games controlled by a very powerful computer."

"This is your choice," Cyclonis adds. "The decision is yours."

Avalan lifts her arms in invitation. "Who would like to be part of the Games?"

Hands shoot up everywhere, even Kai's. The possibility of wielding such power has swayed even the doubters.

The leaders' smiles are identical.

Victorious.

Hayze watches as the teens turn to each other, already discussing what they could be capable of. Two invisible lines have been carved between them, meaning the group parallels the four Quadrants themselves. The Earth teens congratulate each other. The Water teens are hugging. The Air teens look like they're already floating. And the Fire teens are high-fiving, many of them glancing at Hayze.

A sense of responsibility settles around his shoulders. These young lives are here because he and Aura and the others forged the way. They unlocked the Elemental powers woven into their DNA without their knowledge.

Hayze vows these teens won't go through what he did. They won't be little more than a means to an end.

Each one of these souls counts, just like every soul in the Quadrants matters.

Oceania makes her way toward the door. "You must be hungry and thirsty. Come with me."

"We get fed?" Kai asks in wonder.

She chuckles. "Of course. We're here to take care of you."

The leaders exit the room, the teens close behind them. Skylus follows, then Geo, Pace and Tempo also joining. Skylus because she no doubt wants to keep an eye on the new competition, Geo out of cautious curiosity, and Pace and Tempo probably because they aren't ready to trust the leaders.

Hayze lets them leave, allowing the silence to settle around him, wishing peace came with it. Almost fifty vulnerable, trusting hearts just signed up to save the Quadrants. A new wave of Solutions is about to be placed in the Games.

And yet there's only one thought eclipsing his mind.

Aura hasn't returned.

CHAPTER

NINE

AURA

Aura opens her eyes in the forest of the Quakelands. Like the other times she woke in the Games, she feels strong and refreshed.

Except this isn't like them. Because those times she was connected to the pod without her consent. This time, it was her choice.

She stretches out, running her fingertips down arms that aren't real, standing on legs that are nothing more than a simulation. The air smells fresh with raindrops clinging to the delicate foliage of the trees.

Foliage that shouldn't be here after the catastrophic storm...

She steps forward, reminding herself that while the storm crossed the four Quadrants, it didn't reach here. Avalan protected Jewel, keeping her virtual world safe.

So Aura can enter it and blow it all up.

She steps out from beneath the canopy of trees, seeing no reason to delay what she has to do. She needs to get back to Hayze as soon as she can. Hopefully before he wakes, because she's really not sure she said everything she needed to in that hurried message she recorded before climbing into the pod.

Small homes made from timber dot the village before her and Aura scans those at the perimeter, looking for the house Avalan had shown her. They all look the same, so she continues forward, knowing if Jewel is still outside, she'll find Aura instead. Surely Avalan will have inserted her in this world somewhere close to where she needs to be?

There's a squeal of delight and a sudden flash of movement as Jewel comes running toward her.

For a few precious moments, Aura forgets Jewel isn't real and she breaks into a run. As she gets closer, she remembers. But she doesn't slow her steps. She missed her friend. So much. And after today, she'll continue to miss her. It's no different to losing someone you love when they die. Just because they no longer exist doesn't mean you don't ache to see them one more time.

"Aura!" Jewel pants, reaching her and throwing out her arms.

Aura embraces her friend, and they topple over, falling on the grass and laughing as their arms and legs tangle in a mess.

"I can't believe you're here!" Jewel props herself up and leans over Aura, smiling widely.

Aura sits, unable to help staring at Jewel, marveling at what perfection Avalan created. She's just like the little girl Aura saw in the images on the wall. Images of the real Jewel. The one who lived and breathed and was part of the same world as Aura.

"What's wrong?" Jewel takes Aura's hand and squeezes it. "Aren't you happy to see me?"

Realizing she must be frowning, Aura pulls her lips into a smile. "I'm always happy to see you."

"How did you get here?" Jewel asks, looking back toward the forest. "Where's Hayze? Is anyone else here?"

"It's just me," says Aura, unable to help herself from letting go of Jewel's hand to touch her cheek. "You're so..."

"You're beautiful, too, Aura," says Jewel, misunderstanding what she was going to say.

Aura doesn't correct her. How can she tell her she was going to say *real* not *beautiful*?

Jewel's eyes fill with tears and she leans in, pressing her lips to Aura's. At first, Aura isn't startled by this impulsive display of affection. Then Jewel's lips part as she tries to take the kiss to a new level, and Aura pulls back sharply.

"Jewel!" Her fingertips flutter to her mouth. "What are you doing?"

"I thought..." Jewel looks away, a flush staining her cheeks. "You said..."

"Oh, Jewel." The truth of the situation hits Aura, and embarrassment and confusion flood through her, answering questions she never thought to ask.

She loves Jewel.

But Jewel is *in love* with her.

How could she have read this so wrong?

"It's okay," says Jewel. "You love Hayze. I know that."

Aura nods, not wanting to point out that even if she didn't love Hayze, she wouldn't feel the way Jewel wants her to.

"All this time I thought you had a crush on Hayze." Aura smiles, touching Jewel gently on the arm to show she's not upset.

Jewel glances up and bursts into a fit of giggles. "Why would you think that?"

"You always seemed so upset when you'd find us kissing." Now Aura's the one with the flush in her cheeks as it becomes obvious why that was. Then she wonders if it's possible Avalan wanted Jewel to develop feelings for her and why that might be. Although, that doesn't seem possible. Matters of the heart can't be programmed. You either feel that way about someone or you don't.

"Hayze is cute," says Jewel. "If you like that kind of muscled, manly thing, which clearly you do."

"I do." Aura takes Jewel's hand again. "I love Hayze. Very much. And I love you, too. But as my very good friend. Is that okay?"

Jewel nods, avoiding eye contact but allowing Aura to hold her hand. "I'm just happy you're here at long last. I thought I was going to go mad without you."

"I can't stay for long," Aura says, needing to make this clear from the start so Jewel doesn't get her hopes up. "Avalan sent me to you so we could talk."

"Avalan?" Jewel's brows shoot up. "I don't understand."

A group of children walk past a few yards away and Aura gets to her feet, still amazed that this world is virtual.

"Is there somewhere we can talk?" she asks, even though it doesn't matter what the children might overhear, given they aren't real.

Jewel stands and points to the small home directly behind her. "My mother's out trading for food. We can talk in my house."

"Great." Aura's relieved Rateen isn't home. Their past history has been complicated, to say the least. She doesn't think she'll ever get the image out of her head of being attacked by dozens of Rateens at once while trying to escape in a lift.

Jewel leads her to the row of homes, keeping a bit more distance from Aura than she normally would. This makes Aura feel guilty, which in turn breeds slight resentment. She never did anything knowingly to lead Jewel on. She was only ever honest with her words and actions.

"Welcome to my home." Jewel opens her door and steps back for Aura to pass.

"Oh." Aura looks around at the small but comfortable space. Made from the prolific timber of the Quakelands, the room has a square table to one side and two beds with colorful quilts on the other. "It looks different in real life."

"What do you mean?" Jewel plonks down in a chair and motions for Aura to do the same.

Aura tries to think of how to explain, regretting her choice of words as she reminds herself this isn't real life.

"Avalan showed me some videos of you growing up here," she says carefully.

"But how?" Jewel looks around. "And why do you keep mentioning her?"

"Because she's been filming you." Aura leans forward, analyzing Jewel's reaction to this news. "Avalan's your mother."

Jewel's face goes from curious, to shocked, to one filled with horror and disbelief. "No. She's not my mother. My mom's gone to the traders market."

"That woman isn't your mother," Aura says, aware there's no way to take the sting out of these words. "Avalan's your mother."

Jewel shakes her head again, but her eyes remain wide as she waits for Aura to continue talking.

"Avalan was only young when she took over from her father as leader of the Earth Quadrant," Aura explains. "She was pregnant with you and felt she had to choose between her responsibilities as a mother and those she had as a leader."

Jewel crosses her arms as these hurtful words settle in the air.

"So, your father raised you," says Aura. "Avalan wanted you to grow up as a regular citizen of the Earth Quadrant to protect you from any rebel attacks. She wanted you to have a normal life."

Jewel shakes her head as tears stream down her cheeks. "But I didn't have a normal life. Everyone else had a mother. I thought mine came back for me after the quake."

"In a way, she did." Aura drags her chair closer to Jewel. "In many ways, she never left you in the first place. Didn't you ever wonder why your mother was so much older than your father? Too old perhaps, to even have had you?"

"Aura." Jewel's voice turns stern. "Be direct with me. Don't talk in code. What are you really trying to tell me?"

Aura swallows. "When your home collapsed in the quake, two people died."

Jewel narrows her eyes. "You're still talking in code."

"You died, Jewel," she says, each word feeling like acid burning on her tongue. "You and your father both died."

Jewel stares at Aura for several long seconds, before bursting out laughing. "Aura! What are you doing? That's not funny. Be serious."

Aura blinks at Jewel, her expression as dead as her heart feels right now. "I am being serious. You died, Jewel. You're not real."

Jewel stands, raises her hand, and slaps Aura hard across the face.

"Did that feel real?" she asks, her eyes burning with rage.

Aura sits in stunned silence, her only movement to put her hand to her burning cheek. She accepts the pain, somehow feeling like she deserved it. At the very least, she hopes it made Jewel feel better.

"I'm so sorry, Jewel," she whispers. "I didn't want to tell

you. Avalan insisted you'd take the news better if it came from me."

"Take the news better?" Jewel paces around her small home, shaking her head, clenching and unclenching her fists. The walls tremble and Aura draws in a breath, hoping Jewel can keep hold of her Earth powers and not bring the roof down on their heads. "Why would Avalan make up such lies?"

"Because it's true," Aura says, letting her hand fall back to her lap. "It broke Avalan's heart when you died. She said she missed your entire childhood. She couldn't bear to miss seeing you grow up as well. None of this is real, Jewel. She created this entire world for you. It's all a simulation. She even created...you."

"No!" Jewel draws to an abrupt halt and turns to Aura. "I'm real. This house is real. My mother's real. And she's not Avalan."

Aura shakes her head. "The woman who raised you is called Eterna. Sometimes known as Rateen. She's a sophisticated computer. Avalan programmed her—and you—without the other leaders' knowledge. She was so proud of you, she put you in the Games, confident you'd succeed."

"When my mom comes home, she'll tell you this isn't true." Jewel backs away from Aura with each word she spits out. "I don't know why, but you're making this up."

"Avalan calls you Gemma," Aura says, trying to think of some way to convince her.

"You heard her call me that in the arena when the leaders were in there with me." Jewel shakes her head. "Anyone could know that."

"Why do you think Avalan of all people called you that name?" Aura asks. "And she told you she loves you."

Jewel thinks about this but doesn't reply.

"She said Gemma means Jewel in Latin," Aura continues,

hoping she got the word right, still having no idea what it even means.

"Who told you that?" Jewel snaps.

Aura sighs. "Avalan told me. Your mother."

"You're a liar." Jewel makes a dash for the door and sprints out.

Aura leaps to her feet, prepared to make chase, but stops herself at the last moment. That didn't go to plan. At all. Jewel needs time to process this. She'll come home soon enough. Then they can talk some more. Hayze will be worried, but he'll just have to wait a little longer.

Going to the doorway, Aura steps outside, her eyes crinkling as she takes in what she sees.

The forest has vanished. Instead, white nothingness hovers in the distance like a heavy fog.

Aura walks forward, turning to survey the village. She gasps as she registers Jewel's house is the only one that remains. There's nothing here except a small wooden house, sitting in the middle of a world made from fog.

Avalan is trapping Jewel, preventing her from going anywhere except home.

"Aura!" Jewel calls in a shaky voice. "Aura, I'm scared."

"Where are you?" Aura walks forward, afraid to go too far in case she's swallowed by the nothingness. "Jewel? Follow my voice. I'm right here."

Jewel steps out of the fog into the ring of clear air that surrounds her home. She sees Aura and runs to her, seeming to forget she's upset with her.

Aura hugs her friend, making shushing sounds as she holds her close.

"What's going on?" Jewel asks. "I don't understand. We're not in the Games."

"Avalan wants you to talk to me," says Aura. "She's letting you know that what I'm telling you is true. None of this is real."

"I want my mom," Jewel sobs. "Where is she?"

"I don't know," says Aura, knowing she can't leave her yet. "But I'm here. I'll wait with you until your mother returns. Let's go inside."

Jewel links her hand with Aura's. "Don't ever leave me, Aura. It doesn't matter who I am or what I am. I'll be okay, as long as you're here."

As Aura follows Jewel inside. A feeling of intense foreboding snakes through her core, setting every one of her senses on alert.

Avalan didn't send her here to tell Jewel the truth. She sent her here as her companion. A gift for the daughter she felt so guilty for abandoning.

Worse still, nobody else knows Aura's here.

Not even Hayze.

Which means she has no way to get out.

CHAPTER
TEN

HAYZE

None of it matters.

Without Aura, Hayze doesn't have a world he wants to fight for.

Which is why he waits all of three seconds for the others to leave before executing a slow spin, wondering where he starts looking. He'll turn the Sect upside down and inside out to confirm whether Aura's here or not.

And if she's not, then he'll tear the four capitals apart. Then search every inch of the Quadrants.

The earth can continue spinning, the fight for freedom can continue once he's back by her side.

Hayze stops the slow turn. Every panel is the same—a neutral glow that gives the room a soft dawn feeling. Eterna is clearly taking a virtual nap. Not that it matters. She wouldn't help him. She's part of whatever this is.

The door on the other side beckons as he remembers Aura noticing this one contained less data, but he doesn't move. Aura registered a subtle difference and that allowed them to save time and find the way out so they could give Atmos the goodbye he deserved. Is there something he's not noticing? A clue?

Yet each panel is identical, each one containing as much information as it does color.

Hayze stops, frowning. The door behind him leads to the pod room. How long before a new batch of teens are led in there to be tested? He pushes the question away. He can't think about that right now. They've ensured their consent and their safety. Right now, Aura is the priority.

But the thought plants a seed. What if more of these panels are doors? What if they all are more than just a way for Eterna to show her prophecies of doom and destruction? Unwillingly, the images they once contained assault Hayze. They've been branded in his gray matter, painfully embedded amongst the folds. A person can't see that scale of loss and forget.

There wasn't a Quadrant, let alone a life that will be spared.

Hayze finds himself executing another slow turn.

Water.

Air.

Fire.

Earth.

Each one battered and decimated to nothing.

The four quarters of the room were divided into the four Quadrants, mirroring the world beyond. And each time it was the same. Hayze finds himself spinning to the right. Water. Another quarter turn. Air. Another. Fire. And then Earth.

The panels really do mirror the outside world. Does that mean...

He strides forward, focused on the panel directly in front of him. The one that would be the middle of the Earth panels. He pushes on the edge, hoping it'll depress like the other door did. It doesn't budge. Setting his jaw with determination, he scans his Fire tattoo. There's a faint *beep* and his heart jolts with excitement.

Then nothing.

He tries again. *Beep*. Nothing.

And again. *Beep*. Nothing.

He's not allowed to enter. Whatever's on the other side isn't something he has permission to see.

"Damnatus," Hayze snarls. He needs to get into that room. He can feel it in his gut.

"Hayze?" asks a soft voice.

He spins around, registering Pyra standing on the other side of the room, the door to the Sect beyond closing behind her.

"You should be with the others."

She shakes her head. "I wanted to talk." She takes a step forward. "To explain."

"Look, Pyra, I don't really have time to—"

"You know I betrayed the rebels."

"Yes, I do," he says, a scowl drawing down his brow.

She continues to walk toward him, stopping a few feet away. "I didn't have a choice."

He has to stop himself from crossing his arms. "I'm getting a bit tired of hearing that excuse."

Pyra's cheeks flush a dull red. "It's my mom. She's...not well."

"I'm sorry to hear that," he says automatically, trying not to think of the older woman who once proudly gave him a piece of rock with a jagged vein of blue running through it, saying she uncovered it while mining.

He ground that stone down so his paintings could finally capture the shifting shades that are Aura's eyes.

"She was so determined to buy me entrance to Ignis." Pyra's shoulders sag. "But then she started coughing. Every night's been the same. She thinks I don't see the bloodstains on the sheets, but I do."

She won't have long left. Spending hard days underground mining for coal takes its toll, just as mining for edrian does in the Deadwaters. But it's the lungs of the people in the Scorchlands that turn black, not their fingers.

"Look, Pyra—"

She takes another step forward. "And with Dad gone... We needed edrian to trade. Infernos said he'd pay for information." Her eyes turn from sad to pleading. "I couldn't watch her starve to death."

Tell her to come to me. I'll reward her greatly for any more information she can provide.

Hayze's breath is trapped in his chest, cut off by the tightness in his throat. Pace's parents did things they never would've in the name of family. The rebels are willing to start a war in the name of freedom.

Hayze is about to turn his back on this fight in the name of love.

Are any of them that different?

He huffs, pushing the air out along with any anger or resentment he felt for Pyra. "I get it. We do what we believe is right."

Which is what Aura did.

And he has an awful feeling the decision has cost her more than she bargained for.

"Is it true?" Pyra asks, her voice breathy and fragile, as if the truth is as frail as life itself. "Can we..."

Hayze lifts his hand and opens his palm, revealing a dancing flame. Pyra's eyes grow as her jaw slackens. She reaches out to touch it, trembling, as if she wants to nurse it too, but draws back with a wince and a hiss. Pressing her fingers into her mouth, her gaze connects once more with Hayze's.

She's realizing fire is part of him, it can't burn him. When it's deadly to anything and anyone else.

"Aura can do it, too," he says.

And maybe now Pyra, along with the other Fire hopefuls who have been brought in.

She's smiling as a tear tracks down her coal-streaked face, leaving behind a pale, uneven line. "This could change everything."

He doesn't point out it already has.

"Pyra."

Her name cracks through the room with force, making her jump and spin around. Infernos crosses his arms then tightens them, making his newly replaced leather suit creak. Hayze suspects he did that for dramatic emphasis.

"The first eight to enter the Games were just chosen." He scowls. "And you weren't there when your name was called out."

"I'm going in?" Pyra gasps. "I could be able to—" She stops abruptly. Straightens. And nods.

He arches a brow.

"Thank you, Infernos," she whispers, ducking her head and darting through the open door behind him. She glances back once, flashing Hayze the barest of smiles.

He doesn't move. Pyra is about to follow in his footsteps, and he's not sure how he feels about that.

"Why aren't you with the others?" Infernos asks him once they're alone, his scowl returning.

"Where's Aura?" Hayze demands, throwing the question back before the Fire leader is finished.

Infernos draws back, the scowl deepening. "I thought she needed her rest." His gaze darts behind him. "She's not here?"

The response is unexpected enough for Hayze's own scowl to mirror Infernos's. Not only that, it seems genuine. "You didn't know she's gone?"

"When?"

"Sometime after I fell asleep last night," Hayze says. "When I woke up, Aura was nowhere to be found."

"And you're telling me this now?" Infernos almost shouts.

"Avalan told me Aura left to talk to Jewel. Apparently she'll be back soon." Hayze's tone conveys exactly what he thinks of that final statement. He narrows his eyes as something else strikes him. "You and the other leaders never knew where Jewel's pod was."

Which not only means Infernos can't help him right now, but also that Avalan's continuing to keep secrets.

What will the Fire leader do about that?

"We must find her," Infernos states flatly.

Hayze isn't sure whether the urgency is because the Fire leader wants his *Solution*, or whether it's because he actually cares. If it weren't for their time in the Scorchlands where Infernos actually risked himself for his people, Hayze would assume it's the first. In the end, it doesn't matter.

Hayze is going to use it to his advantage.

"I figured the Earth room might be a good place to start." He indicates toward the glowing panel on his right, hoping his bluff pays off. "If Avalan has anything to hide, it could be in there."

"We'll find out," Infernos growls, striding forward.

He swipes his hand over the sensor as Hayze holds his breath. If it opens, then the leaders still have some level of trust.

If it doesn't, Avalan clearly has her own agenda. One she doesn't want the other leaders knowing about.

Beep.

The door clicks open.

Infernos yanks it and steps through, Hayze following. He keeps his face neutral, not wanting to give away that all of this is new. That the existence of a room was nothing but a guess.

It's small, with little more than a desk and a chair. And it's also empty.

Infernos huffs. "It looks exactly the same as my private office, or any of the other leaders'. There's nothing out of place."

He turns to leave, but Hayze steps into the doorway. "Are you sure? Are there any differences, even a subtle one?"

Infernos turns back, looking like he's doing this just to humor him. He scans the room, already shaking his head. "There's nothing—"

He stops. His mouth presses into a firm line. Then he walks toward the desk.

"This is different," he murmurs almost thoughtfully. Maybe in disbelief.

There's a row of buttons on the desk, four with each Element's symbol, but it's the fifth one on the end that Infernos is reaching toward.

Hayze holds his breath, unsure what he's about to witness. Infernos is an unlikely ally, one Hayze is standing beside because he's willing to do whatever it takes to find Aura.

Infernos's finger brushes the fifth button, the one that is blank.

"What is the meaning of this?"

Hayze spins around to find Avalan standing directly behind him. He stumbles back, tense and cautious. Beside him, Infernos crosses his arms. "Hello, Avalan."

She inclines her head, just as Hayze expected her to. "Why are you in my private office, Infernos?"

The emphasis on the word *private* is undeniable.

He simply inflates his chest. "Wondering where you've put my Solution?"

"Aura chose to go after Jewel," Avalan says calmly.

"Where?" Hayze asks, trying not to let the word explode out of him. He jabs a finger at the fifth button. "What are you hiding, Avalan?"

She glances at the button. "You think I have something hidden in here? Jewel? Aura? Some master plan I've kept from you all?"

Neither Hayze nor Infernos answer.

Avalan huffs. She stalks the two steps toward the desk, leans over, and presses it. There's a faint whoosh and Hayze finds himself spinning around once more.

The blank screens that line the wall directly across from the desk are moving. Lifting.

Revealing another room beyond.

Infernos narrows his eyes as he moves closer, clearly not expecting to see this either. "You..."

The room is small, dark and almost empty. All that it holds is a single, still image on the opposite wall. It's a young girl wearing the leather of the Quakelands, smiling as she reaches out as if for a hug.

"Avalan." Infernos says her name with weight. With sadness.

"It's hard for me to be away from any reminder," she says softly. "I miss her."

"I'm sorry," he says, his voice gravelly. He takes Hayze by the arm and leads him out. "We're leaving."

"What?" Hayze demands, trying to shake the iron grip on his arm. "But Aura!"

Infernos keeps dragging him through the office and out into the larger room. There, he lets Hayze go, scowling ferociously. "Those images are Avalan's daughter," he hisses. "She died when she was just a girl in a quake."

That subdues Hayze. He turns to face Avalan as she joins them. "I'm sorry for your loss."

But it only subdues him for a moment.

Pyra lost her father. Then betrayed the rebels so she could have her mother for a few months longer.

Atmos died trying to find a *Solution*.

Avalan isn't the only one to be touched by grief.

Hayze's hands are already fists. "I need to know where Aura is."

To his surprise, Avalan sighs. "Very well." Even Infernos's brows twitch before he schools his face. "Aura's returned to the Scorchlands. That's where Jewel is."

"The Scorchlands?"

It's Infernos who asks, sounding as taken aback as Hayze feels.

Avalan nods, holding her fellow leader's gaze. "As neighbors, I knew I could trust you, my friend."

"You haven't trusted him," Hayze points out. "He had no idea Jewel's there."

"Infernos has lost loved ones himself," Avalan replies. "He understands."

The Fire leader nods back, his lips now tightly shut. Silence tries to take hold, but Hayze steps forward with such force that his footfall sounds like a clap.

"You said Jewel was here," he spits. He's tired of lies.

Her lashes flutter. "Would you have let Aura go if you knew she'd have to leave the Sect?"

The question is rhetorical, which has Hayze's hands curling into hard fists. "For once, tell me the truth. Tell me where Jewel is." If Jewel's there, then Aura is, too.

Avalan gazes back, her dark eyes unnervingly calm. Doesn't

she realize how close he is to snapping? That finding Aura is all that matters?

"She's at the border of the Scorchlands. Near the wall that divides it from the Quakelands."

"I want the truth, Avalan," Hayze grinds out.

"I am telling the truth. The pod is there."

Hayze stares at Avalan for a moment longer, but there's no sign of deceit on her calm face. And the location makes sense— Jewel's true pod is just beyond the border of the Quakelands. Clenching his jaw, he spins on his heel and stalks out of the room.

"Hayze!" Infernos shouts. "You can't leave! The Games are about to start!"

It takes one middle finger to communicate what Hayze thinks of that. He's well aware that a group of teens will be entering the Games. Pyra is one of them. Everyone's about to find out if there are more Solutions.

But Hayze doesn't care. He won't be there to watch it.

For him, the world will keep turning when he's reunited with Aura.

ELEVEN

AURA

Aura knows perception of time is different in virtual reality. And as one day becomes another, it's all she can do to hope this has translated to a matter of minutes or hours for Hayze in the real world. Otherwise, he'll be out of his mind with worry.

She wakes in Rateen's bed and stares at the timber beams in the roof of Jewel's small home. Rateen never returned home, which shocked Jewel and didn't surprise Aura in the least. She's not needed. Not now that Jewel has Aura.

"Did you sleep well?" Jewel asks from her bed a few feet away. "I can tell you're awake."

Aura doesn't reply. She stopped talking to Jewel the moment she figured out what Avalan was up to. As cruel as it feels to treat Jewel like this, it's the only way she can fight back. If Jewel no longer wants Aura here, then maybe Avalan will pull her out. She's already made it obvious she'll do anything to give her little girl whatever she wants.

"Are you still pretending I'm not here?" Jewel asks, only

just managing to keep her voice from breaking. "You can't ignore me forever, you know."

Jewel gets up and perches on the edge of Aura's bed. She responds by rolling over to put her back to the girl she once considered her dearest friend. At least Jewel's stopped crying now, her initial fear at what was happening having morphed into a deep sadness instead. It's easier to ignore a sad person than a terrified one. Unfortunately, that does nothing to appease Aura's guilt.

"I didn't sleep much," says Jewel, seeming prepared to speak enough for both of them. "I've been going over what you told me."

Aura doesn't so much as twitch. But she hangs on every word, silently begging Jewel to ask Avalan to send Aura away.

"I didn't believe you when you told me who I am," says Jewel. "Not at first. I mean, believing that would mean my entire life was a lie. But then I decided to just sit with it for a while. Pretend that what you said was true. And..."

Jewel draws in a deep breath. If Aura wasn't ignoring her, she'd take her hand and urge her to continue.

"And it explains so much," Jewel eventually says. "Why my mother wasn't who I imagined her to be when she came back. Why I never felt like everyone else. Why the world I grew up in was so different to the one Geo described in the Games."

Aura blinks, fighting every one of her instincts to turn around. She brings the image of Hayze to mind, which keeps her in place. Her best chance of returning to him is if Jewel hates her. And she's not going to do that if Aura gives her the hug she so desperately wants to.

"It also explains the fog," says Jewel. "Why the entire village I grew up in has suddenly vanished. It explains why I'm the only one of the eight of us not to wake up in my pod. But do you know what the thing was that really convinced me you might be telling the truth?"

Aura's listening so hard she has to remind herself to breathe. But still, she doesn't say a word.

"It was Avalan," Jewel continues. "Not the way she called me Gemma when nobody knew my mother called me that. It was her eyes. She looked at me in the arena like nobody ever has before. *Nobody*. It was a look of pure, unconditional, deeply abiding love. Like she was living for me as much as she would die for me. It's why I couldn't chase after her. Because even in that moment, long before you told me, I knew my heart had learned to beat beside hers."

Tears well in Aura's eyes and she wills them back into her body. Hearing Jewel talk like this makes her miss her own mother. When she first woke in the Games, it was Tempo's parents she missed. Then by the time she had her true memories restored, so much was happening, she didn't have the chance to miss her mother's arms around her. Or her father's. But listening to Jewel talk now, she aches to see her parents again. Surely, they must love her and miss her as much as Avalan does Jewel.

"Avalan sent you to me." Jewel puts a hand on Aura's leg on top of the quilt, then withdraws it. "She knew how much my heart was yearning to be with you, so she gave me what my heart desired. You."

Aura remains silent, hoping these declarations of love will take an abrupt change in direction.

"And then you told me the truth." Jewel's voice drops to little more than a whisper. "Even though it was clear it hurt you to tell me, you still did. And I didn't believe you. I slapped you and tried to run away. I treated you badly. And yet, still, you're not upset with me. The only reason you're not talking to me is because you're hoping I'll ask Avalan to send you away."

Aura's eyes open wide as if that will help her hear better. Her plan isn't working. Jewel doesn't hate her. It's the opposite. She *understands* her. How can someone who's little more than a simulation programmed to think like a human have figured all this out? Any regular person would assume someone who's not talking to them was upset with them.

But Jewel's different.

She always has been.

She's like a better version of a human than a human is themselves.

Aura rolls to her back and looks up at her friend.

Jewel's eyes fill with tears at the sign Aura's softening toward her, and she shuffles closer on the bed. "I'm so sorry, Aura."

"No." Aura sits up and takes her friend's hand, relief whooshing from her body to be able to be her true self. "You have nothing to be sorry for. You didn't ask for any of this."

"I slapped you," Jewel sobs. "I'm so sorry I did that."

Aura squeezes her hand. "I've had far worse happen to me in the Games."

Jewel sniffs, then smiles. "Did you know the Games were the happiest days of my life?"

"What?" Aura can barely believe this. "The Games were awful. We were fighting for our lives every single day, not knowing what was going to be thrown at us next."

"And I'd never felt more alive." Jewel's eyes shine with excitement. "In the Games, I didn't feel different to everyone else. Everyone was the same. And it was there I found my powers. I had friends. I had...you."

Aura thinks this over. There were aspects of the Games that hadn't been so bad. She rekindled her love for Hayze. She found her own powers. She learned just how strong she really is.

"It wasn't always awful," Aura concedes. "Although, I'm not keen to ever go back."

"Oh, I wish we could." Jewel laughs. "I long for it. Just for one more day so I could really appreciate it."

"Careful what you wish for." Aura lets go of Jewel's hand and swings her legs out of the bed. "Your mother has a habit of making your wishes come true."

Jewel gets to her feet. "Do you want me to ask her to take you out of here? Because as much as I don't want that, I'll do it if you want me to."

Hope lights in Aura's chest and she nods, more guilt seeping into her soul. "I'd like that very much."

Jewel nods, tilting her face upward. "Avalan, can you hear me?"

Silence.

"Mother?" Jewel tries.

Silence again.

"Hello? Mother." Jewel raises her voice. "If you can hear me, please allow Aura back to her pod. Let her return to the real world. To Hayze. I don't want her here if that's not what she wants for herself."

Jewel looks back to Aura, as if expecting her to vanish at any moment.

Aura isn't so confident. Avalan doesn't care what Aura wants. She worked too hard to get Aura here to simply take her away.

"She's not going to do it," says Jewel. "I'm sorry, Aura. I really am."

"I know." Aura gives her a warm smile. "Thanks for trying."

"We can try to make a nice life here for ourselves," says Jewel. "Just the two of us. Perhaps you won't hate it so much after some time."

Aura's smile tinges with sadness. What Jewel just said is

exactly the reason Avalan isn't budging. She knows Jewel doesn't really want Aura to leave.

"You disagree, don't you?" Jewel's shoulders slump. "You'll never be happy here."

"I need to get back to my life. And Hayze." Aura winces, knowing these words will cause Jewel pain, but needing to speak the truth. "I need you to help me figure out how to do that. Preferably with a plan that doesn't involve me being awful to you. I'm sorry I stopped talking to you."

"It's okay. I knew you didn't hate me." Jewel shrugs. "You don't have a hateful bone in your body."

"I'm not so sure about that." Aura thinks of Avalan and how she tricked her into coming here. How she stole Aura's life, treating her as little more than a plaything for her daughter. Let alone all the unwitting teens she sent to their deaths in the Games.

"And I'm not sure how to help you get out of here." Jewel rises to her feet and looks out of a window at the vast white nothingness that stretches out into eternity. "The selfish part of me doesn't want to help you."

Aura goes to stand beside her. "If I don't have any hateful bones, you don't have any selfish ones."

"Nor any bones at all," Jewel says mournfully before her face fills with trepidation. "What if you leave and I'm stuck here like this? I almost went mad when I was left in the nothingness last time."

"Avalan won't do that to you." Aura peers out the window. "And besides, I'm not sure I'll be leaving, anyway."

"There has to be a way for you to return to your pod." Jewel sighs. "Surely, someone has done it at least once."

A memory lights Aura's mind. "Skylus."

"You need to warn me before you say that name." Jewel rolls her eyes. "What about her?"

"When we were looking for your pod in Terra, we came across Skylus and Atmos," she explains. "We asked who got them out of the Games and Skylus said she focused all her energy on her real self until she was able to return her mind to her pod. Then she just disconnected herself, released Atmos and walked right out."

"What?" Jewel's eyes flare. "Really? It can't be that easy."

"It's worth a shot." Aura lies down on the timber floor on her back, mimicking the position her real body is in.

"Hold on!" Jewel crouches beside her. "You can't leave just like that. You haven't even said goodbye."

"Oh." Aura realizes she's right. She was so focused on Hayze, she completely forgot. She sits up and embraces her friend. "Thanks for being the best friend I ever had."

Jewel hugs her back tightly. "I thought Hayze was your best friend."

Aura grins as she releases her. "That's different." She stops short of explaining her feelings for Hayze go far beyond anything that could be described as friendship.

He's the spark to her flame.

The oxygen to her fire.

The fuel to the wildfire that's blazing in her heart.

Aura returns to her previous position and closes her eyes as she concentrates on an image of herself lying in the pod in the secret room in Avalan's office. She pictures every detail of herself, willing all her energy back into her body.

She sees her legs. Her shoulders. Her chestnut brown hair.

She sees her eyelids closed. Her arms by her side. Her toes sticking up at an awkward angle.

But most of all, she sees her soul. The essence that makes her Aura. The part that makes her human in a way that Jewel can never be.

A tingle runs down her spine as a lightness spreads through her body.

Only when she's certain it's worked does she dare to open her eyes.

And sees Jewel's face staring back at her.

Disappointment floods her.

"It didn't work," she whispers. "It didn't work."

"You're still here." Jewel takes her hand, helping her to sit up. "I'm so happy and so sad all at the same time."

Aura is just plain old sad. With a dash of highly confused.

"How did Skylus do it?" she asks. "I put everything I have into doing exactly what she said."

"Maybe she is as all powerful as she keeps telling us," scoffs Jewel. "Or maybe..."

"What?" Aura squeezes her hand, urging her to continue. "Or maybe what?"

"Or maybe she lied to you." Jewel bites down on her lip. "Maybe Avalan did a deal with her."

"What kind of deal?" Aura's mind whirls as she tries to remember everything about Skylus when they found her in Terra.

"The usual kind," says Jewel. "Like letting her out of the Games so she could sabotage what you were doing to find me."

Aura's jaw falls as pieces of the puzzle fall into place. "A trade master gave us a map that led us to a tree where you were supposed to be. Skylus flew up first to have a look and told us she saw you on a platform in the high branches. But when we climbed up, it was an ambush. Later she said she made a mistake. Her story never quite made sense."

"What else?" Jewel asks. "What else did she do?"

Aura swallows. "She lost the power to fly. Twice. Both times when it happened, we were forced to stop what we were doing."

"She was faking," Jewel tuts.

"And she tried to talk us out of looking for you." Aura shakes her head as more memories come back to her. "She said we had Geo, so we didn't need you. Then when we found the stairs to the rooftop of the Sect, she insisted there was nothing up there when there was. And she defended the leaders' actions when Atmos was stuck on the platform in the Games."

"She's a double agent," says Jewel. "She's been playing both sides. I mean, think about it... if it were that easy to exit the Games, the leaders would have done exactly that when you trapped them in the arena."

Aura nods, feeling foolish. Jewel's right. There would have been no need for the leaders to wait for Cyclonis to wake up so they could each run for the colored seats in the arena if they could end the Games by simply willing themselves back to their pods.

"Which means I really am stuck in here." Aura gets back to her feet and goes to the door, feeling the desperate need to be outside. Even the fog of nothingness is preferable to the walls of Jewel's home, which are steadily closing in on her.

She steps outside and walks forward, sensing Jewel is right behind her.

"Don't go too far," Jewel warns. "We might not be able to find our way back."

Aura turns to reply but falls mute when she sees Jewel's small home flicker, then disappear.

"What is it?" Jewel asks, turning to see what has her attention. "My house! It's gone!"

Then something else glimmers to life in the distance.

Aura instinctively links hands with Jewel.

"It's the arena," says Jewel. "Avalan is sending us to the Games."

"I told you." Aura swallows down the bitter taste in her mouth. "You need to be careful what you wish for."

CHAPTER
TWELVE

HAYZE

T he sun beats down with ferocity the moment Hayze steps from the wall surrounding Ignis. The stifling heat is a weight on his shoulders, thickening the air and vaporizing any shred of moisture.

Maybe it's the aftermath of the monstrous fire storm. Maybe it's just because he's been away. But it hits Hayze harder than he expected.

Not that it slows him down.

The oppressive heat is proof he's in the Scorchlands. With each press of his boot into the dusty ground, he's one step closer to Aura. He grabs the small peach he'd tucked into one of his pockets and bites into it. Sweet moisture floods his mouth and he sucks on it hard, willing the energy to suffuse every cell.

He won't be slowing down, no matter how hot or viscous the air is. He'd walk through lava to get to Aura.

Hayze sets up a steady, quick pace. Avalan said Jewel's pod is at the border of the Scorchlands. He's never been there, but he knows it's far. He can't afford to burn out before he reaches it.

So he puts his head down, affording his face what little shade he can, and thinks of Aura. He paints her in his mind. Her eyes twinkling with happiness. Her lips curved in the smile only he can spark. Her face suffused with a delicious flush.

He paints all the Auras he's known. Smart Aura. Courageous Aura. Compassionate Aura.

And then he paints all the Auras he's looking forward to loving. The young woman. The mother. The guiding light who's only become more beautiful with age. Hayze suddenly realizes he's painted himself in those images.

He grows a beard.

He goes gray.

He never stops smiling.

It's those images that he's fighting for. A future with Aura.

"Hayze?"

He jerks to a stop, realizing two things. The sun is high in the sky now—hours have passed. And it's Aura's mother who's looking at him like he's an apparition.

"Vesta." He opens his mouth to speak again, only to realize he's unsure what to say. He hadn't intended to go through his village.

But now he's here, newly-built bunkers scattered behind Vesta, he knows returning to his village had been instinctive. An unconscious curve as he walks steadily west to the border.

Aura's mother's hand flutters to her throat. "We thought you were..."

Hayze jolts into motion again. He doesn't have time to wonder what she's talking about. "Sorry, Vesta. But I need to speak to my parents."

"Brando," she calls out, not tearing her gaze from Hayze. Her hand even tightens around her throat. "Brando!"

He comes running from a nearby bunker, concern etched in the coal dust on his face. "Vesta! Have we lost more?"

Brando skids to a halt as he registers Hayze. His face goes pale and he quickly moves to stand beside Vesta, slipping an arm around her shoulder. "Hayze. We didn't, ah, expect to see you again."

Hayze mentally dismisses their odd behavior. He only has one unknown he's determined to answer right now—Aura's location. "Well, I'm fine, as you can see. Now, if you'll excuse me, I need to speak to my mom and dad."

Brando's eyes pop open. "You can't."

"I am," Hayze says, suppressing a scowl. He wasn't looking for permission.

Vesta shakes her head. "You literally can't."

Her words, the way she says them gently, as if trying to soften their blow, has a fist clenching around Hayze's heart with vicious sharpness. "What are you talking about, Vesta?"

She presses her lips together as her eyes become watery pools of apology.

It's Brando who answers. "They...disappeared, Hayze. The day after the big fire storm."

"Disappeared?" Hayze echoes, his voice feeling as hollow as his mind. "How can they just disappear?"

Brando shakes his head. "We don't know. Everyone woke up the following day and they were just...gone."

Vesta draws in a shuddering breath. "Along with any other rebels."

Hayze takes an involuntary step back, discovering he's shaking his head. "That's not possible."

"Word traveled fast," Brando says. "People in villages all over the Scorchlands vanished overnight. Their bunkers were left untouched, their belongings still there." He shrugs. "Like I said, they disappeared."

Hayze steps around them, his heart now spasming in the confines of his constricted chest.

"Your parents aligned themselves with the Elemental Alliance," Vesta calls after him. "They knew the risks."

Hayze turns around, now walking backwards. "Well, the leaders you've put all your faith in have taken Aura."

Vesta blanches. Brando goes pale.

Hayze spins back. He didn't gain any sense of satisfaction from telling Aura's parents that. He wishes there was a right side in this fight. That he knew which side he was on.

But he doesn't. There's no clear enemy, no obvious winner to back.

Just his heart to follow.

He breaks into a run, heading straight for the bunker he grew up in, one of the few still standing after the firestorm. Barging through the door, he doesn't give his eyes time to adjust to the gloom. "Mom! Dad!"

Hollow silence is his only reply.

Hayze dashes past the rusted metal table, past the rusted metal shelves that still hold cans, and into his parents' room. The bed is rumpled, the gray sheets infused with years of coal dust.

"Mom!" Hayze shouts louder, turning to his room.

He bursts in, taking in his own neatly made bed. The tin with his paints beside it. The emptiness clinging to everything.

"Dad!" he screams. His panic bounces off the walls, seeming to multiply in the confines of the cement walls.

But that's all the bunker holds. Hayze. Rusted furniture. And his congealing fear that Brando and Vesta were telling the truth.

His parents are gone.

He exits the bunker, unable to stay in there. The blazing heat once again engulfs him, making him squint. Where does he go now? He can't leave this unanswered, but he has to find Aura.

"Hayze..."

The croaky voice is faint, but still manages to weave its way through the heavy heat. He turns, frowning in focus. It came from the open door a few bunkers down. A newly rebuilt bunker. Pyra's bunker.

"Hay...ze."

He quickly enters, then gives his eyes a moment to adjust. Pyra's currently dancing along the line between enemy and ally. This could be a trap.

The kitchen is empty so he continues through to the open bedroom door. The smell hits him before the sight.

The smell of death.

The sight of Soleil, Pyra's mother, lying on a bed that's sprinkled with both coal dust and blood.

She coughs weakly, a few more droplets of dark red landing on her concave chest. She lets out a rattly breath as she sees him, falling back onto the filthy sheets. "Ember and Sera..."

"Can you talk, Soleil?" He strides over and kneels beside her. "Is it true? Are my parents gone?"

She nods weakly. "Along with...anyone else...rebels."

The leaders must have taken them in their sleep. Did Pyra know? Was she part of this?

Soleil reaches out and he takes her skeletal hand, registering how cold it is. "There was no...warning. No one came. They were just...gone."

Hayze shakes his head. It doesn't make sense.

"P-Pyra?"

"She's fine," Hayze says, hoping he's telling the truth. Pyra is likely in the Games as they speak. "She's chosen, but you know that."

Soleil's face twists as another wave of hacking coughs wrack her body. Hayze holds her hand, aware she doesn't have long. He's not sure how her frail bones are holding together.

"I hoped..." Soleil's eyes close but she doesn't need to finish her sentence. Hayze knows. His own parents hoped the bargain they struck with the leaders would give their unborn child a chance to rise above the very death she's succumbing to.

"She's part of the Solution," he says softly,

Her lips are cracked, her skin pasty. He reaches into his pocket and pulls out the second peach he took from the Sect, intending to eat it on the final leg to Aura. "Here." He slips it in Soleil's hand and wraps her cold fingers around it. "Eat this."

She shakes her head as tears swim in her pain-filled eyes. "It's too late."

"I want you to have it anyway." He smiles. "Pyra would want you to have it."

Soleil releases a rattly breath, then draws up a weak smile. "You always were her hero." She closes her eyes as she brings the peach to her rattly chest, holding it like a precious gem.

"I have to go," he whispers.

Soleil simply nods, the faint smile still gracing her face. Hayze leaves as silently as he can. The woman's impending death behind him is the reason he was created.

The reason Aura was created.

And Pyra.

He needs to play his part—love Aura.

Hayze angles west and breaks into a jog, setting his jaw as he settles determination into his bones. He won't stop until he reaches Jewel's pod. Until he finds Aura.

He rounds the last bunker, one that's only half built, and lurches to a halt. Brando and Vesta are standing at the end of the cement walkway, the Scorchlands framing them as they clutch each other.

"Is it true?" Vesta asks, clinging to Brando's hand. "Have the leaders taken Aura?"

"Is it true?" Hayze shoots back. "Did my parents just disappear?"

Brando nods. "Without a trace, along with any other rebels."

Hayze's eyes dart beyond the couple, as if the answers are in the endless devastation behind them. He looks back at Aura's parents. "They claim Aura left of her own choice. But they also lied about where she went."

"You have to find her, Hayze," Vesta pleads.

"I intend to," he responds, saying the words as a vow. The irony that Aura's parents are now begging for his help isn't lost on him.

"Everything we did..." Brando swallows, then tears up.

"We did because we love Aura more than anything in the world," Vesta finishes. "We just want her safe and happy."

Hayze doubts she's either of those right now, but he doesn't say it. Once again, he can empathize with the two people standing across from him. They did what they thought was right. In the name of love.

Just like he is.

Hayze steps around Aura's parents, registering that Vesta's quietly crying. "I'll find her."

He breaks into a jog, not looking back, only forward. His world is slowly unraveling and Aura's the only thread that can weave it back together. Finding her is the *solution*.

Hayze's new pace is determined, unrelenting, uncaring of anything but forward momentum. He doesn't pay attention to the heat. To the sweat that's slowly wringing him of moisture. Or the burn that weaves through his muscles and sinew and eventually, his bones.

He angles slightly until he meets the wall that separates the Scorchlands from the Quakelands, then runs dead west.

The sun slowly sinks, failing to take the heat with it. The scenery progressively becomes bleaker and barer.

A small, decrepit hut eventually appears on the horizon.

Hayze tries to pick up speed, only to find there isn't any. His body emptied of anything but mindless determination hours ago. His only saving grace is that he doesn't slow. Doesn't miss a scuffled step in his quest to reach Aura.

The hut grows in size, revealing that it's even more derelict than first impressions. The wood is bleached and sand-stained, the roof is flaky and fragile, the walls are warped and wasted. This is where Avalan put Jewel? Why?

Hayze places his foot on the first step with care and a tired groan is wrenched out of the timber. The entrance is a black hole, the door looking like it rusted open decades ago. A faded sign above reads *The Pod*. Just like Avalan said.

Jewel was certainly safe here. No one would find her this far from anything.

Hayze cautiously takes the next step, then avoids the jagged hole in the next one. "Aura?"

His voice is little more than a whispered croak, so he licks his dry, cracked lips. Only to discover any drop of saliva is long gone.

Aura...

He steps through, then stops. It takes precious seconds for his eyes to adjust to the dusty gloom. In that time, images of what he'll find form in his mind. Just like the decrepit Sect that hid the marvel of the true Sect, this hut will contain spotless technology. Computers.

And a pod.

He's pictured it so clearly, that it takes more precious seconds to register what's truly before him.

A barren hut.

A dirty table.

A blank screen covered in dust.

A sense that this place hasn't been disturbed in decades. Maybe centuries.

"No..." Hayze whispers, his body using its last shred of energy to breathe the denial.

There's no pod.

No Jewel.

No Aura.

As exhaustion and dehydration stake their claim, Hayze crumples.

Darkness wraps its suffocating weight around him, leaving space for two words as consciousness slips through his grasp.

Avalan lied.

"Come on." Jewel tugs on Aura's arm, urging her forward.

Aura's feet remain planted where they are—deep inside the fog of nothingness.

"We can't stay out here," says Jewel. "We have to go to the arena."

Aura knows Jewel's right. But how can she possibly step one foot inside the Games? Every experience she's had inside that arena has been filled with danger, disappointment and death.

"Come on." Jewel pulls on Aura's arm again.

"Why did you have to wish to go back in the Games?" Aura grimaces.

"I'm really sorry." Jewel's shoulders slump. "I swear when I said that I didn't mean for it to actually happen. I just meant—"

"I know what you meant." Aura sighs. "But seriously, couldn't you have wished for something else?"

"I did!" Jewel throws out her hands. "Don't you remember?

I wished for Avalan to take you away, just like you wanted me to."

"Except you didn't mean it," says Aura.

"We have two options." Jewel ignores this last comment as she fixes her eyes on the arena. "We can wait out here forever in the nothingness. Or we can go in there and find out what Avalan wants."

"All I want is to get back to Hayze."

"And you're not going to do that standing out here, are you?" says Jewel. "Maybe we can sit on the colored seats like the leaders did and end the Games."

Hope sparks in Aura's chest, despite knowing they'll need four people for that.

"Okay," she says, hating that she's agreeing to the very thing she wants to do the least. But if it's the one thing that might get her out of here, then it's worth it.

Jewel's face lights with a smile and they walk ahead, Aura's feet feeling like they're made of lead when in fact they're made of nothing at all. As the tall, round structure becomes larger, her curiosity grows. Avalan is clearly up to something.

But what?

It's only then she remembers what happened just before she left the Sect.

"Phase Two," she whispers, more to herself than Jewel.

"What's Phase Two?" Jewel asks.

"The leaders were talking about bringing in the teens who were destined for the Games and fast-tracking them," she explains. "Everyone aged thirteen to seventeen. Two from each Quadrant."

"But that's forty in total." Jewel shakes her head in amazement.

"We insisted it could only happen if we had consent," Aura

116

explains. "As in, we tell the teens what it's all about and ask for volunteers."

"I don't get it," says Jewel. "Isn't the whole idea of the Games that the participants don't know? Like, we thought our actual lives were in danger, which is what brought out our powers."

"That's what Infernos said." Aura shrugs. "But it's too cruel to do it any other way. And besides, we don't actually know that theory is correct. Maybe it will work anyway. I mean, even when we knew the Games weren't real, the challenges were still terrifying. We still felt pain. We still fought to stay alive, despite knowing our deaths would be fake."

"Do you think they're already in there?" Jewel asks as they reach the arena with its impossibly high walls. "The forty teens, I mean."

Aura shrugs. "Hopefully. We'll need at least two others to help if I'm going to get out."

As soon as she's said the words, she wonders if they've made a mistake, revealing their plan out loud. It's clear that Avalan is listening to every word they speak. Then again, they didn't say anything that wasn't already blatantly obvious.

"So, how do we get in?" Jewel asks, staring up at the looming walls. "We need one of those hot air balloons we found in the Stormsphere. It was incredible the way you made that thing fly."

"Or we need a tunnel." Aura tilts her head at Jewel. "Go on. You haven't used your powers in a while."

"Okay." Jewel claps her hands in excitement, then holds them out. "Stay behind me."

Aura takes a few steps back and waits to see what her friend can do. This is what Jewel wanted—the chance to be with Aura and have some fun with her powers. Getting them into the arena is the perfect opportunity to do that.

"I am Earth!" Jewel calls out.

The ground in front of her rumbles, then cracks as it cleaves in two, the tremor spiraling down, creating a space large enough to walk through. Jewel steps forward, continuing to work with her Element to clear the way as she moves. Aura is right behind her, not in the slightest bit afraid as they disappear underground. It's hard to believe she was ever scared of small spaces, like that happened to a different person in another lifetime. She has Hayze to thank for helping her get past that. And her powers. She knows nothing can hurt her. Especially not here.

Aura lights a small flame in the palm of her hand so they can see as Jewel expertly carves out the dirt ahead. They walk beneath what must be the seats of the arena before Jewel begins tunnelling upward.

Daylight floods the tight space and Jewel waves her hands wildly, moving quickly as she emerges onto solid ground. She turns to grin at Aura, pride written all over her face.

"You're amazing," says Aura, stepping up into the arena and spinning around to take it all in. There are huge mounds of dirt around them. As Jewel dug out the tunnel, the soil must have been pushed through on the other side.

Jewel lowers her hands and takes a theatrical bow.

From behind a mound of dirt steps a boy wearing the blue suit of the Water Quadrant. With blond hair and pale skin, he looks about thirteen years of age. The dirt on his face does nothing to hide his curiosity as he peers at them.

Aura realizes she's still nursing a flame in her palm, so she lets it extinguish and gives him a warm smile, wondering if he's the first of the forty teens to arrive.

"Hey there. I'm Aura. What's your name?"

"I'm Kai," he says, wiping his hands on his suit. "I'm from the Water Quadrant."

"I can see that," Aura laughs.

"You can make fire," the boy says. "Like that guy could. Except he turned his entire body into a flame."

"You met Hayze?" Aura takes a step closer, listening closely.

Kai shrugs. "I think that was his name. Oceania said he was from Fire. We didn't see much of him, though. He wasn't there when I went into the pod."

"What do you mean, he wasn't there?" Aura asks.

"I don't know." Kai throws out his skinny arms. "The others like him were there, but he never came back."

Aura thinks about this. Knowing Hayze, he went looking for her. And while she loves his determination to protect her, it's a shame he hadn't waited like she asked him to. If he was watching the Games, she could just tell him where her body is, and he could get her out.

Her head snaps up. Kai said the others like Hayze were there...

"Tempo!" she shouts, looking up at the sky. "Pace! I'm in a pod in Avalan's office behind a secret wall. You have to get me out! Hurry! Please! She tricked me. You can't believe a word any of the leaders say!"

She rushes to Jewel, aware that at any moment she'll be pulled from the Games and away from her friend. She puts a hand on her shoulder. "I promise I won't let them keep you in the nothingness. I'll find a way for you to have a good life."

Jewel's eyes spill over with tears. "Except I'm not alive, Aura. I'm nothing. Please, just worry about keeping yourself safe. Make your life worthwhile."

"You're not nothing." Aura pulls Jewel into a hug. "You're miraculous."

Jewel hugs her back and Aura waits for her body to fade away as Tempo and Pace find her and disconnect her from the pod.

"I don't think your friends are going to save you," Kai says, approaching cautiously.

Aura breaks away from Jewel and looks at him. "It's just taking a bit of time, that's all."

"Can we really not trust the leaders?" he asks, fear having replaced the curiosity in his eyes. "Because I only agreed to come in here when they said they'd keep me safe. My dad will be getting worried if I'm not home soon."

Aura hesitates, not wanting to terrify this boy by telling him the truth, yet not wanting to feed him more lies.

"Maybe your friends can get me out, too?" Kai asks, his small frame trembling. "Because I've changed my mind. I don't want to be in here anymore."

"Neither do I." A tall girl in the flowing robes of Air steps out from behind another mound of dirt. "I want to go home."

"I don't." Pyra approaches. "I want you to teach me how to harness Fire."

"Pyra." Aura's eyes widen. "I didn't realize you were... like us."

Her eyes shine with excitement. "Neither did I. Isn't it fantastic?"

"How many of you are here?" Aura peers around the mound of dirt closest to her.

Five more teens step out, revealing eight in total.

"Where are the rest of you?" Aura asks. "Did only eight volunteer?"

"Everyone volunteered," says Pyra. "Once we saw what the powers could do. We're only the first round."

"What challenges have they given you so far?" Jewel asks.

Aura looks around, seeing no evidence of floating platforms or giant hands made from ice. Then to her horror, she notices something else.

There are no colored chairs ringing the arena.

Which means the leaders have removed her only way to exit the Games. It's just as well she managed to get her message out to Tempo and Pace.

"No challenges so far," says Kai. "We only just got here. Then the dirt started moving and you two appeared. But still, I'd really rather go home."

The ground trembles and the mounds of dirt collapse as they're drawn back into the tunnel, closing it off.

"What's happening?" Jewel asks. "I swear I'm not doing that."

"They're trapping us," says Aura.

The mouth of what used to be the tunnel seems to come to life as dozens of tiny brown insects with red dots on their abdomen crawl out.

"Get back!" shouts Jewel.

"They're just ants," says Kai.

"They're not *just* ants," says the tall girl from Air, taking three steps back. "They're fire ants. Their bites are venomous."

"Then let's fight fire with Fire." Aura smiles, doing her best to keep the teens calm. "We've got this."

Pyra races to her side and mimics Aura's actions as she raises her palms.

A blast of flame bursts from Aura's hands, dousing the tiny bronze-colored creatures and sending out waves of heat.

"I can't do it!" pants Pyra, her face purple as she strains to make a spark.

Aura lets her flame die down. Just as she's about to give Pyra a few tips, the breath is knocked from her lungs as she sees the ants haven't been exterminated.

They've multiplied.

There are at least three times the number of them than there were before, as if her fire has fed them.

"Keep back," says Jewel, ushering the teens away. "Give Aura some space."

Aura tries again, sending out more flames, this time increasing the heat level from orange to white to blue. Pyra remains stubbornly beside her, grunting with her failed efforts to harness her Element.

"Ow!" Aura yelps, jumping back and letting her flame die out as a sharp pain pierces her ankle.

She looks down to see an ant on her ankle and she disposes of it the old-fashioned way by slapping it hard until its crumpled body falls to the ground.

"Aura!" Pyra cries out. "Watch out!"

Lifting her gaze, Aura sees thousands of ants erupting from the ground like a poisonous bronze geyser. Their small bodies shoot into the air then land, forming a shimmering sea of venom.

"What the..." Aura stumbles back, her ankle throbbing in pain and her heart pounding. One bite is agony. A hundred would be certain death.

"Kai," she shouts, trying to keep the panic from her voice. "Get over here. And the Water girl. I need your help!"

Kai and a scrawny girl in a blue suit from Water approach cautiously. Pyra remains by Aura's side, listening intently.

"What do we do?" Kai asks, his voice quivering. "And if I do this, can I *please* go home?"

"Raise your palms and call on your Water powers," Aura instructs. "Imagine ice pouring from your hands. You can do this! Freeze these little guys. You have the power inside you. You just need to let it out!"

Kai and the girl do as they're told and a sick feeling lodges in Aura's gut. This isn't going to work. It's clear that while these two Water teens are terrified, neither of them believes they can do this. And the power of the mind is a vital ingredient when it comes to the power of the Elements, even if it hasn't worked for Pyra just yet.

The Water girl lets out an agonised scream and drops her hands to slap at her feet. Abandoning the mission, she runs back to join the others, leaving Kai standing frozen to the spot, which is ironic given he hasn't managed to produce any ice at all.

"Jewel!" Aura cries as the army of ants swells to become a tidal wave. "Cover them over with dirt!"

Jewel leaps into action, sending dirt swirling in the air as it's picked up from the ground and dumped on top of the ants. Except as the dust clears, it's clear this has only made the poisonous creatures angry.

No. Scratch that. They're furious! They charge erratically at a frenzied pace, swarming on top of each other and surging forward as thousands more pour from the ground. There must be a million or more of them by now. If they don't do something, the entire arena will soon be filled with these tiny but deadly creatures.

"Keep trying, Kai!" Aura urges. "Don't give up!"

The army of ants rises, lifting off the ground in a sheet of bronze, sending the petrified group of teens scattering, including Kai. Only Jewel, Aura and Pyra hold steady.

"What's happening?" Jewel pants. "The ants are making a shape."

"Just remember what Hayze always said," Aura shouts. "We can't die!"

The wave of fire ants swirls into a cone like a tornado, then reforms in the figure of a giant scaly creature with four squat legs, a long body that stretches into a thick tail and two vast wings, casting an ominous shadow behind it. Its brown scales shimmer and quiver, the result of the entire creature being made up of millions of tiny fire ants.

"It's a dragon," says Jewel, giving a name to this terrifying sight towering over them. "They're not supposed to be real. They're only in stories."

"Nothing here is real," Aura reminds her, even though the throbbing pain in her ankle is more intense than any real pain she's ever felt.

The dragon takes a step closer, flapping its wings and baring its enormous teeth. Pyra whimpers as Aura tries to hold her nerve. Dousing the beast with flames is only going to feed it, potentially increasing it in size. Covering it in dirt will anger it. And that's not something she wants to contemplate.

"What do dragons do?" Aura asks. "In the stories."

Jewel steps closer to Aura.

"They breathe fire," she whispers.

"Oh, great." Aura raises her palms, prepared to use the only defence she has.

Pyra does the same beside her, although her hands are shaking so much she can barely hold them up.

The dragon rears up until it's standing on its back legs and holds its wings out wide. It opens its enormous jaws wide and a deep growl rumbles through the arena.

"Watch out!" cries Jewel, shielding her face as flames pour from the creature's mouth.

Aura sends out a blaze of her own and the flames meet in the middle, forming a massive ball of fire that expands and hisses as it floats up, then explodes.

Sparks rain down, showering the arena in hungry flames. They catch on the clothing and hair of the teens as they run in circles searching for somewhere safe to hide.

The dragon continues to pour fire from its gaping mouth and Aura fights back, knowing the battle is as useless as Pyra's attempts to help her. Jewel collapses beside her, succumbing to the intense heat of the inferno she's helping to create.

This isn't working!

Aura waves her hands, turning her flames into a bubble of safety as she casts it over the arena in the same way she did in the Scorchlands with Hayze when the firestorm attacked the village. But fire in the Games is different to fire in real life. It doesn't play by the rules, and it rips through her bubble, devouring Jewel, Pyra and the other seven cowering teens like they're nothing more than dry tinder as it turns them to ash.

Satisfied with its work, the dragon closes its jaw, tucks its wings back down and surveys the damage.

Only Aura has been spared. Her Fire powers saved her, making her body impossible to burn. Not even Pyra or the boy from Fire survived.

Not even Jewel.

The dragon looks at Aura, nods as if giving her a sign of respect. Then its body quivers as the fire ants break apart and scurry along the ground in a river of destruction, until they've woven themselves back into the soil like they were never there at all.

"Pace?" Aura calls out as she surveys the empty arena. "Tempo? Please hurry. I need to get out of here."

A warm gust of wind brushes over her and the air shimmers.

Aura blinks and the eight teens re-appear, along with Jewel.

They look at each other in confusion, patting their bodies, surprised to find themselves alive. Jewel runs straight to Aura and links hands with her.

A voice filters through the arena. *That was Round One. For those of you returning in Round Two, please note that this time if you die in the Games, you will also die in real life.*

A chorus of gasps ripple across the teens.

"I really want to go home," Kai whimpers. "Please."

"What did they mean by *'those of you returning'*?" Jewel asks. "Everyone has already returned."

As soon as the words are out of her mouth, several of the teens flicker and vanish.

Only Jewel, Kai, Pyra, and the tall girl from Air remain.

"Where did they go?" Kai asks, looking around before settling his gaze on Aura. "And why are you still here? Why haven't your friends gotten you out?"

Aura swallows.

"I don't know," she says as a deep sense of déjà vu tingles down her spine.

She's trapped in the Games.

Once again, nothing makes sense.

And this time, she doesn't have Hayze to help her figure any of it out.

FOURTEEN

HAYZE

The wall surrounding Ignis casts long shadows over the packed soil when Hayze finally reaches it again. The energy he sucked from the can of unidentifiable beans he grabbed from his parents' bunker has long faded as he leans against the warm stone. He wipes the sweat from his brow, feeling grit scrape over his skin. He's exhausted. So thirsty his marrow is shriveling in his bones.

And now only Ignis stands between him and Aura.

Pushing away, Hayze keeps his hand on the wall as he confirms the gates are shut. He expected them to be. Avalan would know if he survived the run to the outer border of the Scorchlands and back, returning to the Sect would be his only goal.

Why she sent him away is a question he'll be getting answers to as soon as Aura's back in his arms.

Turning around, Hayze uses the wall for support as he scuffs toward the door Infernos used to get to the stairs that lead to the top of the wall. He runs dirty fingers over the rough stone, looking for the camouflaged pad that opens the door. He finds it, but there's no flush of victory to top up his sapped energy. He doubts this will work.

He scans his Fire tattoo over the pad.

Silence.

A gust of wind sends sand skittering over him.

Hayze tries again, pushing his hand harder against the sensor.

Nothing.

Although he suspected this would happen, disappointment still tugs at him. Discouragement quickly tries to follow, but he forcefully shoves it away. He's so close. No wall will stop him from getting back to Aura.

Pushing away, Hayze straightens, pretending he hasn't run miles and miles in the scorching heat chasing a lie. He only staggers once as he makes his way back to the gates. There, he stands in front of the monstrous metal expanse, the last barrier between him and the Sect.

Between him and Aura.

Hayze lifts his hands, rolling his tongue around in his parched mouth. He's going to shout the words that will call on his powers. It'll be a caution to anyone who hears it.

A mustering of his last shreds of energy.

A promise to Avalan.

Because he's about to melt the gates, hoping there's no one on the other side.

This is no longer the Games. People can get hurt by his powers. Others want him dead.

Destroying the gates could trigger either of those.

Hayze spreads his fingers wide, then lifts his chin. *I am Fire* is a rolling battle cry in his mind.

Except the gates are moving, opening. Hayze staggers a step back, his breath hitching. Using his powers to melt metal is one thing. Human bodies is another, far more horrifying, prospect.

Locking his shoulders, he solidifies his resolve. If Avalan's sent drones and guards, they'll have three words worth of warning.

"I am Fire!" Hayze shouts hoarsely as the gates crack open an inch. A foot.

A body's width.

"Yeah, well, we're Water and those two don't mix."

"Pace?" Hayze gasps. He blinks as he registers his friend isn't alone. "Tempo?"

Pace grins. "Fancy meeting you here."

Tempo also smiles. "We thought we'd be scouring the Scorchlands for ages."

Hayze stumbles forward, grabbing them in a hug with strength he didn't know he had. "But..."

Pace thumps him on the back. When he pulls back, his face is somber. "We had to find you."

"What's happened?" Hayze asks, his stomach already knotted with dread.

Pace glances over his shoulder, then at the gates. "Let's make sure we're safe first." He grabs Hayze by the arm and pulls him inside Ignis.

Tempo darts to the left, glancing briefly at the five guards who are now encased in ice, with only their gasping mouths exposed. Puddles of water have formed underneath, indicating they're already melting. She works a rotating lever and the gates shut once more.

"Come on," Pace says,

Hayze follows, tapping into the burst of energy seeing his friends has gifted. Pace and Tempo were looking for him. It's a show of loyalty that warms his heart. And a clear indication that something bad has happened.

Then they're running through the streets of Ignis. The markets are empty as twilight descends. Even the sconces that light the opening of each black bunker have been extinguished. Eerie shadows stretch over the cement walkways, warping and distorting the flame peaks that adorn each market stall. The scent of coal and concrete has embedded itself in the air.

"In here," Pace whispers, darting between two stalls.

Hayze and Tempo follow, squatting down as they lean against the rough walls.

Hayze watches his friends closely. "What's happened?"

"They started the Games again," Tempo says quietly. "With the first batch of teens."

Hayze nods. He suspected as much. "And?"

Pace's hands ball into fists where they're resting on his knees. "Aura was in there. Along with Jewel."

Hayze leaps to his feet, suppressing the shout of outrage that tears through him. "Aura's in the Games?"

Tempo nods, her eyes pools of anguish. "Aura shouted out, knowing we'd be watching. She said she's in a pod in Avalan's office behind a secret wall."

"She's trapped in there," Pace finishes, his features tight.

Hayze wants to run.

He wants to rage.

He wants to raze the Sect to ashes.

Tempo also stands. "We left as soon as she said that. We came looking for you."

Pace joins her. "And we figured the Scorchlands was the first place to search."

"Why didn't you get Aura out first?" Hayze asks, confused.

"We don't know where her office is," says Tempo. "Is it even in the Sect?"

"It is. Thanks for coming for me," Hayze says, meaning it

with every fiber of his being. "Avalan told me Aura was with Jewel at the border of the Scorchlands. She lied."

"You've run there and back?" Pace asks. "In a day?"

Hayze is already turning to face the Sect. It rises into the bruised sky, a pale specter passively gazing over the four Quadrants it's supposed to be saving. "I will have. Once I'm back in there."

Unleashing his fury.

"Do you need to rest?" Tempo asks. "Maybe you should—"

Hayze is already running. He hears Pace grumble something like "or we could go now" as they sprint to catch up. The markets fall behind as they enter the streets lined with cement homes molded in the shapes of flames. A few people are dotted around, wearing the leather suits of Ignis. They frown at Hayze as he rushes past, then cry out with alarm when they see Pace and Tempo in the blue of Water. Women tuck their children close as men call out to the guards.

The people of Ignis have been warned. And told to raise the alarm.

Rounded doorways slam shut. The flames in windows flare brighter as if to communicate the threat running frantically through their streets.

"Quick," Hayze pants, blinking against the exhaustion stinging his eyes.

Pace gets in front while Tempo remains behind. They're flanking him. Protecting him. Hayze wishes he could tell them how grateful he is.

They race ahead, not knowing the streets they're navigating, but simply focusing on the direction of the Sect. The streets are emptier and emptier with each step, the ripple of slamming doors echoing behind. It's only a matter of time before the drones and guards find them.

The crack that reverberates through the air has them all

ducking. Pace looks up, searching for drones. Tempo glances back, expecting guards. Hayze fills his hands with Fire, ready to attack.

Except this threat is below them.

The ground rips apart in a jagged tear that zigzags up the street they're running along. It starts near Pace's feet and shoots along the cement.

"An earthquake?" Tempo gasps as they skid to a halt.

But the ground isn't shaking and trembling like all the quakes Hayze has endured already. The homes of the Ignis aren't moving, his bones aren't rattling.

Blazing red liquid appears in the crack, a seam of molten rock so hot that Pace leaps back, shielding his face. It rises fast, filling the tear like blood fills a cut.

"This way!" Hayze cries, darting down a side street.

Pace and Tempo follow, shouts of the people in the houses around them bouncing off the looming walls.

"Stop!" roars a male voice. Hayze looks up to see a group of guards standing at the opposite end of the street, guns raised and pointed. "You're a traitor to the Elements!"

Hayze and the others turn and sprint back the way they came. They burst out onto the main street, registering the lava's now overflowing onto the cement. It eats away at the concrete as it spreads, turning it black, then melting it as hungrily as the firestorm devoured the bunkers in the Scorchlands.

"Down here!" Pace gasps, darting down another side street.

This one curves and turns and in a few frantic moments, they're running in the opposite direction to the Sect, but also away from the lava and guards.

"Look out!" Hayze shouts, unleashing a fireball.

It slams into the crackling net that was coming at them,

incinerating it. A dozen more drones that were lying in ambush shoot forward, their whirring filling the dusky sky.

Wordlessly, they turn again, once more returning to the arterial street. They wrench to a halt as they discover it's now a river of lava. A sulfuric stench stings Hayze's eyes as the road is eroded by pure, molten heat.

"What do we do?" Tempo glances back at the approaching drones.

Across the stream of lava, the guards appear. Two line up, side by side, aiming their weapons.

Roaring fills the air as Pace shoots out a barrage of ice. Shades of glacier hit the lava in front of them.

And disintegrates into harmless gas.

"Damnatus," Pace growls, focusing harder.

"I'll help," Tempo says, moving beside him. She joins him in the assault of ice on molten rock.

The frozen waterfall grows. The roaring multiplies.

And so does the steam rising into the darkening sky.

Hayze positions himself on Pace's other side, his heart battering fiercely against his ribs. If they can't escape...

A bullet hits the cement wall above his head. The whirring of the drones grows closer.

"I am Fire," he whispers, drawing the heat toward him instead of unleashing it.

It hits him like a wall, thick and suffocating.

So he invites more. Absorbs it all.

His body is a sponge for the assault. At first, it's overwhelming, singeing his skin, boiling his blood, melting his muscles. But one sharp, indrawn breath, and the heat is neutralized. Accepted as part of him.

Stored alongside the impossibility of Elemental powers.

"It's working!" Tempo cries.

The lava in front of them darkens, going from the color of

fire to blood to brick. A crust forms over the top, black and coarse, crackling as it thickens.

"Come on!" Pace shouts, running out onto the cracked surface. His foot sinks into the newly formed rock, fragile fractures breaking out. But it holds his weight. "Look out!"

He shoots out an ice ball, freezing a net right behind Hayze. It falls to the ground, the electricity short-circuiting in a spray of sparks.

Hayze and Tempo run onto the cooled lava, ducking a barrage of gunshots. Hayze focuses on the stretch ahead of him as he breaks into a sprint. He absorbs the heat of the lava, draws it into his every cell. There's the flash of unbearable fire within. Then a cooling intake of air, taking away the worst of the burn.

Over and over it cycles through him as he leads the way down the street. Behind him, Pace and Tempo create a wall of ice, protecting them from the drones and guards. They've escaped!

"Help!" The wail comes from above them and Hayze looks up to see a woman leaning out of a window, tears coating her cheeks. "Please, help!"

The house molded like a flame shudders and she screams, disappearing back inside. The cement structure groans, then slowly, dangerously leans to the side.

The lava's eating away at the foundations!

"Help!"

This time, it's a man standing in the doorway of the house ahead. A child clings to his legs, burying their face as they try to escape the heat and sulfur.

Hayze stops, already knowing there isn't a choice. Their powers have always been about saving lives. Pace and Tempo do the same, not needing to understand what they have to do next. Standing back to back, they extend their arms and concentrate on the two houses. The buildings go from the color of gray cement to opaque blue as they freeze them, affording the people inside a little more time.

Hayze kneels down and presses his hand to the cooled lava. It's still warm, the cracks revealing the molten pool they're floating on. "I." His fingers curl in. "Am." He closes his eyes. "Fire."

He draws the heat to him, becomes a conduit for it, a vessel to contain it.

"Yes, Hayze!" Pace cries.

He doesn't open his eyes, figuring that means it's working. "Get. Out," he grits through his teeth. "Get everyone out."

"Run to safety!" Tempo shouts.

"Get to higher ground!" Pace adds.

Cries and footsteps surround Hayze and he allows himself a look. The river of lava is now a crusted, dark road. People are fleeing their homes, sidestepping the veins of fiery red running through it.

There's a groaning crash somewhere at the beginning of the street and Hayze registers that one of the houses just collapsed. It breaks through the surface crust, crumbling and sinking into the lava below.

"I'm scared, Daddy!"

Hayze turns back to see the father scooping up the child in the doorway. "I'll carry you."

"But what about Mommy?"

The man holds the child tighter, his face twisted with agony. "She can't walk anymore, you know that."

The man leaps out of the house and runs, his sobs mingling with his child's. Hayze watches, realizing there's a woman trapped inside the house that was just abandoned. Sacrificed in the name of saving her child.

"I'll go," Pace says, already sprinting in the direction of the door.

"Pace!" Tempo cries, following him.

Hayze remains where he is, conscious that keeping the lava cool is his role in this catastrophe. Long seconds drag out. The street empties as everyone flees. Exhaustion drags at every muscle fiber, settling into his sinew. He doesn't have much left in him...

Pace appears in the doorway, carrying a frail-looking woman in a nightgown. Tempo's there behind him, reassuring the terrified woman.

A deep grinding sound rises from the house. A scream rips from Tempo.

Pace looks up, then around. His gaze settles on Hayze, a deep foreboding settling in his eyes. "Find Aura!" He leaps onto the cooled lava, already running with Tempo beside him.

"No—"

Hayze's cry is cut off by the rumble of stone falling, the crack of rock collapsing. The high-pitched sound of terror rising from the woman.

The house crumbles, falling forward as if someone pushed it. Pace, Tempo, and the woman disappear under the avalanche of cement. The downward momentum doesn't stop as the lava crust breaks under the weight. The rubble drops below ground level.

Sinks out of sight.

Leaving behind a stunned, devastated Hayze.

"No..." he whispers.

But the denial is useless. The house, the three bodies that were inside it seconds ago, are gone. Hayze takes a step toward it, wincing at the heat that pours from the pool of lava that's now there. Maybe he could...

Pace's last words rise in his mind. *Find Aura.* That's what his friend wanted him to do. He wanted the fight to end this to be honored.

Choking back a harsh sob, Hayze spins and breaks into a sprint. He no longer has the strength to run and use his powers, so it's a thinning crust that he runs over. A heating ground that his pounding feet sink into.

Hayze doesn't stop until he's passed the refugees of the devastation he's leaving behind. He doesn't stop until he can no longer smell sulfur or hear destruction. It's only then that he allows his momentum to slow and his thoughts to catch up.

When he looks back, panting, it's to a street of molten red far below.

Lava spews from the windows of the few houses that are left, through the holes it's eaten in the tops of others. Each has become its own miniature volcano.

Pace and Tempo...

Hayze doesn't let himself think of what their fate could've been. The impossible has happened more than once since he woke up on a raft, alone in the Deadwaters. The survival of the two friends who harnessed Water is a miracle he'll cling to until he knows otherwise.

So he runs toward the Sect.

Desperately hoping the collateral damage hasn't just begun.

FIFTEEN

AURA

"Do you think the leaders were pleased with how we performed?" Pyra asks. "Is that why they kept the three of us?"

Aura studies the teens the leaders deemed worthy of making it to Round Two.

Pyra. The girl from Fire who tried so desperately to harness her powers yet didn't make so much as a spark.

The tall girl from Air who didn't do very much except correctly classify the swarm of insects as fire ants.

And Kai. The boy from Water who specifically asked to be removed from the Games.

"I think so," says Jewel, nodding enthusiastically. "You did extremely well for your first time in the Games."

"I don't want to be here," Kai whimpers. "And I couldn't make ice when Aura wanted me to."

"But you didn't run away," Aura tells him, thinking how his counterpart from Water had given up the moment an ant bit her foot. "Which means you're brave."

This seems to cheer him up a little. He may be thirteen, but he still seems very much a young boy.

"Do you think they meant what they said?" the Air girl asks. "About us dying in real life if we die here?"

"What's your name?" Aura asks, stalling for time before she answers.

"Mystral." The girl gives Aura a sad smile. "And I really don't want to die."

"The first thing to understand about the Games," says Aura, "is that you can never assume anything. Including that the leaders are telling us the truth. Nobody's going to die. Our friends won't let that happen."

"Why would they say it then?" Mystral asks.

"To scare us," Pyra says with confidence. "If we believe we're going to die, our powers are more likely to come out."

Aura nods. There was a reason Hayze was teaching Pyra to paint. She's a fast learner.

Blinding light flashes into the arena and Aura's hands fly to her face to shield her eyes. As she slowly removes them, she gasps to see five new teens have appeared, sprawled on the ground. Two more are from Earth, there's a girl from Water, and two males from Fire and Air.

They get up and turn in circles as they take in their surroundings.

"Are you here by choice?" Aura asks, wanting to be very clear about the conditions of these Games.

"Who are you?" the boy from Earth asks, stepping forward and narrowing his eyes.

"I'm Aura from Fire. And I've been put in here against my will." She glances around the arena, hoping everyone in the control room heard that.

"We chose to come here," the boy says, tipping up his chin.

"You have to be kidding me." Kai throws out his hands. "Even after what you saw us go through in the first round?"

"We didn't see anything," the new girl from Water says with a concerned expression. "We've been waiting in a room until they called us in."

"Did you see the others come back out?" Mystral asks. "The ones you're replacing?"

The new arrivals look at each other and shake their heads.

"They must be resting," says Aura, glancing at Jewel to find her nodding a little too enthusiastically to be convincing.

"Or maybe they're dead," says Kai.

The teens gasp as their unease becomes palpable.

"Why would you say that?" the Water girl asks. "We were assured of our safety."

Kai plants his hands on his narrow hips. "Because—"

"Because they failed to harness their powers," Aura says, talking over the top of him. "But as you say, the leaders have guaranteed your safety, so I'm sure they're just recuperating before being returned to their families."

This seems to appease the group and Aura shoots Kai a warning look. The last thing they need is for panic to erupt in the arena. They need cool heads to face whatever the leaders choose to throw at them next.

"I thought the arena would be bigger." The boy from Air stands beside Mystral, his regal robes seeming out of place in this barren space.

"It's big enough." Aura glances around, deciding it wasn't just the walls of Jewel's hut that were closing in on her. The arena is too. It really does appear smaller than when they arrived.

There's another flash of light and Aura blinks, trying to adjust her eyes.

"I wish they'd warn us before they do that," says Pyra. "Hey! Where's Kai?"

Sure enough, Kai has vanished. In the exact place he was standing is a boy in a blue Water suit, only he's slumped on the hard ground. He sits up and looks around.

"Cool," he says. "What did I miss?"

"Nothing at all," the Earth girl replies.

"Kai vanishing is *not* nothing," says Aura, already missing the brave boy from Water. She just hopes he's safe. Surely even Skylus wouldn't allow anything bad to happen to an innocent child.

"Is it because of what he said?" Pyra asks. "About the others being dead."

"Who's dead?" the new arrival asks, scrambling to his feet and smoothing down his blue suit.

"Nobody," says Jewel. "There's absolutely nothing to be worried about. The sooner you can harness your powers, the more you'll enjoy it here. Just remember that you can't die."

"They said we could," Mystral points out, turning to the rest of the group. "Before you arrived the leaders specifically said in this round of the Games if we die, we'll die in real life as well."

"I didn't agree to that." The Earth girl jams her hands on her bare hips.

"Me neither," says the Fire boy, not filling out his leather suit nearly as well as Hayze.

There's a general murmur as the rest of the group agrees.

Aura holds out her palms and sparks a flame in each of them. As she hoped, this instantly silences the group as they become transfixed. If she's going to be left waiting in here, she may as well make the most of her time.

"While we wait for the next challenge to start," she waves

the flames dramatically, "why don't Jewel and I teach you to harness your powers?"

"Yes!" Pyra fist pumps the air, her face shining with joy.

"Break into your Quadrant pairs," Aura instructs. "Give each other a little space. You don't want to injure someone if you succeed."

"How do we get started?" the Earth girl asks.

"Hold out your hands and call on your Element," says Jewel. "You all have the power trapped inside you, otherwise you wouldn't be here. You need to tap into that part of yourself and bring it out."

Jewel puts out her hands to demonstrate. "I am Earth!"

She swipes her right hand across the arena, carving out a line in the dirt that divides it in two. Then she swipes it the other way to divide it in four, leaving each pair of teens standing in a separate quarter. Turning in a circle, Jewel then draws a circle in the center around the space she's standing in with Aura, before carving out a larger circle around the outside of them all.

"It looks like we're standing on a map of the world," says Mystral.

"That's right," says Jewel. "Now make your Quadrant proud by harnessing your power."

Battle cries echo around the arena.

I am Fire! I am Water! I am Earth! I am Air!

The teens throw out their hands, swiping the air and doing their very best to bring everything they have inside them to this challenge.

Aura and Jewel go from Quadrant to Quadrant, offering advice, desperately hoping that at least one of the teens will show even just the slightest hint of success. Aura would take a spark, a droplet, a fragment of earth or the gentlest breeze.

But there's nothing.

Surely, they can't all be duds?

As time wears on, so does Aura's dread. The leaders can't possibly be proven right. Is the trick to all of this to really believe that your life is in imminent danger before your powers will manifest?

"Aura," Jewel puts a hand on her elbow. "Can I speak to you for a moment?"

"Sure." Aura does her best to smile as Jewel leads her outside the circle.

"I know what you're going to say." Aura draws to a stop, keeping her voice low. "It's not working."

"That's not what I was going to say." Jewel gives Aura a worried look. "I was wondering if you'd noticed anything unusual about the arena?"

Aura glances around. "No. It's the same old torture chamber we've always been trapped in."

"Does it seem smaller to you?" Jewel asks. "Like, even smaller than when the Air boy commented on it?"

Aura looks again, this time filling with dread. "When you first drew the outer circle, it was several yards from the edge of the arena. But now..." She studies the metal barrier that curves around the arena and rises into the sky, noticing it's little more than ten feet away from Jewel's line.

"It's shrinking, isn't it?" Jewel asks.

"It is." Aura swallows. "It's been shrinking the entire time we've been here. So slowly we didn't notice."

Jewel kneads her hands together. "I'm sorry, Aura. I don't know why I wanted to bring you here. And there aren't even any seats for us to get you out."

"We'll think of something else," says Aura, not certain of this at all.

Jewel paces as she bites down on her lip. "Maybe I can dig another tunnel?"

"Frenius!" Aura grins. "We'll get out the same way we got in."

Jewel nods proudly and they return to the group, clapping their hands to get their attention.

"What's going on?" Pyra asks. "Do you have any better tips for us because this isn't working?"

"No tips for the moment," says Aura. "It appears that our next challenge has already begun. In fact, it began some time ago."

The teens look puzzled, and Aura holds up a hand to keep their attention.

"There's no easy way to say this other than that the arena is shrinking." She tries not to wince as she assesses their reaction to this news.

"But we'll be crushed," gasps Mystral, her eyes fixed on the thick metal barriers, which are only a few feet from the outer edge of the circle. "Unless I can learn to fly."

"It's unlikely you can hone your skills to that extent in time," says Jewel. "Although, you're welcome to try. In the meantime, I'm going to dig a tunnel to get us all to safety."

"Everyone, please stand against the barriers." Aura ushers the teens back to give Jewel space. The edge of the arena is almost touching the larger circle now and as Aura leans against the metal barrier, she can feel it creeping forward.

Jewel stands in the small circle in the very center of the arena and lifts her arms.

"I am Earth!" she shouts, boring her gaze into the dirt below her feet.

Nothing happens, so she calls out again, louder this time.

"I am Earth!"

Vibrating with intense concentration, Jewel curls her fingers into fists.

Still, nothing happens and disappointment shudders into

the pit of Aura's stomach. The leaders are clearly messing with them. There's no other reason for Jewel's powers to suddenly vanish. Unless she's doing this on purpose, like when Skylus *fell* from the sky?

"They're preventing me from digging," says Jewel between gritted teeth.

Aura nods, feeling guilty for doubting Jewel when she's clearly just as devastated her plan didn't work.

"That's not playing fair!" Jewel shakes her fists in the air.

Aura doesn't point out that the leaders never play fair. But Tempo and Pace do. They always do. They wouldn't allow this to happen, which makes her think that maybe they've left the control room to rescue her. All she has to do is wait. Preferably staying alive while she does it. Unless something has happened to them? *No.* She can't think like that. She needs to stay positive if she's going to get out of here.

Pyra fixes her gaze on Aura. "Can you melt the barriers?"

"I can try." Aura moves away from the edge of the arena, already knowing it's not going to be that simple. The leaders prevented Jewel from using her powers, which means they're not going to want Aura to use Fire to solve this challenge. The whole idea of these fast-tracked Games is that the new teens learn to harness their powers. But there's no way she's going to go down without exhausting all options.

"I'll help you." Pyra moves to stand beside her.

"Me, too," says the Fire boy, not wanting to be outdone as he stands on Aura's other side.

"I'm sure I can do it this time." Pyra flexes her hands. "So can Rekka."

Aura has to give Pyra credit for the solid effort she's putting in. She wishes she paid more attention to her back home in their village so she could understand what's driving her desperation to prove herself. Aura knows she doesn't have a father and that her mother isn't well, which could be part of it?

"Ah guys," says Mystral with a tremor in her voice. "We've reached the outer edge of the circle now. You might want to hurry."

"Okay." Aura surveys the terrified faces. "Everyone, get behind us. I'll try blasting this section here."

Nobody needs to be told twice. They rush behind Aura, going as far back as they can, which is only about twenty feet and closing fast.

Aura looks to Pyra and Rekka. "Ready?"

"Ready," they reply.

"I need you to try extra hard, okay?" Aura lowers her voice. "Because I don't think the leaders are going to let me do this. They want you to."

"We can do it," says Pyra.

"I hope so," Aura whispers. "Because everyone's lives are depending on it, including your own."

Pyra's eyes flare. "I thought you said the leaders were lying about that."

"I said they *could* be lying." She winces, hating that she's scaring these two innocent teens but feeling she has no choice. The leaders have been wrong about so much, but it seems that fear really is the key to harnessing powers.

"I am Fire!" Pyra shouts, stretching out her arms.

"I am Fire!" Aura echoes, quickly followed by Rekka.

A flame shoots from Aura's palms and she gasps, causing it to flicker as the shock of her success rushes through her. Gaining control of herself, she focuses harder, increasing the heat of the flame. She steps closer to the barrier, aware that hers is the only flame in the arena. The metal barrier glows orange, then white, then blue as she raises the intensity of the heat. Surely, it will buckle and melt at any moment now.

146

"It's so hot!" someone behind her cries out. "Aura! Stop!"

She lets the flame die and spins around to see the group of teens hunched on the ground with Jewel doing her best to shield them.

Pyra and Rekka are behind her, sweat pouring from their red faces and their hands held out uselessly in front of them.

"It didn't work," Aura gasps, seeing the barrier glowing hot but refusing to bend.

Jewel gets to her feet. "You can't try again. We're like frogs in a pot of soup."

Aura isn't sure what a frog is, but she gets the point. The leaders haven't stripped her of her powers, but they did a great job of making sure they're useless.

There's a flash of white light and Aura cries out, refusing to shield her eyes. It blinds her and when her vision is restored, she's devastated to see both Pyra and Rekka have gone.

"No," she sobs. "They tried so hard. They just needed a little longer. They were close!"

"Um, Aura," says Jewel. "It's not just the Fire teens."

Aura's confused, until she notices what Jewel's talking about. The six teens at Jewel's feet aren't the same ones who were there a moment ago. And there are eight of them.

Eight new faces.

And each of them just as confused and excited as the other.

"What is this place?" says the Air boy, the first to get to his feet. "It can't be the arena. It's tiny!"

"It's an arena for ants," says the Water girl, laughing.

Aura looks at Jewel. If only this girl knew what she'd just said. They've had enough ants to last them a lifetime.

"Do you want to tell them?" Jewel asks, as the barrier approaches the outer edge of the smaller circle, forcing them all together and making Aura feel like she's standing at the bottom of a giant pipe.

"I...umm..." Aura can't find the words. Nor can she find even the shadow of an idea that might work to get them out.

"What's happening?" one of the teens shrieks. "It's hot in here. And there's not enough space."

"We're going to get crushed!" someone else cries as the barrier picks up speed.

Aura finds Jewel's hand and takes it.

Jewel threads her fingers through Aura's and squeezes hard.

The barrier contracts, crushing them all together until their terrified screams are stolen from their lungs.

Agony.

Fear.

Confusion.

Helplessness.

Aura's world turns black.

CHAPTER

SIXTEEN

HAYZE

The moment Hayze steps into the true Sect, the oppressive heat, the drying breeze, the taint of black coal abruptly end.

But the exhaustion isn't going anywhere.

Neither are the images of Pace, Tempo, and that poor woman disappearing under an avalanche of concrete.

Or the knowledge that surviving a pool of lava would only be possible if they were in the Games along with Aura and Jewel.

Hayze descends the stairs, his jaw tight and wired. The Sect is cool and sterile, and the stark contrast to the outside world he just left has him realizing how devoid of *anything* the place is. There's no color. No scent. No noise. Mother Nature's been muted, molded and mastered. Everything is human made.

He narrows his eyes, not slowing, but now far more alert. The non-existence of sound is the part that has unease gripping his spine in a tight fist. There are dozens of teens now in the Sect. Surely they'd be making some kind of noise.

Refusing to falter despite his depleted energy or the harsh

149

grief or the alarm bells, he enters the main room, his palms hot and ready.

Except it's empty.

The screens are once more neutral and blank, the tiled floor unmarked as if no one's stepped in here for days. Hayze strides across them, hoping he's sprinkling coal dust as he goes. Everyone else must be in the pod room, being subjected to the Games. He'll deal with that shortly.

First, he needs Aura.

Turning, he marches to the door leading to Avalan's office. The screen is as colorless and vacant as the others, staring back at him impassively. Probably waiting for him to remember that he can't open it as he isn't one of the leaders.

"Damnatus," Hayze growls.

He spins on his heel and stalks back to the door he just entered through, nursing the anger and frustration. It's the only thing fueling his exhausted body. He presses on the edge of the door and it depresses. Opens.

And reveals what's on the other side.

"What the…"

Hayze blinks, even swipes at his eyes. All that faces him is a black wall dotted with wires and flashing lights.

Slamming the door shut, he works to get his breathing under control. He's more exhausted than he was willing to admit. He just opened the wrong freaking door! Hayze steps back, trying to reorientate himself. He already suspected each of these screens was a door, and he just confirmed that. Frowning, he scans the room. His tired brain still thinks this is the one that leads to the rest of the Sect.

Stepping to the right, he shakes his head, hoping to dislodge the web of exhaustion. He's so close. His mind and body can crumple once he has Aura back in his arms.

Pressing it in, his gut tightens, wondering if his assumptions are correct. Maybe this isn't a door. And even if it is, it could be one that needs a leader's tattoo to open it.

It depresses and springs back out. Yanking it open, Hayze is left stunned once again.

The room is about the same size as Avalan's office, but this one is lined with shelves from floor to ceiling. And each one is stacked, jammed, overflowing with food. Cans, fruit and vegetables in green and orange and red, jars of dried meat. The topmost shelf holds bottles of clear water, the lights from above making them glitter like gems.

Memories of the cave they found in the Quakelands back when this all began flash through Hayze's mind. They'd been so hungry and exhausted, just like he is now, they hadn't questioned it until the surprising buffet was already in their mouths and stomachs. But this time, Hayze doesn't move.

He may not be in the Games, but this still feels like a test. His body cries for the smorgasbord he's only feet away from. His mind is already tugging on his legs, ready to leap into the room.

Hayze slams the door shut, ignoring the way his mouth just flooded with moisture. Nothing happens until Aura's free and safe. And with him.

He moves two doors to the left, not glancing around so he doesn't have to acknowledge that his muddled brain is opening the wrong doors. A sharp push and it opens.

Once again, there are no steps, no way to get to the rest of the Sect.

And this time, he's assaulted by noise.

The monkeys contained in cages screech as light floods the room. They grab the bars and shake them violently, adding the sound of metal rattling to their furious screams. Hayze leaps backward, the memories of being attacked by these creatures who can wield rocks making his breath catch. He slams the door shut, adrenaline he thought was depleted spiking in his veins.

"What the..." he repeats, trying to understand what's going on.

Frowning, he looks around the room again. The sense of shifting sands, the same feeling he hasn't experienced since leaving the Games, is crawling under his skin. Striding over the pale tiles, he makes his way directly to the door leading to the pod room. He's been in and out enough times to know exactly where it is, no matter how exhausted every cell is.

Yet, there's a faint tremble in his fingers as he opens it. Hayze tells himself it's the lack of energy. Not the dread hot on the heels of the unease.

The door opens, revealing another room lined with shelves. This time, there are vials and jars of liquid, bandages, stacks of metal instruments and needles. Possibly what the leaders use to keep teens alive while they're in the Games.

But no pods.

Hayze staggers backward, sways, then catches himself.

What.

The.

Fractal.

He lurches to the right and opens the adjacent door. It's full of the silver pinwheels that dot the Stormsphere. The same pinwheels that collect Eterna's data so she can predict what Mother Nature's plotting.

He lurches to the left. This room's different from the others. The walls are glass, revealing what's on the other side. Ants. Thousands, probably millions of them. They crawl over the glass, the black wall only a few feet behind it, creating the illusion of a moving mass of brown. Each one with a flaming red dot on its abdomen.

Hayze slams it closed like the others, not wanting to know

what ideas those tiny insects have spawned. He already knows how innocuous anything can seem in the Games.

No longer caring which door it is, he opens them in a random panic. Several panes to one side he discovers a room filled with suits from the Quadrants. Blue for Water, red for Fire, purple robes for Air, brown straps for Earth. All hanging. Waiting.

Another is overflowing with vines that he has to shove back in, pushing away the memories of the cave he appeared in when he returned to the Games. Even back then he was willing to do what it takes.

To be where he belongs.

Beside Aura.

This time, Hayze chooses the door on the other side of the central room. This is the one he was sure is Avalan's office. The one he and Infernos entered when the search for Aura first began. The one Hayze assumed he wouldn't be able to access.

He pushes it. It sinks an inch. There's a click.

And it opens.

Wrenching at it, he can't stop the cry that scrapes up his throat and past his lips. There's no office, no desk, no extra button revealing the hidden room that Aura's trapped in. This room is full of edrian.

The precious, blue shards are piled as high as the ceiling, glinting in the soft light that now spills on them. As he stands there, a piece shifts, triggering the tumbling of luminescent blue. The small avalanche collapses like shifting sands on a dune, a few pieces rolling to a stop in front of Hayze's foot. But unlike the food and water, there's no temptation. No urge to enter.

A kingdom of edrian wouldn't be enough to deter him from finding Aura.

Stepping back, he closes the door far more gently than all

the others. His last vestiges of energy are now being used to try and still his whirling mind. He leans a hand against the panel and hangs his head. It's like he's back in the Games... The one place where making sense isn't a prerequisite.

Anger and despair battle within him, both growing with each passing second. Both winning.

Scowling, Hayze lifts his hand, clenches it, and slams it against the panel, deciding to feed the fury. The screen doesn't crack like he was hoping it would, instead pushing in and clicking again. And opening once more.

Hayze is about to shove it closed when he freezes.

"Hello?" a voice gasps from within.

He wrenches it open, discovering the room has changed again.

And this time, he's not alone.

"Hayze!" Geo gasps.

"About time!" Skylus snaps.

Hayze's mind struggles to catch up. This room was full of edrian moments ago. Now, his two friends are in here.

Both behind bars.

Geo has his hands wrapped around the thick, black steel as he looks at Hayze desperately. "The leaders turned on us."

Skylus is standing in the cell beside him, her arms tucked into the sleeves of her robes. "Can you believe it?"

Hayze doesn't answer, deciding not to state the obvious— they should never have trusted the leaders. "But how..." He's not sure what he's asking.

Nothing about this scenario feels real.

"Something in our food," Geo says, his mouth twisting. "They served us a platter of fruit and vegetables, even some dried meat, after the first batch of teens were pulled out. We woke up in here."

"Can you believe it?" Skylus says again, her voice rising.

"The first batch of teens failed?" Hayze asks, keeping his gaze on Geo.

He nods sadly. "I don't know where they took them."

Hayze takes a step forward, his chest tight. "And Aura?"

Skylus huffs. "Of course that's what you'd focus on. Yes, your precious Aura was there. So was Jewel. They tried to help the teens but it didn't work."

Hayze lets out the breath his lungs had been holding onto. "They put more teens in, didn't they?"

Geo shrugs. "We don't know. We were encouraged to have something to eat."

"And we've had so little food since we left the Games," Skylus adds.

Hayze's stomach grumbles with agreement, but it's the least of his concerns. "The leaders now have a war on their hands," he growls.

They've betrayed everything they promised.

Geo glances past him to the room beyond. "Did Pace and Tempo find you?"

Any shred of hunger evaporates as Hayze's stomach knots. "They did. But lava broke through inside Ignis. They..."

Geo goes a little pale. Even Skylus doesn't have a sharp retort.

Hayze clears his throat. "They wanted me to come back here. To get Aura out." He glances at the bars separating them. "And apparently you two. Why haven't you used your powers?"

Skylus rolls her eyes. "We woke up in pitch black. We had no idea what we'd need to use our powers on."

Geo ducks his head. "I was worried I was in the nothing." He shudders. "The ultimate torture."

"But they can't stop us now," Skylus says, pulling her shoulders back and closing her eyes. "Stand back."

Hayze takes a small step backward, but Geo doesn't move. He grips the bars tighter as he stands beside her, determination hardening his features.

A breeze gusts through the small room and Skylus's robes billow. Geo's knuckles turn white. The ground rumbles.

"That's it," Hayze says, his voice as tense as his body. "You can do this."

They've conquered far more.

The wind increases. The bars creak as if the metal's bending. A flush of heat flows through Hayze, possibly his own powers, possibly the fact that something's going to plan for a change.

Skylus's eyes shoot open as she gasps. "Why does it hurt?"

"What?" Hayze asks, stepping closer. "What do you mean, hurts?"

Geo groans, then releases the bars. He stares at his hands, looking pained.

"What's going on?" Hayze demands, now the one to grip the metal. "Are you two okay?"

It's clear they're not. Skylus is shaking, her robes now flapping wildly even though the rest of the room has fallen still. And Geo's still staring at his hands as though he's never seen them before.

"I can't move them..." he whispers.

"I can't stop!" Skylus cries.

Hayze reaches out, trying to understand what's happening, but a scream from Skylus has him freezing. She's now a whirlwind of purple robes and pale hair, her very own cyclone. One that's breaking apart!

"Skylus!" Hayze screams.

Her own cry eclipses his desperate shout. Flecks of purple shear from the edges of her outline, then her strands of hair fracture and scatter.

"Hay—" Geo chokes.

He freezes before he can finish the desperate call for help. As if he just turned to stone.

Skylus's cry splinters along with her body. She becomes a twisting, spinning whirlpool of tiny fragments. Specks that quickly lose any resemblance of a human form, scattering and spreading.

Beside her, Geo's a statue. His eyes are opaque. His skin becomes a sickening shade of umber. As Hayze stares, shocked and devastated, the tip of his friend's finger crumbles. Grains of dirt tumble down, buffeted by Skylus's disintegration. His hand is next, then his arm, the decay gaining speed with each second.

"No," Hayze gasps. He rushes forward and grips the bars, calling on Fire. He has to get to his friends!

Except they're already gone. Skylus has disintegrated. Geo is nothing but grains scattered over the floor.

Destroyed by their own powers.

Hayze takes an involuntary step back, pretending he doesn't hear the crunch beneath his boot. Another and he's out of the room, his stomach an acidic pit of nausea. Silence mocks him, gloating that he's once again alone.

An emptiness that's been created by the loss of Pace and Tempo.

And now fed by Geo and Skylus.

One that was born when Atmos died.

Hayze wills the door to shut, wanting to close off the room he just exited. The emptiness behind the bars is a failure.

Of his ability to save his friends.

Of his understanding of what they're up against.

Of Elemental powers themselves.

There's a faint movement of air behind him, the subtlest of

sounds, but one that tells Hayze another assumption has been proven wrong. He's not alone.

He spins around, registering Avalan stepping through a door at the opposite end of the room. It shuts behind her, cutting off the brief flash of her office on the other side.

She smiles calmly. "This central room rotates," she says almost conversationally. "It's quite clever, really."

Hayze doesn't move. He doesn't need to. The room's already spinning as he tries to keep up.

"So each of these screens can open into any room of my choosing," Avalan continues, waving a hand in a gracious gesture. Her smile grows. "Including my office. The one that holds Aura in a pod."

Hayze narrows his focus on the Air leader. On the woman who's orchestrated this all along.

He clings to consciousness with every shred of willpower.

So he can tell Avalan that if she doesn't get Aura out, he'll kill her.

CHAPTER

SEVENTEEN

AURA

Aura draws in a deep gasp.

She can breathe.

Who knew oxygen could feel like such utter bliss? It's almost as magical as kissing Hayze. Her heart aches with longing as she wonders if she'll ever see him again.

Then her eyes spring open and she looks around, desperately hoping to see the thin membrane of a pod gently pulsing with light.

Except the light around her is stark and blinding.

She blinks, devastated to find she's in the arena. It's back to its normal size, the circles and lines Jewel had carved in the dirt still visible, and the colored tiered seating still missing.

Jewel's beside her in the center circle, sprawled on the ground with her eyes closed. The eight teens crushed by the metal barriers have gone. That's sixteen in total now who've vanished, which still leaves twenty-four others to *fast-track*.

As usual in the Games, none of this seems fair. Kai specifically asked to leave. And Pyra and Rekka tried their best to harness their powers. With a little more work, they might have succeeded. As for the eight replacements put in right at the end of the challenge...they didn't even get a chance to try. What's the point of that?

Jewel stirs, opening her eyes and smiling widely to see Aura beside her.

"I'm so glad that's over." Jewel sits up. "It was gruesome. Probably my least favorite way I've died yet."

Aura doesn't have a least favorite. Mainly because that would imply she also has a favorite.

"Yeah, it was awful." Aura glances up, wondering how many of the leaders are currently listening to her. "If only we could have used our powers."

There's a flash of light as her response and she shields her eyes, knowing what will come next.

Eight fresh teens.

Eight fresh teens who have no idea what they've agreed to.

Eight fresh teens who are very likely to end up dead.

Aura pulls her hands away from her face and lets out a groan.

She was right. There *are* eight fresh teens. Well, she assumes there are eight, even if she can only see six right now.

Two of them are in a cage with timber bars in the quarter of the circle Jewel marked out for Fire. Another two are in the Air Quadrant, trapped in a tall glass cylinder with no lid. Two more are in the Water Quadrant, encased in a hollow cube made from ice. And in the Earth Quadrant, a deep hole has been carved into the ground, which Aura is prepared to bet contains two more teens.

"We have to get them out." Jewel marches forward, only to come to a sudden stop and bouncing back.

"What happened?" Aura asks, moving forward herself only to smack into an invisible wall.

"It's like the wall they put around Atmos's platform," says Jewel. "The one Skylus kept crashing into."

"They really don't want us to help." Aura walks around the edge of the circle they're trapped in, trailing her fingertips across the hard surface. It reminds her of the invisible walls in the maze when they were trying to reach what they thought was the Sect.

"They all look terrified," says Jewel, turning around as she studies each pair of teens.

"That's the idea," says Aura, despising the Games even more. "Look at how they're trapped. Even just a simple use of their powers would get them out."

Jewel nods. "The two from Fire could burn the bars of their wooden cage. Water could melt their way out of the ice. Air could fly straight out of the top of that tube. And Earth could cave in the hole. If they started at the bottom, they could climb right out."

"That's right." Aura clenches her fists. "Simple with powers. Impossible without."

The teens from Water are banging on the walls of their ice prison, trying to break it with their fists. The girl from Air is climbing onto the boy's shoulders to see how close she can get to the top lip of the cylinder. The Fire boy is shaking the timber bars of his cage while the girl waves her hands around, producing more wind than she is fire. And who knows what the Earth pair are doing deep in their hole.

"The Fire girl is the only one trying," says Jewel. "Everyone else has forgotten why they're here."

Aura waves her hands, trying to get their attention so she can mime some instructions. But nobody glances their way.

"Perhaps this barrier also makes us invisible," Jewel says.

"Urgh!" Aura sits on the hard ground and crosses her legs. "They really don't want us to help."

Jewel slumps down beside her. "I don't get the point. Why bring everyone in and not give any of them a fair chance?"

Aura doesn't answer. She doesn't need to. Jewel knows it's an impossible question.

They sit in silence, watching the teens struggle and hating that there's nothing they can do to help. A few times Aura gets up and bangs on the invisible barrier as if it's suddenly going to break away and let her out. But she's as much of a prisoner as the eight terrified teens.

Eventually each of the pairs sit down in their various cages. Aura's not sure how long the two in the hollow block of ice can survive before they freeze to death.

"They've given up." Jewel clenches her fists as she shakes her head.

"Maybe after a rest they'll realize they need to try something different." Aura presses herself against the barrier, trying to get a better view. She wipes some sweat from her forehead. It's getting ridiculously hot. If only Pace or Tempo were around to make some water. She's getting increasingly worried about them. If they were capable of rescuing her by now, they would have. She can't bring herself to consider what that might mean.

"Look!" Jewel is by her side in an instant. "You're right! They're getting up again."

Sure enough, the Fire couple are back on their feet, tugging at the timber bars, while the Water couple are banging on the ice and the two from Air are running their palms along the tall glass.

"Wait." Aura narrows her eyes. "That's not them."

"What do you mean?" Jewel asks. "Oh...I see."

The leaders have changed over the teens, this time without the accompanying flash of light.

"Is this a timed challenge?" Aura asks. "Did the others just fail?"

"I think so." Jewel's eyes spill over with tears.

Aura wraps her arm around her friend, noticing she's coated in a layer of grit.

"How did you get so filthy?" she laughs.

"And how did you get so hot?" Jewel bursts into giggles, realizing how that sounded. "I didn't mean it like that. Even if it's true."

"Because it's boiling in here," says Aura, ignoring Jewel's flirtation. "Maybe the dirt's sticking to your sweat?"

Jewel turns serious. "I have two problems with that. One, if that's the reason, then why are your arms so clean? And two, it's not hot in here at all. In fact, it's a little on the cold side."

"What?" Aura frowns. "You must be kidding."

Jewel's brows tug together. "Aura, it's not hot in here. You're burning up. Do you feel sick?"

"I feel fine," Aura insists. "Just a little hot. Maybe if I cover myself in grit like you, it will protect me from the sun."

Squatting down, she tries to scoop up some dirt, finding it hard like rock. Any loose soil must already be stuck to Jewel.

"You need to rest." Jewel urges Aura to sit down.

Aura resists, slapping at the invisible walls once more. "It feels so wrong to just sit and watch. We have to do something."

Jewel sighs deeply. "Let me know if you think of anything."

Aura sits down, accepting that maybe she isn't feeling as fine as she was making out. Before long, she's lying down with her head resting on Jewel's thigh while her friend periodically presses the back of her hand to Aura's forehead to check her temperature.

"I think they changed them over again," Jewel says.

"Changed what?" Aura's mouth is so dry now it feels like the floor of the forest in the Scorchlands.

"New teens." Jewel's voice sounds a little gravelly and Aura hopes she's not also getting sick. "Although, the Water boy looks like he could be the same. They probably ran out of replacements after taking Kai out early."

"Any of them harnessed their powers yet?" Aura asks, opening her eyes and straining her neck to try and look.

"Not yet." Jewel's voice is so deep it almost sounds masculine.

Aura looks up at her friend and gasps. What she sees is enough to have her sitting up in an instant. "Jewel! You're..."

"Yes." Jewel nods, her movements stiff and awkward. Her body is coated in so much dirt now she's barely recognizable. "I'm turning into earth. You're turning into fire."

"Why didn't you tell me?" Aura clutches at her parched throat. This isn't like when she and Hayze have absorbed heat and fire. It's more like fire is replacing every one of her cells.

"I didn't want you to panic," says Jewel. "I mean, there's nothing we can do about it."

There's a shimmer and Aura struggles to her feet, reaching out her hand to find the invisible barrier's gone.

"Aura, look." Jewel tries to lift her hand, only managing to move it an inch.

Sure enough, the prisons made from wood, ice and glass have gone. Even the giant hole in the earth has been filled in, leaving four pairs of teens in even worse shape than Aura and Jewel.

The Water couple are frozen into position, curled up into each other as they lie on the ground, covered in so much frost their blue suits look white.

The Fire couple are lying motionless, their red leather suits turning black as they spark with tiny flames.

The Air couple's bodies have broken into tiny fragments

that are only just holding together enough to show they were once a human form.

The Earth couple are standing side by side. Two statues made from dirt with their palms raised as if the glass cage they were pressing on is still there.

"This is cruel!" Aura shouts, hoping the leaders can hear her. "This is barbaric! Stop it right now!"

Her words have an immediate effect.

Except not the effect she was hoping for.

Instantaneously, the Fire couple burst into flames, turning to ash. The Water couple freeze into solid blocks of ice that melt, leaving a giant puddle that runs across the parched ground. The Earth couple crumble as their forms disintegrate, sending grains of dirt tumbling into two misshapen piles. And the Air couple spin into a tornado of fragments that scatter across the arena like seeds in a harvest.

Aura turns to Jewel, her own body flaring like she's going to combust at any moment. Jewel's in the same position she was when Aura left her. The only part of her still moving is her panicked eyes.

Just as the inferno sparking inside Aura gets too much, there's a flash of light.

This time it comes as a relief.

Because Aura's had enough of this iteration of the Games.

She blinks, hugely relieved her body has returned to its normal temperature. Running to Jewel, she finds her friend sitting in a daze, her skin clean and smooth, her soft hair flowing in waves.

"I still preferred that to being crushed to death," says Jewel, getting to her feet.

If Aura wasn't so shellshocked by what just happened, she'd laugh. How did her life become a series of decisions about which of their painful deaths they preferred?

"There can't be any more teens left," says Aura. "They've cycled through them all."

"Yet we're still here." Jewel nods.

"I don't want to spend the rest of my days in here," Aura says quietly. "I have a life outside. People who love me. People I love."

"I love you, Aura." Jewel smiles. "And I know that's not enough, but maybe in time you can learn to be happy?"

Aura desperately hopes Avalan didn't hear this. "We can't live in the arena." Aura looks around at the barren space that holds so many memories of pain and death.

"We could see if my house has returned," says Jewel. "I bet now that the Games are over, it's back. We have everything we need in there."

"No, Jewel." Aura clenches her fists. "I'm not going to play into Avalan's hands like that. I'm not going to give her what she wants."

"Even if what she wants is my happiness?" Jewel's eyes spill over with tears.

"I'm so sorry." Aura shakes her head. "I can't choose your happiness at the expense of everyone I love. Hayze will be so worried. And my parents. I have a mother who loves me, too. And a father."

A loud rumble fills the arena, shaking the ground. The barriers vibrate, the noise and intensity increasing until the metal structure falls away, throwing up clouds of dust and leaving Aura choking for air.

A gentle breeze clears the dust, revealing the increasingly familiar white fog of nothingness surrounding them.

Along with Jewel's small home, sitting innocently in the distance.

"Look!" Jewel bounces on her feet as she claps. "My house!

See! I told you it would be back. Come on! We can get clean, have something to eat, then sleep in a nice soft bed."

As tempting as all those things sound, Aura finds herself shaking her head.

"You go," she says. "I'm staying here."

"But...why?" Jewel slips her hand into Aura's and squeezes. "There's nothing here now. You can't stay out here."

"Actually, it's the one thing I *can* do," says Aura.

Since climbing into the pod in Avalan's office, Aura has had no control over anything that's happened to her. Everything has played out exactly the way Avalan wanted it to.

And Aura refuses to play that game.

She wants to go back to Hayze. And going with Jewel to play happy couples in her little hut isn't going to get her there. She'll wait for him in the nothingness forever if she has to.

"You're really choosing to stay out here?" Jewel asks.

Aura squeezes her friend's hand, then lets go. "No, I'm choosing Hayze."

EIGHTEEN

HAYZE

Hayze lifts his arms. He opens his palms. He unleashes a ball of fire in each, letting the flames dance around his fingers.

"Release Aura. Now."

Avalan doesn't move. "You're not going to kill me." Her lips twitch with amusement. "You won't singe a feather on my headdress."

He takes a menacing step forward. "That sounds like a challenge, Avalan."

"It's a fact. Because if you hurt me, you'll never learn how to free Aura."

The twin fires flare alongside his fury as a snarl rips past Hayze's lips. Avalan simply smiles.

She knows she's right.

That it's impotent fury raging through his veins.

Because she's holding something far more powerful than he is—knowledge.

"And my office is no longer behind me," Avalan says, clearly wanting to ram the agonizing truth home with a twist and a thrust. "It's now behind any of these screens and will move each time you open one."

Hayze is seething. The fires in his hands are a split-second away from razing this entire room to the ground.

Except he won't. And Avalan knows it.

Not when Aura's only feet away.

In a direction that could take hours, maybe days, to find. Time his exhausted body doesn't have.

Hayze extinguishes the fires. He drops his hands. He works hard to not let his shoulders follow. "I need her."

He says the words simply. With all the raw honesty he's been stripped down to. Hoping that Avalan has a heart that holds some sliver of compassion.

"So do I," she responds calmly. "Actually, Jewel does."

Hayze frowns. "What are you talking about?"

She waves a dismissive hand. "What matters is Aura's not leaving the Games. Which means we're at a stalemate."

Avalan won't let him get to Aura.

And he has no way of making her change her mind.

Desolation is now his only companion. His friends are gone. Missing or dead. Aura's trapped in the Games. Hayze is alone and out of options.

Except for one.

He settles his gaze on Avalan as resolve hardens in his gut. "Put me in the Games with her."

The Earth leader's brows twitch. "What?"

"You heard me. Put me in the Games with Aura." If he can't get her out, he'll go to her.

Avalan narrows her eyes. "You don't know what you're asking. If you go in, there won't be a way back out."

"It wasn't a request," Hayze says flatly. He's well aware that Avalan has no intention of releasing Aura, which means he won't be leaving the Games, either.

But a fake existence with her is something. A reality without her is death.

Avalan shakes her head as she opens her mouth.

"Take me to the pod room." Hayze tenses, about to say words he never thought he'd utter. "I want to go back into the Games."

Back to Aura.

Avalan straightens. She raises her chin. Her dark eyes glint with something he can't place. "Very well."

She turns right with a sharp move and stalks to the screen nearest to her. There, she swipes her Earth tattoo, then rapidly taps her fingers on the glass in a familiar pattern that Hayze has no chance of remembering.

The door clicks then opens, and Avalan enters without looking back. A few quick strides and Hayze joins her, finding he's in the pod room. And it's empty.

It's like he and Avalan are the only two people in the Sect.

"Where are the teens?" he demands. The leaders are also nowhere to be seen, but that's not his concern.

"You'll have your answers soon enough." Avalan stops beside the nearest pod. "Unless you've changed your mind?"

His only response is a hard glare before he climbs into the artificial cocoon. It's warm and soft and makes his skin crawl. Ignoring the way his body remembers what this means and instantly rejects it, he settles in. The moment Hayze's head hits the white cushion designed to cradle his skull, the exhaustion settles on him like a heavy weight. He blinks, staring up at the white ceiling above. This will be the last thing he sees. His last image of the real world.

Avalan appears above him, injecting herself into the picture. "Your choice has surprised me, Hayze." She's staring at him as if she's not sure whether she's glad or mad. "I'm looking forward to watching what happens next."

There's no opportunity to ask what she means, let alone try to decipher the cryptic words. Hayze's eyes close. His world goes black and his mind welcomes the reprieve. The gentle promise of oblivion beckons him, as tempting as Aura's sweet scent.

He's so tired of fighting...

Hayze yanks his eyes open, battling the darkness. Light floods his vision, as does the realization that he's standing.

That he's in the Games.

"Aura!" he cries, looking around frantically.

"Hayze."

His name is said with such disbelief and joy and tenderness that his eyes sting. A glance to his left and his world realigns once more.

Aura's there, heart-joltingly beautiful, only a few feet away.

Held in a cage, just like he is.

Hayze wraps his hands around the iron bars in front of him, registering he's surrounded by them. The round enclosure containing him is only a few feet wide.

"Holy fractal!"

"Pace?" Hayze gasps, his head snapping the other way.

His friend's also in a cage, pale and shocked. "Tempo, are you okay?" Pace cries.

She's in the next cage along, just as confused and scared. She nods, reaching through her bars toward Pace even though there's almost a yard between them.

Hayze glances around, registering they're all here, all seven teens who must've survived this long. There's no time to try and understand how Pace, Tempo, Skylus, Geo, and Jewel are here. Because they're also in a cage.

Hanging high above the arena, like a circle of canaries from the Scorchlands, just as trapped. Just as helpless.

"What's that?" Geo gasps.

Hayze looks at the Earth boy across from him, then follows his line of sight. Straight down.

He jerks back as the air wrenches from his lungs, making the cage sway sharply. There's *nothing* below them. No arena. No soil. No color or form or substance.

Nothing.

"Hayze."

He drags his gaze away from the endless black, latching onto the anchor Aura's always been.

"What's going on?" she asks, clutching the bars to her cage.

He shakes his head. "I have no idea."

"How..."

He knows what she's asking. "I asked Avalan to put me back in. I'd much rather this than a life without you." And although this isn't a scenario he could've ever imagined, one that he has yet to figure out what it means, the words are still the truth.

He's with Aura.

She's his reality.

"Oh, Hayze."

Those two words are all Aura has to say. Their lifetime of love means he understands the layers they hold. The emotions they capture. The kaleidoscope of meaning.

She's glad he's here.

As she wishes he wasn't now that they've woken up to this.

Whatever the fractal it is.

He turns back to Pace. "Although this isn't a plot twist I'm happy to be part of, I'm glad you survived."

Pace frowns. "We almost didn't. We used ice to protect ourselves, then climbed out before the concrete completely melted."

Tempo's shoulders sag. "The woman who was with us didn't make it."

"And the guards took us prisoner before we could get away," Pace finishes, bitterness twisting his mouth. "And here we are."

"I should've stayed," Hayze says, guilt tugging at his insides.

Pace is already shaking his head. "I told you to go find Aura."

"And you did," Tempo says, her lips softening and angling up. "My guess it's how we're all here."

Hayze glances at Skylus and Geo, now trying to understand how they survived when he saw them disintegrate. Then there's Jewel, still and silent and pale, another mystery he has yet to understand.

"That's exactly why you're all here."

The teens still as the words fill the air. The voice is everywhere and nowhere, but easily identifiable.

Avalan.

Hayze grips the bars of his cage and shakes them, fury burning away any questions. "Let us out, Avalan! The Games are over!"

The soft laughter that ripples through the circle of cages has his skin prickling. "You chose this, Hayze."

"I chose to be with Aura!"

"Same thing," Avalan replies smoothly. "That choice is what brought you all here."

Aura moves forward until her face is almost pressed against the bars. "Whatever this is Avalan, it needs to stop."

Skylus huffs, then spreads her feet and adjusts her center of gravity. "I'm not waiting to be released. The leaders clearly have no idea who they're dealing with."

She closes her eyes and angles her chin up. "I am Air!" Her arms rise, hands poking out through the bars.

Nothing happens.

For once, Hayze wishes it did. Frowning, he adjusts his grip on his cage, flexing his fingers and pressing his palms hard against the metal. "I am Fire," he hisses.

Nothing.

There's no heat. No red glow. Nothing.

"I am Water!" Tempo cries desperately, quickly echoed by Pace.

"I am Earth!" Geo shouts.

Hayze's gaze connects with Aura. She hasn't tried to call on Fire. Because she already knows what will happen.

They have no Elemental powers. In this virtual reality, they don't exist.

Skylus gazes at her hands, incredulous. She's probably wondering if she even exists without her ability to be exceptional. From the moment she discovered her ability to wield Air, it's defined her.

"Now that we've got that out of the way," Avalan says, her voice neutral and calm. "Shall I tell you why you're here? What the true purpose of the Games was all along?"

Hayze stills. Unease morphs to dread. Dread morphs to fear.

Avalan's suggesting this is about to start all over again.

"What's she talking about?" Tempo says, her voice small. Scared.

Pace shakes his bars so hard his cage sways. "No more! Do you hear me, Avalan? No more!"

Geo groans, the sound twisted with pain. Skylus is silent and pale.

"Pace," Aura says softly. "We have to stay calm."

He jerks to a standstill, his eyes wild. Hayze can't blame him. His body may be contained in a cage, but nothing's ever felt more out of control. He glances down before he can stop himself, his stomach wrenching at the sight of what will catch them if these cages fall—nothing.

"Elemental powers were only the beginning," Avalan continues, her voice omnipresent and unruffled. "We needed to ensure Mother Nature could be tamed."

"We never wanted to control nature itself," Aura shouts.

"I proved I could do that," Skylus cries, her hands in her hair. "I *am* Air!"

Pace glares at her. "Right now, we're prisoners."

Trapped.

Helpless.

Waiting to discover their fates.

"The true purpose of the Games was to see if humanity's worth saving."

Avalan's voice somehow whispers and shouts the words at the same time. Somehow makes them sound simple. Straight-forward. As if it was obvious all along.

Shock and confusion are the only two emotions now contained in seven cages.

"Hayze, when you chose to return to Aura, I realized it's time," she continues. "You were willing to sacrifice everything just to be by her side."

Skylus moans as she crumples into a heap of purple cloth and ruin.

"It's time to answer the question that's always demanded an answer—what are you willing to sacrifice so you can save every soul that depends on you?"

Hayze is stunned. Frozen with foreboding.

Feet away, Aura's just as unmoving. Somehow, their love brought them to this moment.

"It's time for the final Games." The smile in Avalan's voice is undeniable. "The ultimate Games."

Hayze has never heard anything more terrifying.

"It's time for you to save humanity."

CHAPTER
NINETEEN
AURA

Aura looks at her six friends hanging in cages over the bottomless pit of the arena. Avalan said they need to save humanity. Which, apart from sounding extremely dramatic, also sounds impossible. Especially without their powers.

"Hey Avalan," Pace calls out. "I don't get it. If you want us to save the world, shouldn't we be out there taming the storms? We can't save anyone stuck in here."

Silence echoes around the arena as his response.

"Pace," Tempo says gently. "Avalan said the Games are to see if humanity is *worth* saving, not for us to save it from here."

"How ironic." Pace shakes the bars of his cage. "They cage us like animals so they can test our humanity."

Aura glances at Hayze and he holds her gaze as a substitute for being able to hold her in his arms.

Tempo threads her hands through the bars of her cage and stretches out to Pace. "Don't let them get to you. You're better than that."

"I'm tired, Tempo," he says on a sigh. "Tired of all this. I just want to build a life. With you."

"I want that too," she replies in a soft voice.

Aura's heart hurts so badly she's certain there are actual cracks forming in it. She can't help but feel responsible for this. If she'd gone with Jewel back to her house, Avalan would never have brought everyone else here. Her daughter would have had what she wanted, and life would have gone on.

Instead, Aura sacrificed a safe, comfortable life for an uncertain future with Hayze. And it wouldn't surprise her at all if he did the same to get back to her. That's how it is between them. It's how it's always been. It's why she fell in love with him, not once but twice. First when she was only young and learning what love is. And then a second time when the leaders stole her memories, only to discover her heart did the remembering for her.

"There will be a vote." Avalan's voice wafts through the bars of their cages.

Aura swallows, breaking Hayze's gaze as she dares to look down. The base of her cage is made up of flat metal slats with enough room between them for her to see the gaping black abyss that's replaced the hard ground of the arena. She looks up again as her stomach flips over.

"One of you must leave the Games immediately," Avalan continues.

They wait for her to explain further, but only silence bounces back.

"What happens to the person who leaves?" Skylus asks. "Do we return to the real world? Or do we..."

"*Die* is the world you're looking for," says Pace. "Do we die?"

Again, no response is offered.

"This isn't fair," Geo growls. "We need more information."

"We can't vote for something when we don't know the outcome," Jewel adds.

"That's right." Hayze nods, his dark blond hair falling into his eyes. He swipes it away and glares at the sky. "Why did you put us here if you're not prepared to explain?"

"Hayze," says Avalan, sounding annoyed. "May I remind you that you requested to be returned to the Games?"

"I wanted to be back with Aura," Hayze says. "And for the record, this doesn't count. I can't even reach her."

"The arena is the last place you should have come back to," Aura sobs.

"Aura," says Avalan. "May I also remind *you* that you refused to leave the arena, despite a far easier life having been offered to you. You are also here of your own choice."

Hayze's eyes flare as he shakes his head in denial.

"This triggered the Games," says Avalan. "This simple act of a person choosing another over themselves. When both of you did it, at the same time no less, I knew it was a sign. It would be hasty to write off the human race when it's clearly still capable of selfless love."

"Gee, thanks guys," Pace grumbles.

Tempo shoots him a glare that despite the distance between them manages to shut him up.

Aura returns her eyes to Hayze and words pour from their souls as they search each other's faces. She knew their love was exceptional. But is it really strong enough to save the entire world?

"Avalan," says Jewel, her voice shaking. "Mother?"

"What the fractal?" Pace presses his face to the bars of his cage. "Did Jewel just call Avalan *mother*?"

"Mother," Jewel repeats. "You've done so much for me, and I'm grateful. Really, I am. But I need you to tell us what's going on. What's this vote about? What will happen to the person who gets the most votes? Stop avoiding our questions. Please."

"*Mother?*" Pace mouths to Tempo, who shrugs in response.

"She means Mother Earth, you idiot," says Skylus, rolling her eyes. "She's not her actual mother."

"Oh right," says Pace. "I knew that."

"The person who gets the most votes will lose the bottom of their holding cell," says Avalan.

"You mean cage," Pace corrects.

"And yes, death in the Ultimate Games will result in the loss of your life." Avalan adds.

"And if we refuse to vote?" Aura asks, already deciding she can't possibly take part in anything so brutal.

"Refusing to participate will result in casting a vote for yourself," Avalan replies, sounding like she's reading from a list. "A tie will result in two or more of you being selected. Once cast, your vote is final. Each Quadrant gets two votes. And you have two minutes to decide, starting now."

There's a short crackle of static and the seven teens turn to each other with jaws hanging open. A timer appears in the sky, made of fluffy, white clouds that immediately begins counting down.

"Skylus can't have two votes," Geo complains.

"It appears that I can." Skylus pulls back her shoulders.

"I'm not voting," says Hayze, his hands balled into fists.

"That means you vote for yourself," Tempo reminds him.

Tears sting Aura's eyes, even though she expected this from Hayze. She wants to protest, but knows she has no argument to offer. She can't exactly suggest anyone else, except herself, and there's no way Hayze will vote for her.

She looks across at Jewel, who stares back at her with sad eyes. Jewel isn't real. She's nothing more than a simulation, which can never compete with an actual human life. Or can it?

Because in all the time Aura's known Jewel, there's been nothing fake about her. She feels pain, love and hardship just like anyone else here. Perhaps even more acutely. Which makes Aura wonder what the definition of *real* is.

But there's more to this decision than that. Avalan is running these Games. And she's made it very clear to Aura that she'll go to any lengths to protect her daughter. Voting for Jewel could have consequences Aura isn't prepared to face. Not when Hayze's life is hanging in the balance alongside her own.

She crosses her arms. "I'm not voting either."

"But..." Hayze groans, coming to the same conclusion she just did. There's nothing he can say to change her mind.

"Don't be fools," snaps Skylus. "It's no wonder the leaders only gave you one vote each if you're going to waste it like that."

"Avalan," Aura corrects. "Not the leaders. We don't know where the other three are or if they're in agreement with this."

"Cyclonis would never allow Avalan to rule," says Skylus. "Everyone knows Air is the superior Element."

"Oh, shut up, Skylus," Pace growls. "Honestly, have you ever listened to yourself? You're obnoxious. Hayze and Aura are just as entitled as you are to use their votes as they wish."

"In that case, I vote for Pace," Skylus huffs. "Twice."

"No!" Tempo gasps. "You can't do that."

"I just did." Skylus scowls at Pace. "He's the obnoxious one."

"I vote for Skylus," says Tempo quickly. "So does Pace."

Pace nods his agreement. "Yep. Skylus it is."

Aura tries to stop her head from spinning as she catches up to what just happened. She turns to Geo and Jewel, the only two yet to vote.

Jewel's eyes fill with tears as she drops her face. "I'm so sorry, Hayze, but I vote for you."

"Jewel!" Aura inhales sharply. "Please don't."

Jewel turns away, her body shaking as she refuses to look at Aura. The betrayal stings hard. She never expected this from her friend, especially after Aura chose not to vote for Jewel, despite knowing exactly who and what she is. And Hayze has always been so good to her, in the Games and outside them when he spent countless hours searching for her pod.

"Well, that's two votes for Pace, two for Hayze, and two for me," says Skylus, brimming with confidence. "Geo, the power is in your hands."

He looks between his three choices, knowing that to refuse to vote, or to vote for anyone else will result in all three dropping from their cages.

"A friendly reminder that Hayze is responsible for us being here," says Skylus.

"And also a friendly reminder that Skylus is a complete pain in the ass," Tempo replies without missing a beat.

Aura shoots her a grateful glance.

Hayze reaches out a hand to Aura. "No matter what happens, always remember that I love you."

"You're not going anywhere," says Aura, doing her best to appear calm. "Geo isn't going to vote for you."

Hayze nods.

"Jewel," Aura begs. "Ask Avalan to stop this. It's not necessary. She already knows humanity is worth saving. She said as much herself. You're the only one she'll listen to."

Jewel continues to refuse to look at Aura.

Geo mutters under his breath, giving the impression that he's counting. But what could he possibly be calculating?

"You need to hurry," says Tempo, her desperation rising as the timer hits thirty seconds. "If time runs out, your vote will be cast for yourself, and it will be a three-way tie."

"Tempo," says Pace, reaching out for her. "I only have one regret."

"What's that?" she asks.

"Not meeting you sooner." He bends his head to rest his forehead on the bars of his cage. "It shouldn't have taken the Games for me to find you. I should have—"

"You should have nothing," she cuts him off. "None of this is your fault. You found me now and you're stuck with me. Okay?"

Aura watches this exchange, desperately hoping these words are for nothing. Then guilt punches her in the gut as she realizes this is the same as hoping for Skylus to die. Which she doesn't. As irritating as Skylus can be, Aura doesn't wish her dead.

"Hurry, Geo!" Tempo begs. "Ten seconds!"

Geo nods. Glances at everyone in turn, still seeming to be calculating in his head. Then he looks to the sky. "I vote for Pace."

So many things happen at once that Aura doesn't know where to turn her attention first.

Tempo lets out an ear-piercing scream that vibrates through the arena.

Skylus staggers backward, clutching her chest in relief.

Hayze rattles the bars of his cage, desperate to help his friend.

Jewel's shaking intensifies.

Geo hides his face in his hands.

And Pace emits a garbled gasp.

His cage groans.

The base opens.

And Pace's legs swing out. He grips onto the bars, trying to hold on to his last seconds of life. But the metal is slippery and it's only a matter of seconds before gravity pulls him down and he's forced to let go.

And now he's falling.

Aura forces herself to watch, sending him all the love and compassion she has in her heart, promising never to forget her courageous friend from Water.

Pace's face is a contortion of confusion and regret as he plummets with his hands grappling above him. He vanishes into the darkness and Aura focuses her attention on the girl Pace loved. The best way to honor him is to take care of her now.

"It's over now, Tempo. He was so brave."

Tempo looks across at Aura, her face riddled with horror. Then she turns to Geo.

"Why?" she asks him. "Why did you have to choose him?"

Geo shakes his head, reverting to the silent guy they first met on the rafts.

"Round Two commences now." Avalan's unwanted voice fills the arena as the timer in the sky resets, then immediately begins counting again. "You have two minutes."

"That's why I voted for him," says Geo quietly.

Aura lets this sink in. Geo guessed this would happen. He knew there'd be multiple rounds and must have calculated his chances of survival were better to vote with Skylus than Pace.

"How many rounds will there be?" Hayze shouts. "Tell us, Avalan."

She doesn't answer, which is no surprise.

"The two minutes have started," says Skylus. "Stop wasting time."

"I vote for myself," says Tempo, her voice filled with pain. "Twice. Please, everyone else vote for me, too. I want to be with Pace."

Aura had forgotten Tempo now gets the two votes for her Quadrant, and her already broken heart crumbles. She shakes her head, despite knowing she'd do the same if Hayze had fallen into the abyss.

"I'm sorry, Tempo," Aura says. "But I still refuse to vote."

"Please, Aura!" Tempo pleads. "Vote for me."

"All votes are final," Skylus reminds her. "Aura has voted for herself."

"Hayze, please," Tempo begs, turning her attention to him. "Vote for me."

"I'm sorry." He winces. "I also refuse to vote. I'm not playing this Game."

Jewel straightens her back and the pain in Aura's heart turns to dread as she silently begs her not to vote for Hayze again.

"I vote for Tempo," says Jewel.

Aura despises how relieved she feels.

"Thank you," Tempo says, tears streaming down her face, almost as if her Water powers have returned.

Jewel turns to face Aura. "I'm sorry I voted for Hayze in the first round."

Aura blinks at her, neither accepting nor rejecting her apology.

"I vote for myself," says Geo. "Skylus, if you also vote for yourself, the decision has been made."

Aura bites down on her lip, wondering if Geo had predicted exactly this scenario. He seems so confident with his vote.

Skylus tilts her head, studying Geo. "You know, Geo, I expected better from you."

"What do you mean?" he asks. "Just hurry up and vote. Let's send the message that we're refusing to play this Game."

"But you *are* playing," she replies. "You're trying to vote

Tempo out without it seeming like you're casting a vote her way. You're already thinking about how you look to everyone else before the next round starts."

Aura breathes in, desperately hoping two rounds is as far as this will go but knowing that won't be the case. "Just vote for yourself, Skylus. It makes no difference what Geo does. Use the opportunity to send Avalan a message."

"Or you could just vote for me," Tempo says, bracing herself for her fall.

Skylus nods, giving Tempo a warm smile. "I'm ready to vote."

"Well," prompts Hayze. "Let's hear it then."

Stepping near the front of her cage, Skylus leans forward. "Two votes for Geo."

There's a loud bang as the bottom falls out of both Geo and Tempo's cages, drowning out any reaction either of them might have had.

Tempo falls quickly, gone without a fight as she hurtles toward the person she loved the best. Aura cries out, even more devastated than she thought she'd be. She knows better than anyone how much Tempo's parents will grieve her loss.

Geo holds onto his cage in the same way Pace did, reminding Aura of when he clung to the upturned safe zone in the Quakelands to stop himself from falling. Only, back then, he had Aura and Hayze to help him. Here, he has nobody.

He lets out a strangled groan and tumbles after Tempo into the darkness.

Aura spins around to face Skylus.

"You did this," she growls. "Geo didn't need to die."

"Can't you see what's happening here?" Skylus spits out. "Saving Geo would only have meant needing to dispose of him later."

"What are you talking about?" Aura fires back, not wanting to accept what she's hearing.

"This is a game of last person standing," says Skylus. "And it's a game that I intend to win."

TWENTY

HAYZE

"Round Three. Now that we're down to four participants, there will be one vote per person in all future rounds."

Avalan's voice is calm, dispassionate. Hayze isn't surprised. She can't have a shred of humanity in her if she's watching this. Orchestrating this.

The irony that she says she's doing it to save humanity only makes him more furious.

"Avalan!" Hayze roars her name as he shakes the bars of his cage. "No more! Stop this!"

His only response is the floating numbers above them resetting.

2:00

1:59

1:58

Skylus half-wails, half-shrieks. "You can't take my extra vote away!"

Except Avalan can do whatever she wants. This world is hers. She makes the rules.

"Hayze." Aura's voice cracks and she draws in a shuddering breath. "We need to..."

He stills, even though the fire of fury is licking at his very soul. He needs to stop fighting this, no matter how wrong it is. The only way he'll be leaving this cage is if the bottom falls out and he plummets into non-existence.

Or if he wins.

Raising his gaze to Aura, he realizes there's a single outcome he's willing to consider. One outcome he'll do anything for. Sacrifice anything for.

Aura's survival.

He nods. "We need to do this."

They need to play Avalan's sick game.

Skylus huffs. "You've always struggled with acceptance, Hayze." She glances between him, Aura, and Jewel. "The sooner you realize what needs to be done, the better."

"Skylus," Aura says, her hands flexing around the bars of her cage. "Avalan's pitting us against each other. We have to be better than this."

Skylus glances up at the timer.

1:40

"I haven't come this far to lose, let alone die. The people of the Quadrants need me. They *need* Air."

Hayze shakes his head. "And you're saying I'm slow on the uptake."

"The people of the Quadrants need more than that, Skylus," Aura says. "They need to be united. And not just by the Elements. By their humanity."

Hayze glances at Jewel, noting the way she's watching Aura with rapt focus. He remembers how she voted for him in the first round. How she apologized to Aura. Realization dawns as the seconds continue to count down, making him wonder if Skylus was right—he's slow to figure things out.

It's Aura who stole Jewel's heart, a feeling he's more than familiar with.

No wonder she wanted Hayze out of the picture. He's a threat. How could he have not seen this earlier?

"Please, Skylus," Aura continues. "You're better than this. If we all vote for ourselves, it's a tie. We show that all our lives count, just like those in the Quadrants."

"Except then we all die," Skylus points out.

"If that's what Avalan chooses, then we die standing for what matters—our people's right to live."

Hayze's chest swells with warmth. Aura's embodying the very essence of humanity—love no matter what. This is what he returned to the Games for. But even as pride fills him, he resists the fierce urge to rattle the bars again.

He returned to fight for that. Fight for love.

Not to watch Aura sacrifice everything for it.

She turns to him, her ocean eyes a tumultuous storm of everything he's feeling. He wanted to at least touch her one more time. Taste her. Breathe her in, even in this fake reality.

He mouths two words. "Near far…"

Aura's lips move soundlessly. "Wherever you are."

"Thirty seconds," Avalan announces.

Hayze presses his forehead against one of the bars, inviting the bite against his skin. The Game is continuing as inevitably as time is. Jewel has her arms wrapped around her middle, her face pale. Skylus has withdrawn into her cage, chewing on her lip as she glances at the others.

0:22

Hayze resists the urge to look at Jewel. This is her opportunity to either side with the cause Aura pledged herself to…or kill Hayze. He opens his mouth, already knowing what his decision will be.

Except it's Skylus who shifts her weight, leaning forward so her face is between the bars. "I've always liked you, Aura." She glances at Hayze. "And you, Hayze. You believe in things like kindness and compassion and love."

Hayze holds his breath, hoping they've finally reached her.

Skylus turns to the third person trapped in this nightmare. "Which is why I vote for you, Jewel." She lifts her chin. "We all should."

Aura gasps. "Skylus, no! You don't know what—"

The bottom of Skylus's cage falls away and she drops in a writhing mass of purple robes.

She screams the entire way down, arms flailing and legs kicking in vain. She slices through the very air she was so proud she harnessed, a dead weight as she no longer has the ability to defy gravity.

The terrified cry abruptly stops. The image of her fear-filled face is swallowed by black nothing. Skylus has disappeared. Died if Avalan's to be believed.

Leaving Hayze, Aura and Jewel.

"What the fractal?" he whispers. He looks up at the timer and finds it's disappeared. "Avalan! We never voted!"

His answer is hollow silence. Callous silence.

"It's because she voted for Jewel," Aura says quietly. "Skylus voted for Avalan's daughter."

"Her daughter?" Hayze is puzzled. "That's why she called her mother?"

Aura nods. "It's true. Jewel is Avalan's daughter."

Hayze's eyes snap to Jewel, realizing that's exactly what just happened. This has been rigged from the start.

"You can't die," Hayze says, his throat aching as he looks at Jewel. "You've been safe all along."

She flinches, then looks away.

"It's more than that, Hayze," Aura says, drawing his attention. "Jewel...isn't like us."

He frowns, hating the uneasy sensation scuttling up his spine. "What do you mean?"

Aura glances at Jewel, then back at Hayze, her gaze heavy. "Avalan's daughter died when she was a child. An earthquake took her life and her father's."

Hayze looks between Aura and Jewel, trying to understand as he remembers Infernos telling him about this. How could Jewel be dead and have been part of the Games since the beginning...

"Avalan loved Jewel more than life itself," Aura continues, watching the realization both dawn and drag him down. "Still does. So she created a reality where she still exists."

"You're not even real," Hayze breathes, looking at Jewel. He knows he shouldn't be shocked. Not after everything he's been through.

The girl in the cage across from him is nothing but virtual reality. A program like the rest of his surroundings.

She's not human.

A tear trickles down Jewel's pale cheek. "I didn't know," she whispers, tightening her arms around herself. "I thought..."

Hayze staggers back a step, making his cage rock sharply. Jewel grew up believing she's real?

"Round Four," Avalan announces smoothly.

"Enough!" Hayze roars. "Avalan, this game isn't even close to fair!"

The timer appears.

2:00

1:59

1:58

Jewel whimpers as she crumples to the floor of her cage. "Mother, please..."

1:56

1:55

1:54

"We have to see this through," Aura says, her own tears shimmering in her eyes.

They're playing the final Games, the *ultimate* Games, whether they like it or not.

Once more, Hayze finds himself staring at Aura. Wishing this wasn't their reality, even as it is. Instead, he tries to tell her without words what he's already decided.

He won't vote for Jewel, and not just because doing so would ensure his death just like it did Skylus's. Jewel may be a computer program, but she's a product of a mother who couldn't face a future without her daughter.

She's a virtual creation who fell for the same girl he has.

She's a symbol of the very thing that brought him back here.

Love.

Aura nods, understanding. She already reached the same conclusion.

They speak simultaneously.

"I vote for myself."

They choose to die rather than be the death of someone else.

Even if that person doesn't exist beyond this realm.

Jewel shoots to her feet. "What?" she gasps. "No, you need to choose me!"

Hayze and Aura don't speak. Their decision has been made. Their fates sealed.

Even when he knows it'll mean his death.

Because Jewel will never choose Aura. And Jewel's already chosen Hayze once before.

Aura gasps, gripping her bars so tight her knuckles are pale moons. "No," she moans, realizing what's going to happen next.

Jewel's a computer. Of course she'll choose Hayze.

"No regrets," he says, devouring Aura with his eyes. "I love you more for choosing yourself."

Aura could've chosen Jewel, knowing she's virtual reality. But that would've meant either her own death, or choosing to end the girl she befriended and cares for. Jewel may not be real, but everything Hayze and Aura have experienced in the Games is.

Falling in love all over again.

Forging friendships.

Finding the truth.

And Jewel was a part of that.

Which means it's just her vote now and this will be one step closer to over.

0:15

0:14

0:13

The timer above reveals how much time these moments have both gifted and taken. Peace and grief, anger and acceptance all find an uneasy truce in Hayze's heart and mind. This isn't how he wanted to end, but it's also an ending he's strangely proud of.

This is worth dying for.

Love is worth dying for.

A sob erupts from Aura. "Jewel, choose me," she says, her eyes begging as she looks at her friend. "You know I don't want to live with the alternative. Please."

"What?" Hayze gasps. "No! I'm the one you need to choose!"

Jewel simply whimpers as she clamps her hands over her ears. She tucks into herself, a tight ball of misery.

0:05

0:04

0:03

"Just do it, Jewel," Hayze cries. "Don't make this all for nothing. Say my name!"

If she doesn't choose, the final Games were for nothing. His sacrifice, Aura's, was for nothing.

And that's not how this can end.

Jewel shoots to her feet, presses her face between the bars, and shouts, "I choose me! I vote for myself!"

Hayze freezes. His heart stutters. A new silence invades the space. Silence as profound and unfathomable as the nothingness beneath them.

Jewel just...

0:01

"Do you hear that, Mother?" Jewel cries to the sky. "I choose me!"

Jewel, the girl who's as virtual as everything else, just chose to sacrifice herself rather than hurt someone else. She chose humanity.

She acted with more compassion and selflessness and love than Skylus did.

Hayze waits, knowing this is significant. Unexpected.

And that it changes everything.

They've either won.

Or the floors of their cages are about to disappear.

Dropping them to their deaths.

CHAPTER
TWENTY-ONE

AURA

J ewel just broke all the rules.

She chose herself.

The Ultimate Games weren't supposed to end like that. Which makes Aura think they're not going to end at all. Not until Avalan has found a way to ensure Jewel wins.

"Why isn't anything happening?" Jewel asks, her eyes glued to the bottom of her cage. "It was a three-way tie. We all lost."

"You can't lose," Aura tells her. "You can never lose."

"But we were testing humanity." Jewel clutches the metal bars. "And I chose humanity over...whatever I am."

A flash of bright, white light has Aura shielding her eyes. She feels the slats of the base of her cage disappear from beneath her feet. Yet she doesn't fall. Instead, she's floating, just like Skylus when she learned to harness Air.

The light fades and Aura pulls back her hands, blinking as she tries to focus. She's standing on the dirt floor of the arena. The abyss has vanished, just like her cage.

Hayze is standing to her left.

Jewel is to her right.

Her heart tells her to run left.

Her head tells her to run right.

Instead, she remains where she is and waits for them to come to her. She's unsure who moves first. Both come charging at her and she opens her arms, embracing them together. Hayze reaches out, drawing Jewel in closer and they form a tight circle.

Aura releases her hold with no idea how this will end, only that Jewel will be victorious. Which means both Aura and Hayze will lose. She can't help feeling that they've already lost anyway.

A holographic image lowers into the arena, like a screen with no substance. On it is a video feed of Avalan.

Hayze's spine straightens. "Why don't you get in a pod and come here to talk to us yourself? Or are you too afraid?"

Avalan seems to find this amusing as she smiles at Hayze. "You're closer to the truth than you realize."

Aura frowns, trying to make sense of this.

"It's time to show it to you. The truth." Avalan's face fades away and is replaced with a video of a younger version of herself.

Aura wonders what this has to do with anything. She already knows Avalan's backstory. She was the daughter of the leader of the Earth Quadrant who was forced to take over from him before she was ready, because she was pregnant with Jewel.

Except Avalan's home in this video is like nothing Aura's ever seen before in any of the Quadrants. Or the capitals. For a start, it's enormous. The walls are smooth and painted pale blue, the floor is coated with something woven from white thread and the windows have black fabric billowing from them. Avalan must have been extremely wealthy to have access to so many resources.

Avalan's clothes are strange too. She's wearing blue trousers made out of a heavy fabric with faded patches and a tear in one knee, and a long soft coat that looks more like a blanket with sleeves. She doesn't have a single feather in her shoulder-length hair.

Young Avalan exits her house via a heavy timber door with glass panels in it, stepping out onto what looks like the deck of a barge, except it's on the ground. Planks of timber cover the area with a perfectly rectangular pond in the middle of it, inflatable plastic chairs floating across the shimmering surface.

Beyond the strange pond is a field of the greenest grass Aura's ever seen. Each blade is the same height, making it look like someone has trimmed it, although that can't be right. A forest stretches out behind the grass, with colorful birds circling the canopy as they call to each other.

A furry four-legged creature runs up to Avalan. Aura gasps as she waits to see if it's going to attack. But instead, it licks Avalan's outstretched hand as its tail wags furiously. Avalan pets the creature, and Aura sees it's wearing a red collar with silver studs and a metal tag.

"Where is this?" Hayze asks, seeming just as confused. "This isn't the Sect."

Jewel shakes her head. "It looks like paradise."

A man walks out of the home and stands behind Avalan, wrapping his arms around her as the furry animal wanders off to sniff at a bowl filled with more food than many people would eat in a week. Avalan turns to the man, her face glowing with wonder and love as she stretches up to kiss him.

Aura glances at Jewel, noticing tears streaming down her cheeks.

"What's wrong?" Aura asks.

"That's my dad," she whispers, unable to tear her eyes away from the scene.

"Oh." It's now that Aura recognizes him from the videos she was shown of the man who raised Jewel.

"I almost forgot what he looked like," says Jewel. "I miss him so much."

Avalan breaks from the kiss and Jewel's father puts a gentle hand on her belly, revealing a soft curve.

"That's you, Jewel," says Aura. "She's pregnant with you."

Jewel shakes her head. "It could be another baby. This doesn't feel right."

Jewel's father points up at the sky, seeming concerned by the gray clouds that are quickly gathering.

"Go inside," he tells Avalan, letting go of her as a loud rumble pierces the idyllic scene. As she scurries into the house, he rushes to the furry creature, stooping to pick it up as the tag on its collar glints in the dwindling light of the storm.

A bolt of lightning leaps from one of the clouds. Its jagged form shoots out like an arrow of fire and strikes the metal tag with deadly precision. The creature lets out an agonised yelp as its fur catches fire and the man staggers toward the rectangular pond. He throws the animal in the water, despite it being clear it's far too late to save it. The water hisses as steam rises from it and the man opens his mouth wide, gasping for air. His hands fly to his chest and clamp down as he tumbles forward, landing in the pond beside the dead creature and sinking beneath the surface.

"That's not how it happened!" gasps Jewel. "That's not how he died!"

Aura nods, equally confused. They saw Jewel and her father die in an earthquake when their house collapsed. This isn't right.

But her attention is quickly stolen by the image of Avalan running from her house and diving into the pond like she's from the Water Quadrant, instead of Earth. She disappears under the surface then reappears, dragging Jewel's father to some stairs at the end of the pond. Except she isn't strong enough to haul him out.

Rain pelts down, soaking any part of Avalan that wasn't already wet and she turns her face to the sky as she cradles the man she so clearly loves. She opens her mouth just like Jewel's father had, only instead of gasping for air, she lets out an ear-piercing howl.

The image fades and the Avalan of today appears in its place, her feathered headband adorning her dark mane of hair once more.

"What was that?" Hayze asks her.

"Didn't you recognize me?" Avalan asks.

"Of course I did." He plants his hands on his hips. "But who was the man? Where were you? Was that Jewel you were pregnant with?"

"Such a curious mind," Avalan replies.

"Where are the other leaders?" he asks, not giving up. "What have you done with them?"

"You just asked me five questions, without the chance to answer one," she says, her condescending tone hard to miss.

"Then start talking," says Jewel. "Because we all need answers."

"That man was my husband," says Avalan, her voice strained. "I loved him. What you witnessed just now was his death. His real death, not the one I made up for you in the Quakelands. And yes, I was pregnant with Jewel at the time. Or Gemma as she was called then."

"When was *then?*" Aura asks. "You looked like you were on another planet."

Avalan laughs at this, and Aura sincerely hopes she isn't right. Although, she's prepared to believe almost anything at this point.

"No," says Avalan. "That was Planet Earth. Back in a time before the rage of Mother Nature ruled our lives. A time before Quadrants, and capitals, and a secret Sect. It was before edrian, and pods and Games, and powers. In those days Mother Nature was merely throwing a small tantrum, instead of her murderous rampage that came after."

"It couldn't have been that long ago." Jewel runs a hand through her dark hair. "I'm only eighteen."

"You're not any age, my daughter," says Avalan. "In fact, you're not even my daughter. My real flesh and blood daughter was born centuries ago. That's what you saw just now. A calmer time when people lived in large homes with gardens, and pets and pools. Although, admittedly Mark and I had more than others. He ran one of the most successful tech companies the world had ever seen, and it was all his own creation. He taught me everything I know. Oh Jewel, he loved me so much. I just know he would have loved you, too."

"But I remember my father," says Jewel. "He raised me. How can I remember that if he died before I was born? And how are you still alive if all this happened centuries ago?"

Avalan shakes her head as she fades away, replaced by the image of her younger self, sitting at a large timber desk, surrounded by screens. She's typing furiously at a keyboard, her screens lit up with long lines of data that's flashing by so quickly Avalan barely has time to blink as she adds to it. She looks different to the last video of her. For a start, she's rail thin, like she hasn't eaten in weeks. Her hair is limp and greasy, her skin sallow, and she has dark circles underneath her blood-shot eyes. Aura's not sure she'd have recognized this version of her so quickly.

"Can you hear that?" Hayze asks Aura quietly.

She nods. "A baby's crying."

"Is that me?" Jewel asks. "Why isn't she going to me?"

"I don't think she can hear you," says Aura. "She's too involved in her work."

Avalan throws up her hands in victory and lets out a whoop of joy that momentarily drowns out the sound of her baby crying. She leans back in her chair, and one of her screens lights up with an image of Jewel's father, standing in a white fog.

Avalan gets up and crosses the room, pulling back a curtain to reveal something a lot more familiar to everyone watching.

A pod.

She climbs in, still ignoring the sound of her desperate child calling for her and closes her eyes as the glowing membrane cocoons her.

"Look at the screen," says Hayze.

For a moment, Aura's confused. They're all looking at the screen. Then she realizes he means the screen on Avalan's desk. The one that had held the image of Jewel's father. Because now Avalan is standing beside him. Not the exhausted, malnourished version of her, but an image of her best self. Sleek hair, strong curves, clear skin. She's just as beautiful as the older version of herself is now.

Jewel's father opens his arms wide, and she steps into them.

All the while, baby Jewel continues to cry, her wails climbing in pitch before eventually turning to an exhausted sputter.

"Turn it off," says Jewel, looking in danger of crying again now. "Avalan! Turn it off!"

Aura notices she didn't call her *Mother*. She can't blame

her. The behavior they're witnessing isn't how a mother cares for her child.

The scene continues with a virtual Avalan embracing Jewel's father, while the child they created in real life falls quiet.

"That's awful," Aura whispers, a tear of her own streaking down her face.

The image blinks as if time has passed and shifts to Avalan climbing out of her pod. She stretches, smiles and looks at her screens with proud satisfaction, trailing a fingertip down the one that contains Jewel's father, who's now standing alone.

Then shaking her head as if she just remembered something, she walks quickly out of the room. The camera angle changes and now they see a smaller room with a strange small bed that has high sides on it, like a prison cell with no roof. There's a baby in it, lying perfectly still and silent.

Aura slips her hand into the comfort of Hayze's, already knowing what they're about to see will be difficult to witness.

Avalan runs to the small bed and lifts her very still baby to her chest, collapsing to the floor and sobbing in the same way she had when lightning stole the man she loved.

"She left me to die," Jewel says with a hard edge to her voice. "I was only a baby."

Aura lets go of Hayze to put her arm around her friend. "I'm so sorry that happened to you."

Jewel nods. "I've never been real. Not since that day. Not since she left me."

The image fades and the older Avalan returns.

"You made up my entire life story." Jewel clenches her fists. "Why?"

"I'm so sorry." Tears pour down Avalan's perfect face. "I can't tell you how sorry I am. I wasn't thinking straight in my grief. What happened to you was entirely my fault."

"It was," Jewel spits out. "You killed me."

"I really am so very sorry," Avalan repeats. "You'll never know just how sorry I am."

"You created a simulation of me in virtual reality," says Jewel. "You gave me a virtual existence, thinking it could replace the life you stole from me."

Avalan nods. "I took so much from you. It was the only way I could give you something back. You had a beautiful life in the Quakelands, getting to know the father you never had the chance to meet."

"Then you took him from me, too," says Jewel. "And sent me nothing more than a simulation in his place."

Avalan nods. "Your father was doting on you too much. You were never going to win the Games if you didn't learn to be independent. Rateen gave you the preparation you needed, even if you weren't aware that's what she was doing."

"But what are the Games?" Aura asks. "How did the world get from what we just saw to the world as we know it now?"

"You don't understand, do you?" Avalan shakes her head in disbelief. "After everything you've lived through, you still don't understand."

"Then tell us," Hayze growls.

"Jewel isn't real," she says. "None of this is real. Everything you've ever experienced and everyone you've ever met was put there by me."

Aura lets go of Jewel to look at Hayze.

"Are you saying we're not real?" she asks, not taking her eyes from the only real thing she's ever known.

"Not exactly," says Avalan. "You're real. At least you were real when I created this world for you to live in. You should be gratef—"

"Grateful?" Hayze booms. "For what exactly should we be grateful?"

"Keep your vest on," says Avalan. "Let me show you."

The screen fades and Aura, Hayze and Jewel contract closer, with no idea what they're about to witness.

"Pods," says Hayze, stating the obvious as the screen lights up again.

"So many pods," Aura adds as the image pulls back to reveal not just one but dozens.

"Humans were destroying the planet," Avalan's voice filters into the arena. "Temperatures were rising. Icecaps were melting. Forests were burning. There were hurricanes, and tsunamis, and earthquakes as volcanoes erupted and cities were swept away. So, I came up with a Solution. The Ultimate Solution."

"I thought we were the Solution," says Aura. The camera sweeps across the pods as if it's being filmed by a drone. She falls silent as she tries to take in the scale of the scene before her. There aren't just dozens of pods, there are hundreds of them. As the drone continues to pull back, hundreds become thousands.

"People could take their chances on a dying planet," says Avalan. "Or they could purchase a pod that would perfectly preserve their body for however long it took for the world to regenerate. To keep your minds active, I created a world of Quadrants. One where you'd learn to respect the environment so that when you finally woke up, you'd never mistreat your planet again. Your memories of your previous life were put on pause while these lessons were learned. Put simply, the Games are a test of humanity. They're designed to see when it's time to wake up."

Aura is speechless. It has been difficult in the Games to accept that nothing that was happening to them was real. But this is a whole new level. If they can believe what Avalan is telling them, their entire lives have been a fake.

"Are we in those pods?" Hayze asks.

"That's right," says Avalan. "Everyone you've ever met is in one of them. Tempo. Pace. Skylus. Your parents. Everyone. Well, everyone except Jewel. And Rateen."

"Are you in one of them?" Jewel asks. "Did you choose to live, even though you let me die?"

"I am," says Avalan. "I needed to see if my Solution would work. And despite how much we've figured out about the world, none of us really know what happens after we die. The only guarantee I had of spending time with you was by joining you in this world."

"In a fake world," Hayze mutters.

"But so much of it was real." Avalan's voice takes on an emotional edge. "Your parents chose to be your parents again. World leaders became leaders once more. Even you and Aura were drawn to each other again."

Aura turns to Hayze to find he's not at all surprised by this. Neither is she. Their love is their constant.

"Three times," he whispers. "Not two."

"What do you mean?" she asks.

"I fell in love with you three times." He draws her to his chest. "Once in our real lives. Once in the Scorchlands. And then again in the Games. Three times you've stolen my heart."

Aura wraps her arms around his waist, turning her face from the devastating image on the screen. Evidence of so many people desperate to escape their dying planet, including themselves. She lets go of Hayze as another thought occurs to her.

"What happened to those who couldn't afford a pod?" she asks.

Avalan falls unusually silent, which is an answer itself. She allowed the elements to exterminate them. Only the wealthy survived, who ironically were the ones to have killed the planet in the first place. Aura can only hope that she and Hayze did as much as they could to set that right before they climbed into a pod themselves.

"If you won't answer that," says Hayze, "then answer this. If you're in a pod, then who's controlling the world? Who's regulating the pods? Who's been deciding what happens in the virtual lives you've created us for hundreds of years?"

"The one I trust the most," says Avalan.

"Who?" Hayze growls.

"Eterna," says Avalan. "But she already told you that."

"Rateen." Aura's brows shoot up. "We're being controlled by artificial intelligence."

"That's right." Avalan laughs again. "The non-playable character is playing us all."

TWENTY-TWO

HAYZE

Nothing.
    Is.
    Real.

Hayze has lost count of how many times that revelation has shattered his very existence, but this time, he's not sure it can be put back together.

Because there's nothing to resurrect.

No pieces.

No truth.

No phoenix to rise from the flames.

Because none of it existed.

He looks down at his hands. "There's no such thing as Elemental powers, is there?" he asks hoarsely.

Avalan chuckles. Or should he call her Eterna? Or Rateen, seeing as they're all the same person. The mastermind of the world he thought was real. The owner of every truth he's ever believed. "No. They were part of the simulation, like everything else."

"Simulation," Aura whispers.

Jewel crumples to the ground. "But..."

Hayze wonders which part finally brought her down. The grief of her father's death. Or the truth of her own sad ending. Or the weight of knowing the world she was trying to save was never real?

Hayze blinks. In some ways, he and Aura are as real as Jewel is. They don't exist in this realm any more than she does.

The only difference is Hayze and Aura have bodies tucked into pods somewhere, along with thousands of others.

Along with Avalan's.

Drawing Aura to him, Hayze turns back to the screen. Avalan's looking at Jewel as if she wants to step out of the screen and take her in her arms. Technically, she could seeing as this entire reality is her own making, but she doesn't. Hayze draws in a sharp breath as he realizes why.

Jewel may have been her virtual creation, the only way for Avalan's daughter to grow up, but she became more than that. She developed her own thoughts. Her own emotions.

She learned to sacrifice for love.

The computer simulation Avalan birthed would never have chosen herself in the final Games. She would've chosen Hayze so she ensured she kept the one she loves by her side—Aura. In the same twisted way Avalan chose to build something of such monumental proportions so she could keep her daughter from the non-existence of death.

"We won," Hayze breathes. His arms tighten around Aura as he straightens. This time, he says the words with more force. More certainty. "We won, Avalan."

Aura's spine also uncurls, shedding the shock the ultimate lie their life has been. "Humanity won."

"That's why you created all of this," Hayze says, sweeping an arm to indicate not only the arena, but everything else beyond it. The Sect. The capitals. The Quadrants.

All fake.

All virtual.

All a *simulation*.

"To test whether humanity was ready to return to the world we took for granted."

Avalan stiffens, her dark gaze snapping back to Hayze. "The world humanity destroyed with ignorance and greed and selfishness."

The same world that took Avalan's husband. The same world she was escaping when she neglected her daughter.

Hayze releases Aura as he takes a step forward, watching her closely. "It's healed, hasn't it? That's why the Games were started. Because we can go back."

"We can wake up," Aura says, sounding like she's trying to assimilate the ramifications of that as she joins him.

Hayze is trying to do the same. Avalan said centuries have passed. What does Earth look like now? What world will they return to?

"They're right." Jewel gets to her feet, coming to stand beside them. "Aura and Hayze have shown they're ready to live for what matters."

Their hands instinctively find each other's. Their fingers intertwine. Their gazes don't leave the woman who laid down the ultimate gauntlet.

The one they picked up.

And refused to use.

Avalan's lips settle into a firm line. "Yes, they did."

Jewel spins to look at Aura. "I knew you would." A blinding smile splits across her face. "You saved everyone."

Aura reaches out to clasp her hand. "We all did."

Hayze nods, extending his own even as he wonders whether Jewel will take it. She didn't wish him dead in the end, but that doesn't mean she's willing to accept his token of truce. It's Aura who Jewel ultimately chose.

Jewel takes his hand, then squeezes it. "I only chose me because I couldn't be the one to tear you apart. I realized the love you two have isn't one I could come between." She looks over her shoulder toward the screen. Toward her mother. "I realized I couldn't be the one to end it."

Hayze's breath evacuates his body. He gazes at Aura in mute shock. They really did win.

Their love, the one that time and reality couldn't destroy, won.

Which means they're about to wake up from the dream they didn't know they were living in. They're about to live and love all over again.

Aura nods, a sweet, mesmerizing smile playing along her lips.

Hayze mirrors her, a sweet, mesmerizing joy singing through his veins.

"It's time, Mother," Jewel says, squaring her shoulders and raising her chin. "Humanity has earned its place back in the world."

Hayze ignores the faint flash of irritation. He's not sure who decided Avalan was the one to decide that, but he's not going to argue. Not when he's just won the Games he never wanted to play.

And is gaining more than he could have ever imagined.

"No."

Avalan's single word is a blunt blow. One that leaves Hayze reeling for long seconds.

"No?" he eventually gasps.

"What do you mean, no?" Aura demands.

"It's pretty self-explanatory," Avalan responds flatly. "I'm not ending this."

Hayze shakes his head. "Humanity won. We chose."

Aura's free hand twists into a fist. "It's time to wake everyone up."

It's time to end something that should never have begun.

Avalan's gaze falls on her daughter, softening. "Jewel's shown that the world doesn't need humanity. Virtual humans can be more compassionate and loving than real ones."

"What?" Hayze shouts.

"You can't..." Aura cries.

Jewel runs toward the screen. "Mother, you have to—"

Everything flashes a blinding, painful white.

Hayze shouts in anger and alarm, grasping for Aura. And touching nothing.

Because that's all there is.

Nothing.

He spins one way, then the other, desperate and terrified in a way he hasn't been since the Games began. He's scared for his life. For Aura's. And every soul who was depending on them.

All he sees, hears, tastes, is nothing.

"Avalan!" he roars, injecting red hot rage into the one word.

The white nothingness swallows it. Absorbs it.

Nullifies it like it doesn't exist.

Maybe even reduces it to a string of data to be filed away somewhere under 'humanity behaving badly.'

Hayze breaks into a run, knowing there's nowhere to go, but too full of desperate denial to do anything else. His legs move. His arms pump. His lungs spasm in and out.

But there's no wind on his face. No horizon to be seen. No shred of hope.

"Aura!" he gasps.

He tires almost instantly. So quickly that he knows it's not natural. His own body isn't becoming fatigued, the pod containing it is shutting it down.

He stumbles, tries to right himself, only to discover he can no longer feel his legs. He barely feels his torso crashing to the non-existent floor beneath him. He's vaguely conscious that his head bounces on the endless white that shouldn't have substance.

One moment he's throwing himself through the nothing, the next he's a barely-conscious pile of limbs lying in it. Hayze blinks, realizing what's happening.

He's becoming a part of it.

His lips twitch, wanting to voice how much every cell in his body rejects that. That through all of this, he's been *something*.

The one who protected Aura with everything he had.

The heart that beat for her.

The soul that fell for her, over and over again.

Except this moment is the undeniable culmination of exactly who's in control. Of who decides exactly what he is. His body doesn't move. His heart rate slows. His breathing is so faint he can barely hear it.

Avalan's shutting him down. Putting him to sleep.

Possibly worse.

Hayze's eyes flutter closed against his will, hating how helpless he feels. Hating that Avalan's no doubt watching this. The virtual Avalan. The woman who created this world centuries ago intended for it to be temporary. For it to last as long as the Earth needed. And for humanity to learn to do better.

But the computer version that's her legacy has decided otherwise.

The mother who's nothing but code and algorithms. The one who was probably never going to give up the daughter that's as virtual as she is.

White is all Hayze can see behind his eyelids. White...nothingness. The same absence of anything is slowly taking over his mind. It's already swallowed his body.

Will this all start again?

Will he live for centuries in the same reality, like Jewel has?

Will his consciousness cease to exist?

As he fades fast, Hayze hates that this helplessness is a reminder of who was really in control all along. He can't cry. Can't say Aura's name one last time. Can't stop the realization that he lost the Games he never wanted to win.

And it cost him everything.

TWENTY-THREE

AURA

Aura is no longer in the nothingness.

She is the nothingness.

The arena has gone. Her body has gone. Her mind is hanging on by a gossamer thread.

Avalan went rogue. Not the flesh and blood woman who's lying in a pod, waiting to be woken when the planet is healed, but the artificial version of her. This was something not even Avalan could have predicted—that her creation would develop an independence capable of overruling her own desires. And she unwittingly gave it the opportunity to seize control and change the course of her future. Of all their futures. Because there are no humans left to wake them up.

They're at the mercy of a machine. One who's shown herself to be cruel, manipulative, and relentless. *Eterna*. If Aura had lips, she'd smile at the appropriateness of the name. Eterna's rule will be forever, holding their fate in hands made from lines of code.

Aura drifts, trying desperately to replace thoughts of Eterna with thoughts of Hayze but finding herself unable to as the white fog invades her consciousness. She's not sad. Not angry. Not lonely. Not…anything.

She just is.

"Aura," a voice whispers. "Aura!"

She doesn't ignore the voice. It's more that she has no idea what to do with it. Moving is beyond her. Listening is a challenge. Thinking is only just possible.

"Aura." The voice is louder now. More insistent. "Aura, can you hear me?"

Yes.

"It's me, Aura. It's Jewel. Please answer me."

How?

"Wake up!"

I'm asleep?

"Open your eyes, Aura!"

I have eyes?

"Aura, you have to hurry. Skylus was right when she said you need to focus all your energy on your real self until you can return your mind to your pod."

Who's Skylus?

"The reason it didn't work in the Games was because the body you focused on wasn't your real self. The one being held in suspension is. Do it, Aura. Hurry!"

Do what?

"I can't stay, Aura. Eterna's looking for me. I've encrypted myself using a cipher. She'll find me eventually, which is why you must wake up. Now, Aura! Wake up!"

What's a cipher?

"Go to the pod, Aura! End all of this. Do it now. Find Hayze and go to the pod!"

Hayze? Hayze… Hayze!

A current of electricity ripples through Aura's awareness. It jolts something deep inside her consciousness.

Her legs can't move.

But they exist.

Her arms are like weights at her side.

But they're there. And she can feel them.

Her chest rises and falls as her heart beats in a slow, steady rhythm.

And the smallest toe on her left foot twitches to life.

Aura focuses on that toe, stretching her mind to encompass the entire foot. She travels all the way up her leg, rushing down when she reaches the top to sweep her right side. When she gets to her toes on her right foot, she moves up again, keeping her focus on both feet. Both shins. Both knees. Both thighs. She drifts across her pelvis, her stomach, counts each rib inside her chest, until she's at her shoulders. Left arm. Left hand. Four fingers and one thumb. Then up again. Right arm. Right hand. Four fingers and one thumb. She moves up, keeping her entire body in her mind until she finds her neck, then her jawline, taking in both sides of her face at once. There's her nose. Her ears. Her blue eyes with pale lashes closed. And her forehead; the warehouse of her thoughts and hopes and dreams.

She enters her brain, finding blood vessels and nerves and the parts of her that make her human.

Human.

She's human.

She's Aura.

And it's time to wake up!

Aura's eyes fly open, and she gasps for air. She's in a pod, exactly like the one she found herself in during the Games. But this one is different. It's not how it looks. It has the same pulsing veins of light over the thin membrane cocooning her. The difference is in how it feels. Or rather, how *she* feels.

"I'm real," she whispers. "This is me."

She knows without a doubt every word Avalan said is true.

Because she remembers it.

She remembers being born in a time where people lived in homes like the one in Avalan's footage of Jewel's father's death. They had lawns, and decks, and pools, and pet dogs who wore collars around their necks.

She remembers the weather becoming unpredictable. Freak storms and floods wiping out entire towns. Tsunamis and earthquakes swallowing human lives like giant hungry beasts demanding to be fed.

She remembers her parents. The same people from the Scorchlands, except they weren't called Brando and Vesta. They were Ben and Vanessa and their home made from bricks was filled with just as much love as the underground bunker that didn't exist.

Aura had a different name too.

"Alice," she says. "I'm Alice."

Yet too much has happened since she was Alice. She lived an entire life that didn't take place. Except somehow it did because she's held onto everything she learned and lost in that reality. The Quadrants may have been a figment of Avalan's mind, but the experiences within it were real to all the people trapped inside.

Including falling in love with Hayze. Or Hayden, as she knew him when they first locked eyes over a Bunsen burner in the chemistry lab at their school. But while that romance had been cut short, the one they had in the Scorchlands was long enough for her entire soul to become immersed. It was no wonder she fell for him yet again in the Games.

The virtual world was the one where she came to life, shedding all parts of her that were Alice. Which means she's Aura now. Just as Hayden is Hayze. Because they're not the same people as the terrified teens who climbed into their pods.

She remembers that moment too. How their parents

reserved them a place in Eterna Incorporated's controversial high-tech storage facility when so many kids in their neighbourhood couldn't afford to do the same. It was no different to needing enough edrian to live in one of the capitals. Except Aura had been on the other side of privilege that time. And strangely it hadn't felt any more comfortable. A world of haves and have-nots is only easy to live in if you do it without your heart.

Aura and Hayze resisted accepting their places in their pods, wanting to live out the remainder of their numbered days in the natural world. But when a tornado wiped out their homes, they ran with their parents to take refuge in their pods.

The choice was to live in the future or to die right then. Fifteen-year-old Alice had no idea how complicated this simple decision was. Avalan somehow inserted her into the virtual world as a baby, stretching out hundreds of years to feel like only eighteen of them had passed. And as Aura prepares to emerge from her cocoon and stretch her newfound wings, she wonders if Avalan was right to put them through what she did? Because Aura's learned so much. She knows exactly how vital it is that humans care for the earth so it can continue to sustain life.

She takes a deep breath and extends her arms. She's still wearing the white bodysuit she slipped into when she climbed into the pod. Her arms move freely, having waited centuries for this moment. Her fingertips caress the membrane of the pod and slowly it retracts.

Blinking in the artificial light, Aura sits up and looks around.

The enormous warehouse is lined with rows of pods as far as she can see, all gently pulsing with veins of light.

When she first entered this room, it was filled with people saying their goodbyes as they scrambled to find their allocated pod before it was too late. But not now. Aura's the only conscious soul in here. Likely the only conscious soul in the entirety of Earth. Which makes her humankind's final hope.

"No pressure," she mutters, swinging her legs out of the pod.

She takes a few steps down the empty aisle, surprised to find her legs are strong and sturdy. The pod kept her muscles functioning as well as the rest of her. Overwhelmed by a sense of déjà vu, she realizes this is how she felt when she woke up on the raft in the Games.

Alone.

Scared.

Confused.

Except unlike that time, now she's strong.

Confident.

Brave.

She can do this.

Turning around, she recalls her parents' pods are on either side of her own. Except, she's not ready to wake them yet.

First, she needs to wake Hayze.

Stretching her mind back, she remembers saying goodbye to him when their families had parted at the end of the aisle. Their parents hugged, promising to continue their friendship when the world was safer. Hayze pulled Aura into his arms, holding her fiercely as if he never wanted to let her go. But he had. He had to. He kissed her lips and walked between his parents as they went to the next aisle.

Aura runs down her row of pods, trying not to think of all the lives trapped inside. She reaches the end and heads up the next aisle. The one she knows Hayze is in. But how will she know which pod is his?

"Jewel!" she shouts. "I did what you asked. Now I need your help. Which one holds Hayze?"

Slowing her steps, she holds out her hands, concentrating on each pod she passes, looking for a sign as she desperately hopes Jewel heard her.

When she's halfway down the aisle, her hope begins to ebb. Jewel is hiding from her mother in lines of code. There's nothing she can do for Aura now. She may have to wake every last soul in this long line of pods, which she's fully prepared to do if it means she finds Hayze.

Then she sees a flicker.

Spinning to her right, she studies the pod in front of her.

The lights blink again, so quickly she's not sure if she imagined it.

She goes closer, holding out her palms, aware her heart is beating faster.

"Hayze?" she whispers. "Is that you?"

The veins in the pod's fine membrane pulse with the same light as the others in the long line. But surely, she went to this one for a reason. Because there's something else she learned in the Games, and that's to trust her gut. And right now every one of her instincts is telling her this is Hayze's pod.

Reaching down to a small glowing button on the side, she presses it.

The pod whirrs softly and the membrane begins to retract.

Aura holds her breath.

She's either managed to use everything she learned while suspended in Avalan's reality to find the guy she loves.

Or she's about to learn her biggest lesson yet.

TWENTY-FOUR

HAYZE

A wareness claws at the tattered edges of Hayze's consciousness, but he resists it. There's nothing to wake for. Literally.

Endless white waits on the other side. Empty.

Lifeless.

Bleached death.

There's no Aura. No family or friends. No way to fight for them.

Yet his mind continues to sharpen. To wake.

Once again, his body isn't his to control. His *world* isn't his to control.

Still, Hayze fights it. Tries to cling to oblivion, which is preferable to nothingness. Preferable to a world without Aura.

"Hayze?"

The whispered, tremulous voice carrying his name is all it takes to go from helplessness to action. From hopelessness to movement.

From welcoming non-existence to rejecting it.

Hayze's eyes fly open. His mind registers he's in a pod. His body leaps out, shoving past the sides that are still retracting.

And there she is. Her own smile mirroring his. Her own hope taking flight in the beautiful depths of her ocean eyes.

"Aura."

Hayze says her name with reverence. In a hushed whisper. Like a prayer.

She launches forward at the same time he does. They crash together, arms wrapping tightly, mouths seeking, hearts pounding. Everything that is Aura assaults Hayze at once, how she tastes, feels, smells. He pulls her against him tighter, needing more. He sweeps his tongue into her waiting mouth, craving more. He draws in a deep breath, cherishing more.

Aura pushes up on her toes, increasing the pressure as her hands spear into his hair. Hayze groans. She echoes the sound of willing surrender.

His knees almost give out.

Instead, he holds onto the most amazing sensations he'll ever have the privilege to experience. He holds onto Aura.

Because this moment is real.

She's real.

This kiss is *real*.

When they finally pull apart, Hayze vaguely registers what else is real—his surroundings.

Thousands and thousands of pods.

Pushing away what that means for a few seconds longer, he rests his forehead against Aura's. They're both breathing as if it's been a frantic, desperate run to this moment. As if the other is their oxygen. As if they can absorb their essence and make sure they'll always carry a part of the other.

"We're both awake, aren't we?" Hayze whispers.

Aura nods. "Like, really awake."

No more lies. No more Games. No more virtual reality.

"Are you okay?"

She sighs. "I'm holding you, and that's what counts."

Hayze closes his eyes as he props his chin on her head. "It feels good. Really good."

Aura sighs in agreement, burrowing in so her cheek is pressed to his chest. He finally allows his eyes to open to take in the fact his surroundings are going to be a shock.

And they don't disappoint.

It's like the world is on repeat—rows upon rows upon rows of pods. The colossal space they're in makes him feel tiny. The gray ceiling is high above, the distant walls barely visible past the endless cocoons of white. It's a warehouse. A monstrous one.

Full of lives held in suspended animation. Each mind currently trapped in virtual reality, clueless that it's all a lie.

"You haven't remembered yet," Aura says, watching him closely.

He blinks. "Remembered what—"

Hayze is assaulted by images. No, by memories!

Sitting with Aura in their favorite park, enjoying a sunny day, surrounded by vibrant green trees and blooming flowers. Everything blurs and pales in comparison to the future they're planning.

A terrifying storm ripping through their suburb. Hayze and his family huddled in the basement while Aura texts him frantically from her own home. They're both so scared, both comforted by each other's messages.

Sitting at a desk in a classroom when a weather alert pierces the air. There's chaos, fear in everyone's eyes, finding Aura in the crowd and holding her hand as they're led to the gym.

The first heatwave that struck long before summer was due. The air was thick and oppressive, even long after dark, so he and Aura snuck to the public pool. They'd laughed and kissed and enjoyed the stolen moments despite the promise of doom clinging to the air as much as the heat.

Joining a local protest against the government's inaction on climate change. Hayze and Aura made signs together, chanted with the crowd, enjoyed the sense of purpose and action amidst the crisis.

The panic and urgency of evacuating their homes because of an approaching wildfire. Hayze helping his parents pack essential items, the sky an eerie orange glow, worrying about Aura's safety until they could reunite at the evacuation center.

A sudden, severe blizzard that trapped everyone indoors. Hayze and Aura connecting over a video call, both wrapped in blankets, sharing stories to keep each other company, their smiles the only thing keeping them warm. Their friend Patrick's farewell after his parents decided to leave for somewhere safer. Aura's neighbor, Tegan, bringing candles during a power outage so they could sit around and tell ghost stories.

The day Hayze and his family learned the term *supercell storm* alongside *tornado* and knew they had to flee. That was the same day they stepped into this warehouse with its endless rows of pods. The tearful goodbye with Aura, promising they'd find each other again somehow, the lingering feeling of her hand slipping from his a moment before she walked away.

No, not Aura. Alice...

Hayze blinks, now gazing at the girl who also led a life she didn't know about. "My real name is..."

"Hayden," Aura finishes, a smile ghosting over her lips.

"And you're Alice," he breathes. Hayze shakes his head. "We're no longer those people."

"No, we're not." She brushes her fingers over his cheek. "I loved you as Hayden. And now I love you, Hayze."

"Alice. Aura. The names never mattered," he says, once more pressing his forehead to hers. "I love *you*."

Their lips gravitate to each other once more, this time allowing themselves the time to revel in the past they've just uncovered, in the present they're discovering. In the future they're now forging.

This kiss is tender. Deep. Delicious.

It may be because Hayze now knows all the other kisses were simply a movie playing out, but these are more intense. More moving. More... Just more. He's never felt so awake, so alive. He can't wait to touch and feel and taste—

Hayze straightens, conscious any other exploration is going to have to wait.

His gaze flickers to the pods, then back to Aura. "We have to wake them up."

He realizes his parents are here. Patrick, who was Pace, and Tegan, who was Tempo.

She also tenses, the passion banked for now as her hands tighten their grip on his shirt. "All of them."

It's time for humanity to exist beyond the confines of lies.

Hayze's brow contracts as he starts to understand the ramifications and responsibilities that come with those words. "How are we awake? How did we escape the nothingness?"

"Jewel," Aura says. "She's hiding from Avalan amongst the virtual reality code. She woke me up, then led me to you."

Hayze nods, letting this digest. Jewel's proven that human qualities like kindness and compassion and selflessness can be captured in lines of letters and numbers. It's staggering.

Except now a fellow computer program, one infused with a mother's fierce protectiveness, is proving how far they're willing to go to keep her alive.

Aura glances around. "It's going to take days to wake everyone up."

Hayze nods, realizing she's right. He scans the pods containing his parents, not Seraphina and Ember, but Sarah and Emmanuel. Somewhere Pace and Tempo and Geo and Atmos, even Skylus, are being held in a timeless balance between existence and non-existence. Their memories waiting to be acknowledged. Waiting to be real again.

"We need to find Avalan," he says. She's the one who started this. She's the one who can end it.

Aura scans the endless rows. "We have no idea which one she's in."

She's one woman. And there are thousands of pods.

"Or what she'll do when we wake her," Hayze adds, the truth settling into his bones like stone.

It's likely the fierce protectiveness that Eterna has is a reflection of the real Avalan. If she learns her daughter's existence becomes nothing but the virtual program it is when humanity wakes, she may make the same choice her alter ego has.

To keep every last soul in suspended animation.

Aura stiffens as she realizes the same. "We can't wake her. Or anyone else."

It would not only alert Eterna, Avalan's virtual self, but Avalan the mother could be a threat.

Avalan can't end this.

Eterna won't.

Which means they have to.

Hayze and Aura disentangle as they slowly turn. Their arms brush, then their backs. Then they're standing shoulder to shoulder, registering two massive doors in the distance. "We have to destroy Eterna," Aura breathes.

"Then the virtual world will cease to exist," Hayze finishes.

Everyone will wake up. Every last soul will regain consciousness.

But how?

They remain motionless as the two words seem to ricochet through the vast warehouse. The task is as daunting as the colossal space itself. They've gone from trying to find a needle in a haystack, to needing to find a way to destroy the haystack because it was never real.

Aura frowns, then rubs the furrows on her forehead. "Jewel said something to me when she woke me up…"

Hayze turns to grip her arms as he watches her closely. "What?"

"She said…" Aura rubs harder, as if massaging the memory to life. "Go to the pod, Aura. End all of this. Find Hayze and go to the pod."

He glances around, his eyebrows hiking. "Helpful."

So far, all that tells them is even Jewel knew that waking Avalan wasn't a good idea. She didn't say Avalan's pod. She said *the* pod.

And they're surrounded by thousands of them. They don't have time to find out which one is *the* one. If Eterna finds out they're awake. If she finds Jewel tucked amongst data and code…

The chances they find the right pod in time are slim.

Hayze draws in a sharp breath as one word sticks. Then practically slaps him in the face.

Pod.

He finds he's rubbing his temple, mirroring Aura's actions from moments ago. His own memory is coming alive. A moment in the Games that suddenly has layers of meaning.

"Hayze?"

Aura's looking at him as if she knows something significant has sparked.

A derelict hut on the edge of the Scorchlands, bleached and

decaying. Wood groaning as he steps onto it, a door that rusted open decades ago. A faded sign above it...

"The pod," he breathes.

The place Avalan sent him to when he was searching for Aura. The place she said Jewel could be found!

Aura's hands clasp his face, bringing his focus back to her beautiful face. "What pod, Hayze?"

"It's not a pod, but a hut at the furthest point of the Scorchlands called 'The Pod'," he says, swallowing hard. "I ran for an entire day due west to get to it."

Aura's eyes widen. Then stretch wider again. "The pod."

He nods, enjoying the sensation of her palms cupping his cheeks. "The pod."

They say the next word simultaneously. Together.

"Frenius."

Their smiles bloom at the same time, starting at their lips and ending in their hearts. A shared memory rises between them, the first moment they used that word.

Hayze and Aura in their former life, watching the riots over food shortages on TV. Hayze picking up the rotten tomato that was now a scarce commodity. Aura smiling as she took it from him and split it open to reveal the precious seeds inside. The shared understanding of the solution.

They needed a garden. A plot in the backyard to grow their own food.

They said the same word all those lifetimes ago. "Frenius."

Their hands reach out, their fingers intertwine. Together, they turn to face the massive doors waiting at the end of the long row of pods.

The world they haven't seen in hundreds of years waits beyond.

It'll hold freedom.

Or the end.

TWENTY-FIVE

AURA

Aura holds her finger to the green button on the wall beside the giant double doors, noticing the back of her hand looks different.

Her Fire tattoo is missing.

Because it never existed in the first place.

"Are you ready?" Hayze asks.

She looks across at him.

He existed.

He always has, no matter which world she's lived in. He's the only thing that's remained constant.

"I've never been more ready." She presses the button, and the doors slide back, revealing the same set of stairs Aura and Hayze scurried down with their parents when the tornado hit. The concrete is still solid, despite the inevitable cracks and discoloration from the years that have passed. But Aura's memories of that day are unchanged.

Running to the bunker as the world around her was torn apart.

Bursting into the stairwell with her heart pounding.

Descending each step with mounting dread, unsure if she'd ever have the chance to climb them again.

Saying goodbye to Hayze with her heart screaming at her to never let him go.

Climbing into the pod and closing her eyes...

"I can't believe this is happening." Aura squeezes Hayze's hand as they take the first step.

"We actually made it," he says.

"Now to make sure everyone else does, too."

"They will." He sounds more confident than she feels. "We'll make sure of it. We haven't come this far for nothing."

They ascend the stairs in silence, both aware of how enormous this moment is. If they succeed, humans will populate the earth once more. Only this time, they'll take better care of it. Because if they don't learn from their mistakes, Eterna was right, and they really don't deserve to survive.

The doors at the top of the stairs have been secured with a long metal bar and Aura heads to one end as Hayze goes to the other. Together, they heave it out of position, place it on the floor and get to work on the other bolts and latches.

When the door is clear, Aura holds her breath as Hayze jerks on the handle. It swings open with a loud creak, revealing the world Avalan never intended them to see.

Every one of Aura's senses is overloaded as she takes in the sight.

Bright, natural sunlight. Fresh, crisp air. And a sound she missed more than she would have ever believed possible.

Birdsong.

Clutching Hayze's hand, they walk out of the warehouse, into the cacophony of chirping and tweeting and twittering as they step into the dense forest that's grown around them.

"It didn't look like this when we first came here." Hayze's eyes are wide.

Aura shakes her head. "It really didn't."

Eterna Corporation's warehouse had been constructed in the middle of a vacant field with half of it buried underground and the other half now covered with a mass of climbing vines. The patchy brown grass that once surrounded it is blanketed by trees that stretch into the sky, the thickness of the trunks proof of just how long the world has been left untouched by humans.

"It's amazing." Hayze's voice is a whisper. "So much more beautiful than the forest in the Quakelands."

"That might be because of the lack of killer monkeys." Aura laughs.

Hayze lets out a chuckle. "What kind of sick mind creates a world with killer monkeys?"

Aura pulls Hayze further into the trees. "Don't forget the killer dolphins."

"And vines that come to life and suffocate you," he adds.

"Not to mention dragons made from billions of tiny fire ants," she says, realizing by the shocked look on Hayze's face he doesn't know about that. She pauses, squinting up at the sky. "Which way is west?"

Hayze points. "That way."

"How can you tell which way the sun is moving?" She tilts her head, trying to see how he figured that out. "I have no concept if it's morning or afternoon."

"I'm just naturally smart, I suppose," he says, winking.

She punches him playfully on the arm. "You sound like Skylus now."

"Eep!" He grimaces. "No, we came to the warehouse from the other direction and our houses were in the east. So, west must be that way. Which means it's morning."

She nods, impressed. "Actually, that is quite smart."

"Frenius?" He quirks a brow.

"Don't push it." She laughs again, loving how content being with Hayze makes her feel.

They set off with the sun slowly rising behind them. Walking feels good after lying so still for such a long time and Aura's legs surge forward, the feet of her bodysuit protecting her from the forest floor.

They pass through several clearings littered with piles of rubble that must have once fitted together to form someone's home. Before the supercell tornado and the ones that must have followed. Before Mother Nature evicted her tenants and reclaimed her planet as her own.

"How far do you think it is?" Aura asks when they stop at a running stream to quench their thirst.

"I have no idea." Hayze splashes some cool water on his face. "It took several hours to reach the pod in virtual reality, so hopefully it's much the same."

"Hopefully." Aura doesn't point out that not much in the real world has lined up with the virtual one, but it's not like they can do anything about that.

"Avalan wouldn't have wanted the pod too far from the warehouse." Hayze stretches his legs and Aura feels heat race to her cheeks at the sight of his strong thighs in that tight suit.

"What?" He catches her gaze.

"Nothing." She smiles shyly as she crosses her arms. "It's just that I thought red was your color, but now I'm not so sure."

"You've seen me in this suit before," he says, confused. "In the Games."

"Hmm." She gathers the courage to scan him from head to toe, pausing at his broad chest. "But I've never seen you wear it this well."

He laughs, sweeping his own gaze over her body. "Speak for yourself."

"I'd kill for a pair of jeans right now." Aura pulls at the stretchy fabric encasing her legs.

"And my trainers," Hayze adds.

"I wouldn't mind a bra either." Aura crosses her arms tighter for emphasis.

Hayze smirks. "Not sure that's necessary."

Aura's about to slap him again when a huge deer wanders up to the creek several feet away. They freeze, not wanting to startle it.

The deer laps at the water then looks across at them, tilting its head as it tries to figure out if they're a threat.

"It's never seen a human," Aura whispers.

"It's okay, deer." Hayze holds up his hands. "We won't hurt you."

The animal's eyes widen and it runs into the trees, kicking up dirt and fallen leaves behind its hurried hooves.

"Poor thing," says Aura. "It was terrified."

"It's good for it to learn to run away." Hayze wraps his arm around her. "Not everyone will be as nice as us."

Aura nods, a wave of sadness washing over her. Hayze is right. While they've learned the lessons of their generation's mistakes, not everyone will have. There will still be shades of clever and kind amongst Earth's population. She just hopes it's an improvement on last time. Because the Earth has managed to regenerate itself into something quite spectacular, echoing the beauty of how it must have been before humans had spread like a cancer, consuming every available resource. Even the weather seems to have stabilized.

"Are you okay to keep walking?" Hayze asks.

"Of course." She nods. "Are you?"

"Yep." His arm slips down so he can take her hand. "I needed that drink though."

They walk on, with minutes stretching into hours until

eventually they break through the tree line to discover a long stretch of red sand that touches the horizon. Plump rabbits dart between low shrubs that dot the landscape, and a flock of bright pink birds sweeps across the sky in a triangular formation, before abruptly changing direction and soaring away. It's a stark contrast to the overgrown forest they just emerged from but has a magic of its own.

A gentle breeze caresses Aura's face and she draws in the warmth of the sun that's begun its descent as it leads them toward the inevitable darkness.

"I think we're getting closer." Hayze pulls on Aura's hand. "If we hurry, we can make it there and back before nightfall."

Aura swallows down her nerves, and they march forward. The sand is more difficult to move across as her feet sink into it with each step. Her legs begin to ache, but she presses on. Too much is at stake to give up now.

"There!" Hayze points. "Look!"

Aura blinks ahead, unable to make out whatever it is Hayze thinks he's spotted. But his eyesight was always better than hers, so she's prepared to take his word for it. Besides, she *needs* him to be right. She can't walk much further without taking a rest.

After trudging on for a few more minutes, Aura sees it.

A small hut on the horizon with crooked walls that lean to the left. Could this derelict building really contain humanity's last hope?

"How is it still standing after all these years?" Aura increases her pace with excitement. "Even if it withstood the tornado, this isn't possible."

"It's different from the one I saw in the Quakelands." Hayze squints as he tries to get a better look. "That one was made from wood. This is made from something else."

"How can you be certain it's the right hut?" Aura asks, panting as they break into a run.

"I'm not certain." Hayze grins. "I'm just pretty sure."

"I guess that will have to do." Aura keeps her eyes on the hut as they close the gap, gasping for breath when they reach it.

While it looks far bigger when standing in front of it than it had when it was nothing more than a dot on the horizon, it's not large. Aura's family home in the suburbs had a shed in the backyard around this size. Hayze was right about it not being made from timber. It's constructed entirely from a black metal that Aura doesn't recognize. And while it's stood the test of time, it's only just. The lean is more severe up close, like it might topple over in the next big wind. If Jewel hadn't helped release Aura from her pod when she did, it may have been too late.

"*Pretty sure* was just upgraded to *certain*. This is definitely it." Hayze walks up to the door and touches a sign hanging above it.

The Pod.

"How do we get in?" Aura steps up beside him.

There's a click and the door slides open.

"What the fractal?" Hayze looks from the door to Aura. "How did that happen?"

Aura shrugs, not complaining one bit.

Hayze steps inside first, momentarily disappearing into the darkness before Aura follows.

A light blinks on, revealing a room with nothing but a desk and a closed laptop.

"Did it look like this last time?" Aura asks.

"No." Hayze walks to the desk and stares at the laptop like it might bite him. "Well, not really. It was an empty room like this, but it was dirty. There was dust everywhere and a screen on the table, not a laptop."

"This hut must've been sealed." Aura glances at the open door, hoping it doesn't close as mysteriously as it opened, leaving them without air.

"Hello Aura." Jewel's voice filters into the room. "Oh, and Hayze."

Aura spins around, looking for her friend.

"Jewel?" Hayze instinctively draws closer to Aura, threading his fingers through hers. "Did you open the door for us?"

"I did," says Jewel. "You two are a good team. I gave the clue to Aura, then Hayze was able to find the pod. Neither of you could have done that alone."

Aura glances at Hayze, both remaining silent as they wait to hear what else Jewel has to say.

"It was your final test," she says. "The first and only one set by me."

"What were you testing?" Aura asks when Jewel falls silent.

"My mother was testing humanity." Jewel's voice spills over with emotion. "But I was giving it one last shot."

"Jewel, please don't talk in riddles." Hayze throws out his free hand. "That's what Avalan does. We're your friends. Just say what you mean."

"I wanted one last shot with Aura," Jewel says, talking quickly. "If she stayed in virtual reality, I could have found a way to have a life with her. But I knew she didn't want that. And when I helped her wake up, she proved that to me by passing my test."

"How?" Aura winces as she already knows the answer.

"The first thing you did when you woke up was look for Hayze," Jewel replies. "You held each other. You said words I would die a thousand times over to hear just once from your lips. But I never stood a chance."

"Jewel," Aura pleads, unable to deny this. "I couldn't give you my heart when it already belonged to someone else."

"I know." Jewel's voice is little more than a whisper. "I've accepted that. Which is why I need you to open the laptop."

"Why?" Aura places her palm flat on the laptop, keeping it closed.

"Because you trust me, don't you?" Jewel asks. "You may not love me the way I want you to, but I know you trust me."

"I do." Aura glances at Hayze, who nods. She opens the laptop and the screen comes to life, revealing a flickering image of Jewel.

"Hi." Jewel waves, her sparkling dark eyes smiling at Aura.

"Hi." Aura returns her smile, knowing she'll never see her friend in any other form again.

"Hi, Jewel." Hayze leans into the screen. "For what it's worth, I'm really sorry."

Aura frowns, then realizes he's apologizing for Aura having chosen him.

"You have nothing to be sorry for," says Jewel. "You've always been good to me."

"I still am sorry," he says. "If loving Aura's a crime, I'm just as guilty as you."

"Are you going to help us wake everyone up?" Aura asks, not entirely comfortable being caught in the middle of this.

Jewel nods as she looks away, but not before Aura sees a glimpse of fear creep into her eyes.

"What's wrong, Jewel?" Aura brings her face closer to the screen. "What aren't you telling us?"

"Waking everyone up is easy." She draws in a deep breath and locks her eyes on the screen as she pulls herself together. "All you need to do is hit the *escape* key."

Aura lets out a small huff of amusement. "How appropriate."

"It appears my mom has a sense of humor." Jewel rolls her eyes.

"What exactly happens when I press the button?" Aura asks, tired of surprises.

"Everyone will wake up," says Jewel. "Including my mother. The virtual reality will end. But you need to be sure, because once you press that button, there's no going back."

Hayze nods, instantly on board with this plan. Except there's something he hasn't realized.

"What about you, Jewel?" Aura asks. "What happens to you if the virtual world no longer exists?"

Jewel gives Aura a sad smile. "I won't exist either."

"No!" Aura steps back from the laptop. "There has to be another way."

Hayze slips his arm around Aura's trembling frame. "Aura, we have to do it. There's too much at stake."

"He's right," says Jewel. "I've thought about this for a long time. It's what I want."

"You can't want that!" Aura's eyes flare. "How can you choose not to exist?"

"Because I never existed in the first place." Jewel speaks plainly. "I haven't since the day I died in my cot, too weak to call out for the mother who didn't come to me until it was too late."

"You exist." Aura's hand flies to her heart. "In here. You're part of all of us. We know you. We love you."

Jewel shakes her head. "There's nothing left for me here. The only part of the life Avalan created for me that was worth living for was the people in it. My father. You two. Pace and Tempo. Even Skylus was worth living for at times." She laughs softly, clearly remembering some of the more ridiculous things Skylus came out with.

"No," Aura says again. "I won't do—"

"Aura." Jewel's voice is stern. "If you don't press the button, humanity remains asleep. Waking them up one at a time will take too long and Eterna will realize what's happening and override the system. It's the only way."

Aura collapses against Hayze, burying her face in his chest as she struggles to accept this.

"What do we do?" she asks, looking up at him.

He blinks once.

Twice.

Then draws a breath.

"We have to press the button, Aura."

"Can you do it?" she asks, unsure if she has the strength.

He nods, releasing his hold on her as he steels himself.

"Aura," says Jewel. "I want you to be the one to do it. It's time for you to let me go, like I did with you."

Aura swallows, trying to gather her strength to fulfil Jewel's final wish.

Hayze steps back, putting a hand on Aura's arm, reassuring her he's right beside her.

"Please, Aura," says Jewel.

Aura returns to the laptop, her finger hovering over the *escape* button. She looks at the screen and Jewel nods at her.

"You're the bravest person I ever met," says Aura.

"I'm not a person," Jewel whispers.

"Yes, you are. And I love you."

Aura presses the button before Jewel can reply, wanting the last words her friend hears to be words of love. Words that confirm just how real she is.

The screen goes blank.

Jewel has gone.

And just as she said, there's no going back.

The decision was made.

Which means it's time to find out exactly what that means for everyone else.

CHAPTER
TWENTY-SIX

HAYZE

For an endless second, nothing happens.

Long enough for the realization of Jewel's sacrifice to leave Hayze reeling.

Long enough for a blink to feel like it just wiped away everything that was, leaving a blank slate.

Long enough to wonder what the fractal that's going to look like.

There's a small *pop* that feels like an explosion. Hayze and Aura flinch and leap back, gripping each other's hand with the strength of two people who've triggered a chain reaction they're still trying to understand.

If this is the end...

The second *pop* is followed by a flash of light as the laptop bursts into flames. The fire burns hot, red and orange, quickly turning to blue and white. The plastic warps and melts, the screen cracks and liquifies. The machine that held Jewel's last image only moments ago turns to a misshapen blob, then acrid smoke, then pale ash. A slow circle of flames expands from the pile of gray, eating away at the desk.

Hayze blinks, then remembers to breathe. The connection to the virtual world that's sustained thousands of lives was just destroyed. Severed.

Ended.

Even the black walls of the hut seem to shudder with the enormity of everything that means.

"Hayze!" Aura gasps, tugging his hand as she looks around frantically.

Because the walls weren't metaphorically shuddering. They're moving!

Spinning on their heels, they sprint for the door. Hayze half expects it to start closing, a punishment Eterna built into the system for those who dared to trigger the end. He pushes his feet into the ground, desperate to inject as much speed into the few steps they need as possible.

Fire power sure would be handy right now...

Except the door remains open and Aura leaps through, quickly followed by Hayze. They keep running for a few more steps, the rattling and groaning behind spurring them on. Only when they're a safe distance away do they stop and turn to look back.

In time to see the walls of the hut collapse inward, the roof quickly following.

The crash ricochets through the forest, reverberates deep in Hayze's chest. The twisted pile of black shifts and creaks, then starts to smolder. Gray tendrils turn into inky smoke as they multiply. Small, sluggish flames turn into larger, hungrier ones.

It's not just the laptop that's self-destructing. The whole hut is.

Realization hits Hayze hard. If Avalan wanted to destroy this once the VR ended...

He turns to Aura, seeing the same dread blooming over her face. "The warehouse," he breathes.

"We have to—"

They twist and break into a run. It doesn't matter that their bodies are exhausted. It doesn't matter that they're hungry and thirsty and dashing through a world they've only just discovered.

Getting to the warehouse before...

Hayze shakes his head, not allowing the thought to finish. This can't be the end.

Their arms pump, their lungs struggle to keep up, their feet pound the ground. Birds cry in alarm while animals scurry away. Hayze keeps his focus on two things—Aura and momentum. His throat burns. Sweat blurs his vision. But all that matters is keeping the sun behind them.

And reaching the warehouse before the orange orb sinks below the horizon, robbing them of a way to judge east.

They barrel through trunks that are steadily growing darker. A mantra quickly establishes itself in Hayze's mind, a loop that accompanies his mad sprint, a rhythm as relentless as time itself.

This can't be the end.

This can't be the end.

They leap over a fallen log and Aura stumbles. Hayze reaches out and steadies her, neither of them slowing. He knows she wouldn't want him to. Not when they've come this far. Not when they're so close.

Not when the alternative is...the end.

One moment they're dodging trunks and branches, the next the warehouse looms before them, tall shadows already creeping up its sides. The doors are open, just like Hayze and Aura left them, but they're also ominously empty.

"Where is everyone?" Aura gasps.

There are no people in matching white suits standing around, astounded at the evolution that unfolded while they were sleeping. No one sitting on the leaf-littered ground, bewildered and confused. No one hugging loved ones they haven't touched in longer than they ever thought possible, crying and laughing and crying some more.

Hayze and Aura burst through the open doors and run down the stairs into the warehouse. There's a flash of blinding white light, just like in the Games. They stop, memories of all the times that's happened before rushing at them, fear clawing through their veins. It takes precious seconds for their eyes to adjust to the gloom, but then they widen. And widen some more.

The veins on the pods are flaring bright white, making the sides translucent. The bodies within become visible—dark, still shapes. No, dark, *moving* shapes. Hayze and Aura walk carefully down an aisle, heads swiveling as they watch the birth of humanity unfold.

Triggered by their return to the warehouse.

Bodies shift. Hands twitch and rise. Heads jerk with surprise as consciousness sharpens and reality hits.

The sides of the pods slowly retract, revealing blinking eyes and confused faces. Each is a flower blooming, unfolding, releasing the precious life it's kept alive. Hayze wishes there was time for people to assimilate everything—that they're awake, alive. How many years have passed...

But there's not.

Not if the same thing happens to the warehouse as the hut.

Not if Eterna is planning on destroying every last shred of evidence that her VR existed.

"Go to your parents," Hayze tells Aura, already striding toward his own pod. "Everyone needs to get to the forest."

Aura nods, hesitates, brushes her hand against his, and

darts to the next aisle. Hayze jogs to the two pods that are now completely open beside his own empty one. His father is the first to climb out. He quickly goes to the adjacent pod to help his wife. She clambers to her feet and they clasp each other wordlessly. The enormity of the moment is obvious in the way they cling to each other.

The last time he tried to see them, he was told the Rebels had all disappeared. But it was Avalan removing them from her VR world. All that fear and grief was for nothing.

"Mom," Hayze says quietly. "Dad."

They spin around, eyes bursting wide, smiles bursting wider.

"Hayze," his mother sobs, opening her arms.

He falls into them, feeling his father clasp them both.

"Hayze. My boy," his father murmurs, holding his family tight.

They used his name, Hayze. Not Hayden. Seems he's not the only one who was forever changed by VR. He suspects they'll be Sera and Ember in this second chance at life, even though it's no longer defined by Quadrants or Elements.

He pulls back, wishing there was more time. "You have to get out of here." He points to the end of the aisle. "The doors are open."

His mother frowns. "But why the rush?"

"Son, we need to understand what we've woken to—"

His father's words are cut off by a *pop*. Then another.

The pods they just left burst into small, scorching flames. Orange and red blaze to white and blue. Hayze's heart stutters painfully.

It's happening again.

He spins as he registers more people exiting their pods. Some slowly. Some almost leaping as if scalded. A few stay where they are, no doubt wondering what's waiting for them.

"You have to get out!" he shouts, trying to keep the panic out of his voice. "Go!"

Aura's voice carries from the next aisle. "The door is this way!"

"Hayze?" his mother asks, worry furrowing her brow.

"Mom, you need to trust me. Get out and into the forest. Tell everyone else as you go."

His father straightens, then nods. "You never needed Elemental powers, son. I should've known your strength was simply a part of you."

Taking Hayze's mother's hand, he turns and runs. A woman stands not far away, cradling a baby as her eyes dart around, scared and lost. They scoop her up with their momentum, taking her toward the doors.

Pop. The pod the woman was standing beside bursts into contained flames, the white cocoon shriveling to black. It crumples in on itself, quickly disintegrating.

Hayze turns away, already running to the next person along. "To the doors! This way!" The middle-aged man runs a hand over his balding head, hesitating, only to be jostled by a panicked woman darting past. It triggers a flash of fear, then he's rushing after her.

Over and over, Hayze tells people to run. He points in the direction of safety and freedom. Then he hears his mother and father doing the same, sees a flash of Aura's hair as she sprints to the next aisle. Once the flow gains momentum, once the panic reaches critical mass, the surge is inevitable. People follow blindly, running toward the door in a desperate stream.

The warehouse steadily evacuates as the pods steadily self-combust.

Hayze runs to the far end, the furthest point from the doors, wanting to make sure no one's been missed. No terrified child torn from their parents. No disorientated soul unable to process so much so fast. He stops when he sees someone climb out of their pod, far later than anyone else.

He freezes when he recognizes the slight frame and dark hair.

Avalan.

She straightens and draws her shoulders back as she takes in the world she's woken up in. She doesn't look confused or disoriented. She looks...calm. Almost calculating.

Does she know? Is she aware of the legacy she spawned? That the computer she left in charge had no intention that this moment would ever be born?

Avalan turns, sees him staring, and smiles. She *smiles*. "Hello, Hayden."

"It's Hayze," he growls, the questions still slamming through him.

She nods as she walks toward him. "Yes, I do know," she says. "Eterna showed me everything when I woke up, just like she was programmed to."

"I suppose at least she followed those directions." He watches her closely, trying to gauge her reaction.

To the world and lives she saved.

To the amount of time that should never have passed.

To the pain and suffering she inadvertently caused.

To losing Jewel all over again.

She glances up at the ceiling far above, still calm, still calculating. "We'd best get out. This warehouse won't be standing for much longer."

As if to corroborate her statement, her pod pops and bursts into flames. Followed by a rumble that rolls through the walls.

Hayze breaks into a sprint and Avalan does the same. They run past rows of burning pods, fracturing the curls of dark smoke curling and rising as they pass. The walls groan and creak louder.

The end is here.

The open doors are now only slightly lighter than the warehouse as twilight claims the forest. A body appears and he already knows who it is. Who's waiting anxiously, ready to run back in if she needs to.

"I'm coming, Aura!" he calls out, injecting more speed into his muscles. Thank fractal for adrenaline.

As he draws closer he can make out her hair, wisping in a slight breeze. Then her relieved smile. Then her ocean eyes, calling him to her. His heart soars as he pushes forward, then slows enough to take her hand and keep going.

They run together, feet pounding in unison, palms clasped tight.

Ahead, through the trees, are dozens, hundreds—no doubt far more—white-suited bodies. Tall and short, old and young, frozen and staring. All alive.

All free.

All watching the sight Hayze and Aura are running from.

They slow, then stop, then turn. There's a screech of metal. A hideous tearing of massive sheets and beams. Violent cracks split the corners of the warehouse. The walls wobble and shudder, now cast adrift.

Then the sides are falling in, one side toppling like a dead weight, the other starting at one side and dropping, a wave of inevitability dragging the rest down. The roof collapsing will be next.

Then a fire that will leave nothing behind but ash.

Hayze squints, registering the outline of someone still far too close to the warehouse.

"Avalan," Aura gasps.

The woman who couldn't let go, the mother who loved too much and not enough, the leader who saved them and masterminded their torture, turns to gaze back at them. Her dark eyes connect with Aura, then Hayze.

She mouths two words. "I'm sorry."

Then she turns and runs.

She darts into what's left of the warehouse the moment the roof caves in with a greedy roar. It crushes everything, the walls, the massive beams that once held it up, the burning pods.

The person who built it all.

The sun sinks below the horizon the same moment the flames flicker to life. Small and scorching, they dance over the twisted, dead metal, devouring and destroying. It won't take long for them to die, too, leaving behind ghosts and ash.

"She's with Jewel now," Aura murmurs solemnly, leaning into Hayze.

He presses a kiss to her temple, acknowledging she's right. This is why Avalan was calm. This is what she was calculating.

How to finally be at peace. How to finally lay her daughter to rest.

How to be with her once more.

A sob erupts behind them. Followed by a shout. Then laughter.

Hayze and Aura spin around, seeing the people finally start to realize. To process.

And celebrate.

Tears are running freely. Smiles are so wide, they dazzle. Men and women hug and cry and laugh. Families reunite. Lovers reconnect. Children run, weaving and squealing, their bodies finally experiencing the same thing their mind is.

"Hayze, look," Aura whispers, pointing to their left.

The others are here. Alive.

Pace and Tempo are hugging and kissing in a way that's grossly reminiscent of the Games. Not far away, Skylus has crumpled in a heap, crying. Atmos leans over her, looking terrified. Geo is holding a young girl with the same dark hair and lanky frame as him, an older version of him supporting an elderly woman not far away. Even Infernos, Cyclonis, and Oceania are there, as vulnerable and displaced as everyone else. Turns out, reality was the great equalizer.

They all made it. There was a price to pay—pain and loss that's forever changed them—but they made it.

Hayze and Aura turn to each other simultaneously. Their soft smiles echo the other's. His hands come up to cup her face, hers wrap around the back of his neck.

Their lips brush.

Their hearts thud with emotion and joy and truth.

The earth has healed. Humanity has a second chance.

Their love he found has a future.

As Hayze deepens the kiss, as he holds on tighter, he realizes this was never the end.

It's the beginning that was always waiting for them.

CHAPTER
TWENTY-SEVEN
AURA

Five Years Later

Aura tilts her face to the sun, her body humming with magic far superior to anything she experienced in virtual reality.

She stretches out her arms, remembering the flames that once sparked from her palms. Her Fire powers made her feel invincible. They also made her feel a bit clever. There's a part of her that will never feel whole without them.

Bringing her hands to her stomach, she molds them around the growing bump that's stretching her dress to its limits.

Her baby.

Hayze's baby.

The miracle that has her glowing with joy.

After the people escaped the warehouse, they headed into the forest to forge their new future, only to discover that while the land was fertile, humans were not. It was an irony that was lost on nobody. They'd done the impossible and risen from their pods, only to wonder if Eterna had played one last trick on them. Did she intend for humans to never repopulate the earth, even if they woke up?

But whether their infertility was Eterna or just a result of being held in suspended animation for so long, Aura and Hayze refused to let this ruin their happiness. They made the decision to care for the planet that humans had almost destroyed, so they could leave a legacy for the other plentiful forms of life that depend on it for survival.

They built a simple hut from the rubble of the homes the tornado ripped apart. They learned to forage for food, collecting and planting seeds for future harvests in a garden, just like they had centuries ago. They propagated herbs and fruit trees, fertilizing them using compost from their food scraps. Nothing is wasted. They weave blankets, make mattresses stuffed with dried moss, produce electricity from the wind, and draw water from a well.

Most of all, they appreciate every single moment of life.

Then, as unexpectedly as a tiny flame had flickered to life in Aura's hand in the Games, a new life sparked within her belly.

She hadn't believed it at first, no matter how ill she felt or how many cycles she missed. Hayze had believed it though, certain of it from the start. It wasn't until her stomach expanded and she felt the quickening of her baby's first movements she dared to accept he might be right.

It was the first true magic she ever harnessed.

A baby.

Half Aura.

Half Hayze.

Totally and completely loved.

"Hey, beautiful."

Aura spins around to see Hayze walking between two tall rows of corn stalks. He smiles and her heart melts as it always does when he's near. Her baby is one lucky kid to be inheriting his genetics.

"Hey, you." She reaches out and Hayze wraps his arms around her, careful not to squeeze her too tightly, despite her telling him a thousand times she won't break.

"I told you to rest." He does his best to look stern. "I can do whatever needs doing out here. Where should I start?"

"It helps to move around," she says. "Besides, the fact you have to ask what needs doing out here shows how much you understand the garden."

He laughs, knowing she's not taking a shot at him. He does more than his share of the work at their little house. If it weren't for him, they wouldn't have a house at all.

And Tempo, who deserves some credit. She turned out to have exceptional building skills with a natural understanding of exactly how to fit materials together so they don't fall down. That is when Pace isn't busy chasing her around their garden trying to steal another kiss.

They built two huts right near each other, along with their parents, who constructed small homes of their own. It's a little community, with other similar ones popping up nearby. Even Pace and Tempo's parents have managed to repair their friendship, made easier by the fact the betrayal never actually occurred in real life. Nor did Ondine's injuries, which means Pace has his mother back, and Tide struts around their village like the luckiest man alive. Although, they've returned to their original names of Olivia and Tony, given Olivia hasn't retained much of her memory of life in Aqua.

Sometimes Aura and Hayze take a walk to visit Geo and his cute little cousin, or to help Atmos who seems to have just about as much of a knack for construction and farming as he did for flying.

Their relationship with Skylus is more complicated. She prefers to live in isolation, having built herself a treehouse in a large elm in the middle of the forest. They check on her from time to time to make sure she hasn't leapt from the branches, convinced she can still defy gravity. She's often asleep—or pretending to be—as she grieves the world they left behind. The world where Skylus was able to do something nobody else could. If only she could see she's still unique. They all are. There's still plenty of good Skylus could do in this world.

Occasionally they even run into one of the leaders. Not Avalan, of course. Or Cyclonis, who succumbed to his advanced years within months of escaping his pod. But Infernos lives in a village nearby, trying to assert the power he had in his former life. For the most part it works, with his followers happy to be relieved of the heavy burden of deciding how they should live. Oceania, or Olive as she's now known, is determined to blend in with her little community, claiming she wants to live a normal life.

"Aura!" Tempo calls from the other end of the garden, tripping over her feet in her haste to reach her. Pace is right behind her.

Hayze's back stiffens as he steps closer to Aura and glances around for danger.

"I think it's good news," Aura tells him. "They look happy."

Tempo flings her arms around Aura, while Pace grins widely.

"What happened?" Hayze asks. "Are you okay?"

"I missed my cycle." Tempo beams. "And you know that never happens."

"I do?" Hayze lifts a brow and chuckles.

"She was talking to me." Aura rolls her eyes, then returns her attention to her friend. "Do you think—"

"I do think!" Tempo squeals. "Aura, I'm pregnant!"

"Just to be clear," Pace says to Hayze, "the baby's mine, not Aura's."

Hayze laughs and gives Pace a hug. "Congratulations!"

"I'm so thrilled for you." Aura reaches out and squeezes Tempo's hand.

"We were so hopeful after your news that we might be blessed as well." Tempo returns to Pace's side, and he gives her a lingering kiss.

"You deserve this." Hayze winks. "Especially given all the practice you put in."

Pace hoots with laughter. "Practice makes perfect."

"Have you told your parents?" Aura asks. "Your dad must be a foot taller."

"We wanted to tell you first." Tempo beams. "We're so excited your little one will have a cousin to grow up with."

Aura's heart swells with love for these friends who have truly become family. And now that Mother Nature has finally deemed humans to be worthy of their right to continue to live upon her soil, their family can continue to grow.

"Go and tell your parents," says Hayze. "News like this shouldn't wait."

Tempo and Pace nod their agreement. This was another lesson they learned in the Games—to live for the moment, as you never know when it will be your last.

Aura watches Tempo and Pace walk back through the garden, remembering one woman who knew when her last moment was approaching. Because she chose it herself.

Avalan.

A woman who was guilty of loving her husband so much that her grief sent her into a spiral. One that would see her neglect her daughter with the worst possible consequences as she created a world that would ironically save everyone else.

If Avalan hadn't done all of that, Aura and Hayze wouldn't be standing here right now. Their baby would never have been conceived. And who knows if the planet would have survived if it wasn't given the chance to regenerate.

Which makes Avalan the most controversial figure in the history of humankind. She was a killer, a savior, a genius, and a fraud.

But underneath all of that, she was a mother.

Like Aura is soon to be.

Aura looks at Hayze as he takes a shovel to dig up some potatoes. She understands how losing someone you love can destroy you. She had a taste of what it was like to lose Hayze in the Games and she never wants to go through that again.

Except, she could never do what Avalan did to Jewel. The tiny human she created with Hayze is the thing that matters most in this world. And they can give that child the life Jewel never had the chance to experience.

Aura takes a step closer to Hayze. "If she's a girl, I want to call her Gemma."

He pauses his work turning over the soil and, instead, turns this idea over in his mind.

"Gemma?" he asks. "Not Jewel?"

She shakes her head. "Gemma was her real name. That was who she never had the chance to be."

"Gemma." Hayze sets down the shovel and goes to Aura, putting his hands on her shoulders. "I like it. I just have one question."

"What?" She presses up on her toes.

He pulls back slightly. "What if he's a boy?"

"Then the next one will be a girl," she says. "Or the one after that."

His eyes flare. "Just how many babies are you planning to have?"

"I'm not sure. But we should do our bit for humankind and have at least ten."

Aura kisses him, catching his surprised laugh with her lips.

She doesn't have to tell him she's joking. Although, she wouldn't complain about having ten babies with Hayze. As long as she has him by her side, she'll take whatever life throws at them.

They hold each other tight, her belly between them. Their baby kicks and Hayze reaches down to press his hand to her middle.

"Near far..." Aura whispers.

"Wherever you both are," he replies without hesitation.

Because two are about to become three. And while life has been filled with so much confusion and uncertainty, Aura knows one thing for sure.

Hayze will always be with her. Just like he'll always be with their child.

When she's with him, everything feels right.

And while love like this exists in the world, there can be no argument that humankind was worth saving.

THE END
Ready for another series
by Tamar Sloan and Heidi Catherine?
Check out The Sovereign Code
http://mybook.to/HarvestDay
Or The Thaw Chronicles
http://mybook.to/RisingThaw

THE SOVEREIGN CODE

Humans saved bees from extinction...
and created the deadliest threat we've seen yet

The loss of bees was heralded as the sixth wave of extinction.
Economies crashed. Ecosystems collapsed. Wars were waged
as countless starved. Luckily, humans were able to alter bees'
genetic code to deal with the hazards of pesticides and disease.

Inadvertently making their venom fatal to humans.

River grew up in the Green Zone, a haven for those who are
Immune. Bees are free to fly, pollinating their prolific crops.
Echo was raised in the Dead Zone where bees are exterminated

so vulnerable humans like her can live. Stealing from the heavily guarded Green Zone is a necessary part of survival.

River and Echo are both in their seventeenth year. They're both about to have their immunity tested. And they're both about to have their futures forever altered.

Ultimately, they're about to become part of the final fight for human survival. Are bees really the enemy they need to defeat? Or is mankind a far greater threat...

Grab your copy now.

https://mybook.to/HarvestDay

THE THAW CHRONICLES

Tamar Sloan and Heidi Catherine are the authors of the bestselling series, The Thaw Chronicles.

Get your free prequel now!
http://mybook.to/BurningThaw

WANT TO STAY IN TOUCH?

ABOUT THE AUTHORS

Tamar Sloan hasn't decided whether she's a psychologist who loves writing, or a writer with a lifelong fascination with psychology. She must have been someone pretty awesome in a previous life (past life regression indicated a Care Bear), because she gets to do both. When not reading, writing or working with teens, Tamar can be found with her husband and two children enjoying country life in their small slice of the Australian bush.

Heidi Catherine loves the way her books give her the opportunity to escape into worlds vastly different to her own life in the burbs. While she quite enjoys killing her characters (especially the awful ones), she promises she's far better behaved in real life. Other than writing and reading, Heidi's current obsessions include watching far too much reality TV with the excuse that it's research for her books.

More Series to Fall in Love With...